CRITICS HAIL
MONTGOMERY'S CHILDREN
BY RICHARD PERRY

"SIMPLE GRANDEUR . . . abounds in fine, vernacular turns of phrase . . . reading it reminded me how much a writer can make of our language."—*The Washington Post*

"Perry has written from the heart, and from a place that is harder to define—the soul."—*St. Louis Post Dispatch*

"A BEAUTIFUL NOVEL, ELEGANTLY WRITTEN."
—*Los Angeles Times*

"Perry has some of the imagination of Toni Morrison, the whimsey of Ishmael Reed, even some of the wacky magic of Gabriel Garcia Marquez as well as some of the good sense of recent history."—*Essence* Magazine

"PERRY'S . . . AN ORIGINAL FROM WHOM MORE BOOKS WILL BE EAGERLY AWAITED."
—*Publishers Weekly*

RICHARD PERRY was born in 1944 and grew up in Monticello, New York, the oldest of eight children. By the time he was twelve he knew he wanted to be a writer. He graduated from The City College of New York and holds an MFA from Columbia University. His first novel, *Changes*, was published in 1974. He is also the author of short stories and a novelization of a screenplay. He teaches literature and creative writing at Pratt Institute in New York.

MONTGOMERY'S CHILDREN

A NOVEL

BY
RICHARD PERRY

A PLUME BOOK

NEW AMERICAN LIBRARY

NEW YORK AND SCARBOROUGH, ONTARIO

This is an authorized reprint of a hardcover edition published by Harcourt Brace Jovanovich, Publishers.

The quotation on page 29 is from *Treasures of Tutankhamun,* New York: The Metropolitan Museum of Art, 1976.

The original hardcover edition was designed by Dalia Hartman.

Library of Congress Cataloging in Publication Data

Perry, Richard, 1944-
  Montgomery's children.

  Reprint. Originally published: San Diego: Harcourt Brace Jovanovich, 1984.
  I. Title.
PS3566.E715M6   1985   813'.54   84-22658
ISBN 0-452-25674-7 (pbk.)

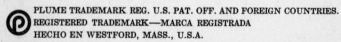 PLUME TRADEMARK REG. U.S. PAT. OFF. AND FOREIGN COUNTRIES.
REGISTERED TRADEMARK—MARCA REGISTRADA
HECHO EN WESTFORD, MASS., U.S.A.

SIGNET, SIGNET CLASSIC, MENTOR, PLUME, MERIDIAN AND NAL BOOKS are published *in the United States* by New American Library, 1633 Broadway, New York, New York 10019, *in Canada* by The New American Library of Canada Limited, 81 Mack Avenue, Scarborough, Onatrio M1I 1M8

First Plume Printing, April, 1985

1 2 3 4 5 6 7 8 9

PRINTED IN THE UNITED STATES OF AMERICA

For Jeanne

PART ONE
1948

CHAPTER
1

In 1948, people in Montgomery, New York, did not understand that natural resources are limited. So although the opposition to the racetrack was vocal and well organized, none of its energy was directed to the preservation of trees. Only one voice was lifted when that magnificent forest, which had taken several hundred years to grow, was leveled inside of six weeks, and that voice was raised where no one could hear it, at night, on the slope of one of the hills that overlook what is now the grandstand.

They began clearing the trees on a Monday in March. When the crew entered the forest they were greeted by a stillness deeper than death. Investigation revealed the absence of animals. Animals had been there; the signs were unmistakable: empty nests, droppings the size of green peas, spoor whose breadth and variety spoke of exodus. But as for the creatures themselves, nothing, not even an earthworm.

In 1948, between that forest and the heart of Montgomery (a distance of one and a half miles) was mostly undeveloped land. Now, connecting the town and the track is a four-lane highway, the sides of which are lined with restaurants, gasoline stations, and motels. The motels feature waterbeds and X-rated movies. You can find in almost any bar men and women who for a price will indulge the most complicated of your sexual fantasies. This in a town in which, before 1948, pornographic would have been the mispronunciation of the machine on which records are played, and a prostitute having the whole of the metropolis to herself would have starved to death. So would a dope dealer. Before the track, the very term "dope dealer" would have given birth in most people's minds to the confusing image of a man who trafficked in imbeciles. Now, of course, you can get anything you want.

Alice Simineski, who with her partner in 1960 established the drug industry in Montgomery, grew up on the east side of Syracuse, New York. Her immigrant father, bewildered by his failure to achieve the American dream, took his life by hanging the day that his wife told him she was three months pregnant with their second child. In the next five weeks, Alice's mother efficiently mourned him, buried him, and found a replacement. Her womb scraped clean by the midwife's instrument, she took up with a black man in the numbers racket. Her daughter was four years old.

For Alice, it had been an ordinary childhood. Her mother seemed happy; her stepfather was not unkind, simply, in the manner of most American fathers, not inclined to display affection. In fourteen years he had touched Alice only once, and that by accident. As a provider, however, he was blameless. There was enough money for her mother to put aside something for her daughter's future; Alice had thought vaguely of becoming a schoolteacher, but by the time she was old enough to go to college, the public schools in Syracuse had succeeded in disabusing her of this notion. Still, she was aware of the need to do something with her life, or, as her stepfather had said, "to make something of herself." This expression had charmed Alice in a way that its companion "pull yourself up by your own bootstraps" had not. A literal child, she had attempted the latter and found the levitation it suggested impossible to achieve. But making something of herself—that was another story. The words encouraged the movement of her hands; she would knead her face into different faces, rearrange her limbs, experiment with make-up. Not content with her mother's wardrobe, she dressed in her stepfather's clothes, from underwear to hat. One day he came into a room to find her stretched across dining-room chairs five feet apart. "Gal, what you doing?"

"I'm a bridge," she said.

The warmth of his laughter startled her. It was rich and strong and brown, like him, and he carried it with him to the kitchen. On his way past, his hand accidentally touched her head.

Although she was in no way gifted, Alice was perceptive enough, and what she saw occurring openly in the schoolyard and on street corners, what she witnessed passing over the counter in pharmacies and advertised in magazines told her that Americans would do anything in an effort to avoid life. Why not tap this market? She used her "future" fund to buy her first shipment of marijuana and diet pills, and to set up a system of distribution. Her stepfather was outraged, but her mother pointed out to him the salaries of teachers as compared to the money from an occupation that paid more and was less hazardous. Besides, owning your own business—supplying products people wanted and, in the process, providing jobs—was in the best of American traditions.

Alice arrived in Montgomery with a partner, a man named Hosea Malone, or Hose-ee, as people there call him. While Alice, who developed a passion for chocolate, resembled a species of miniature whale, Hosea is short, thin, with skin the complexion of a spoiled mushroom. He'd been an elevator operator in a hotel Alice stayed at on frequent trips to Manhattan, and, against everyone's advice, she had fallen in love with him, taken him in, and eventually made him a full partner. She fell in love with him for three reasons: the way he did not allow his eyes to avoid her face when he talked to her, the way he wore hats, and his privacy. There are people whose privacy you recognize because they inform you of it, or because they are cold and stand-offish. Their privacy makes you uncomfortable; you never know when you are wandering into their space. As a result, you are required to do your own computation, one that usually results in a distance you're forced to shout across. Alice had come to understand that these people are masking insecurity and powerlessness. They do not command the space around them, precisely because they are unsure of how much they need, and whether, if gained, they can handle it.

Hosea was different. There was an aura about him, almost visible, a magnetic field that, if it had vibrated any more rapidly, would have turned to light. There was nothing dangerous about it; it did not imply even the mildest of warnings. It was more like the kind of statement made by a good-looking man when he fingers his wedding band in a room full of women.

Overweight and unattractive, Alice had characterized herself as a woman who did not listen to her heart. It was not until she began living with Hosea that she realized her heart had never spoken. The only impediment in their personal relationship was Hosea's refusal to make love to her, although he would sometimes consent to lie naked in her arms. This occurred when he was upset and allowed her to comfort him, or when he read in her wistful, isolated eyes her unspoken need to be held. There is no record of what levels of frustration Alice reached on these occasions, but if they were painful, they did not diminish her affection. Hosea was considerate and honest,

6

he was not ashamed to be seen with her in public, and, despite the lack of sex, he treated her as a woman, never forgetting holidays or her birthday, or the date that he'd first looked, unflinchingly, into her bloated face. All of this was so gratifying to Alice that she did not mention her disappointment when he stopped wearing hats.

Hosea had been an exemplary member of the black community in Montgomery, a deacon in the church, husband to a fine, brown-skinned woman named Meredith, and father to a half-dozen daughters. Although Hosea loved his girls, he craved a son who would carry on his name, whom he could teach to catch a ball, and fish, and build things. He and Meredith prayed for this to happen, but when the prayer was answered, it seemed the mocking reply of a God who was less than merciful. Hosea, Jr. was born blind, with a head that would eventually grow to the size of a small watermelon.

This event caused to be born in Hosea's heart the most nagging of human questions: Why? He was God-fearing, long-suffering. Why? He'd been building an addition to his house on evenings and weekends; now he laid his hammer down. Why did he slave so hard on that construction crew? He decreased his output, gave up working overtime, and, at the core of his idleness, came face to face with a paralyzing realization—that life had no meaning, that it was empty, that he had filled it with the fathering of children and his obsession with work, and, in the few hours left between those and sleeping, with the church. None of the tremendous energy he exerted *went* anyplace, nothing could be affected, all was chance. Despite his paralysis, he felt a momentary triumph. He'd done it. He'd peeped life's hole card. Then he began to be afraid.

In silence, Hosea and life regarded one another—he confused and frightened; life just there, like a rock, or sky, or old age, calm, unmoved by the fact its existence had finally been recorded with an impact that stopped hearts, too cool to even say "I told you so." Hosea understood his options. He could rail against it or he could close his eyes. Or he could just stand there, looking.

One Sunday afternoon when the baby was four months old, Hosea sat in his living room. He was wearing his favorite hat, a gray Dobbs that had cost him seven dollars in 1935. Now, as if to hide from what he saw, he pulled the brim down over his eyes. Outside, it was raining; the children infested the house, running, screaming, leaving toys, shoes, and pages of the Sunday comics in their wake. Meredith roamed the kitchen singing at the top of her lungs, making dinner. Their youngest daughter, Donna Lee, a two-year-old, finger in her mouth, stood in the middle of the floor unceremoniously peeing on the rug. Hosea was watching with the expression of a man who has just missed the last train out of Poughkeepsie when the need smashed him in the chest. Sweat collected on his forehead; his skin crawled. This was a longing he had never felt, and the discovery left him baffled. He needed privacy. He needed to be alone, to be responsible to no one but himself, to have space that he could turn in without bumping against the edges of things. Stifling panic, he struggled to his feet; chest burning, he negotiated the room littered with children and stood in the kitchen doorway watching the slimness of Meredith's legs. He made himself think about how those legs opened for him, how her ankles locked around his waist when her love came down, but when his heart began to race, it was not with desire, but terror. He lurched into the bedroom, stood over the crib where the hideous child lay sleeping, a fist in one blind eye. Hosea considered how seldom the infant cried, as if, aware of the problems he'd caused, he was trying to keep a low profile. Hosea wanted to vomit.

He wanted to inhale one unimpeded breath. He retraced his steps, went out the front door, down the porch steps into the yard. He lifted his face into the rain, into the gray, indifferent sky, and let it crush him.

"Look at Daddy," the girls said, giggling. "Silly Daddy."

Meredith came to the door holding a long wooden spoon. "Hose-ee," she called. "You'll catch your death of cold, man. We ain't got no money to bury you."

There was concern in her voice, but Hosea heard only the laughter. He slumped back into the house, in his head a pleading directed at Meredith, the kids: *Please. Don't touch me.* When Meredith put her hand out to caress his face, he slapped her across the room.

He left the next morning. Three weeks later, in the hour before midnight, he came back. That was the night before the Monday morning they began clearing trees for the racetrack. He stayed for twenty-seven minutes, which was all the time it took him to collect his clothes and his son. Then he went away again, leaving people to wonder what kind of care a man could provide for a blind baby with a watermelon head.

When Hosea returned to Montgomery twelve years later, wearing wine-colored shoes, a silk suit, and hatless, he had a small fortune in dope taking up the trunk of his two-toned Chrysler, and Alice, the floor around her strewn with chocolate-bar wrappers, taking up most of the back seat.

CHAPTER
2

Montgomery is still a pretty place. Named without the least exercise of imagination, Broadway is, nevertheless, broad, about four Cadillac lengths wide. As yet, no one has cut down the trees that line it, and at the height of a summer's day, the shadows of those trees meet like old friends in the center of the avenue.

Domed and columned, replete with stone lions regal in their immobility, the courthouse sits at the crest of a sloping hill, the lawn that stretches indolently down to Broadway so green it appears at first glance artificial. Where there once were stores that sold overalls and nails by the weight, there are now boutiques featuring designer jeans and jewelry interchangeable between the sexes. There are two black barbershops. The five-and-ten, in which as a child Gerald Fletcher could buy for a nickel enough candy to ensure a stomach ache, is now a McDonald's and the site of an Off-Track Betting emporium; in neither place can you get anything for a dime. The Key Food grocery has matured into a supermarket the size of a football field and moved across the street to the north side of Broadway next to the X-rated theater. Taking its place is the black-owned Duewright Funeral Parlor, business for which is brisk.

In the streets, black policemen regulate traffic with an impunity indistinguishable from that of their white colleagues, and apprehend, with a lack of frequency alarming to black residents and white, those, grown legion, who break the law. Perhaps this concern with crime is the reason people don't stop and chat along Broadway the way they used to. They all seem to be moving with a furtive quickness, like that of businessmen leaving pornographic bookstores. Except the teenagers. They, black and white, the former bearing only the slightest resemblance to their grandparents, congregate at corners, where they smoke marijuana and listen to music that their elders find unfathomable. They all seem to be waiting for something to happen, but it is a waiting without expectation. They wear the expression seen on the faces of workers waiting for paint to dry, the attainment of which will mean the tedious application of a second coat.

The population of Montgomery in 1948 was 4,500, about 150 of whom were Negroes. Their presence represented the fallout from the migratory patterns that mark the history of black people in the United States, patterns created almost always by calamity. The first group came to Montgomery in the years just before World War I; the next two followed hard on one another's heels: one around 1933, during the Great Depression, the other in the early years of World War II. They came from places whose names had the kind of elegance associated with red dresses and gold teeth. Northern white people didn't know how to name places. Woodridge, Fallsburgh, Poughkeepsie. What kinds of names were they that you couldn't roll them on the tongue, bite down hard and spit, sing them? Call a place Slidell, Zachary, Bolatusha, Natchez, or Valdasee. Then, when you said a name, you'd be saying something.

They came north, these Negroes who understood the power and responsibility inherent in naming things, for the same reasons black people had been coming north since Reconstruction: the hope for jobs and a better life for their children. Most of those who ended up in Montgomery had spent a brief time in Philadelphia, Newark, or New York City. Many black people had adapted to these environments. Having lived all their lives with music, they simply switched to the upbeat urban tempo and began to improvise. But others found themselves too often longing for a piece of earth to dig the toes of a bare foot in, for sight of a tree that had not been whipped into submission. For these, the requisites for a place to live were that it be rural, that it be northern, and that it have jobs. Montgomery had all of these. It was in the heart of a resort area, and black men and women cooked and cleaned and waited on tables in the hotels. Later, the ground was broken for the superhighway to New York City, and the men took their places in construction crews, diverting the courses of streams, swinging hammers through heat and cold, through gray days and days delirious with sunshine, easing, with the gentlest of fingers, cylinders of dynamite into fissures of rock.

They considered themselves, even by the standards black people can set for one another, to be extraordinary. They were thrifty and industrious. They raised their children to have respect for their elders and a fear of God, and the church operated at the center of their lives. None of them, however, discussed with their children (some because they never thought about it, others because they did) the fact that they were an African people and, through little fault of their own, were recently descended from slaves. Nor were the children aware that social scientists made a living demonstrating their inferiority, or to what extent they and their parents operated in the national imagination as the ultimate in the comic, and the darkest, most labyrinthine symbol of evil.

There was no *Jet Magazine* in 1948, no *Negro Digest*, no *Essence*. Black-studies programs were still some twenty years away. For black (and white) schoolchildren

12

in Montgomery, nearly a generation would pass before they seriously questioned what they had been taught: the majority of people in the world were white, and the stone of "civilization" had been hewn and polished by men of European descent. In a bit of surgery that put organ transplants to shame, Egypt was carved out of Africa. The vast Chinese landscape was nothing more than a theater for the indomitable Marco Polo, peopled by creatures so given to overpopulation that they had barely managed to invent noodles and gunpowder. Although every black person could tell you who Booker T. Washington was, few knew what W. E. B. Du Bois stood for, and those who'd heard of Marcus Garvey thought he'd been a madman and a thief. Nobody subscribed to the *Amsterdam News* or the *Pittsburgh Courier*; they read the *Daily News*, in which, for the longest time, black people were featured in two places only: on the back page as athletes and on the front page as crooks.

These were images that had to be resisted, and in a series of contradictory ways, black people in Montgomery did so. Negroes were comic and evil? They would be serious and good. They viewed their relationship to the world as one between "it" and "us." If they came to exaggerate that world's viciousness, it was because they feared that to do otherwise would leave their children susceptible to disillusion. So they did not teach the children who they were and where they'd come from; they taught them what they couldn't be and the places they must not hope to enter. The politics of this condition were never raised. The world was wicked less because of white men than because of its failure to embrace Christ. Only the qualifying word "less" measured their inability to deny all of their experience.

In this system of opposites they had erected, there was the inevitable attraction. Driven into the arms of

Christ, repelled by the white world, they were, nevertheless, drawn to it, shared some of its values, chose from it the symbols of success and beauty to covet in their not-so-secret hearts. Prosperous white men were held up as models. Children were not to "act like niggers"; neither were they to look like "them." Washing thoroughly behind one's ears and using oils and lotions to conquer the ash that visited between the fingers and attacked the knees were achievable. But this was not the essence of what looking like a nigger meant. The traveling salesman who sold skin lighteners did a steady business in Montgomery, thanks to the husbands who used their wives' ointments on the sly. Women practiced breathing through their mouths so their nostrils wouldn't flare and call attention to their magnificent African noses. Several boys severely burned their scalps with hair-straightening compound, the major ingredient of which was lye.

In 1948, most black people in Montgomery lived on the southern outskirts of town about a mile and a half from the courthouse. They occupied an assortment of frame houses built in the last half of the nineteenth century, when Montgomery was little more than a general store and a blacksmith's shop. By the time the town became the county seat, in 1910, the white people who'd originally lived in those houses had moved into the bigger ones near the foot of the courthouse hill.

Back then, black people in Montgomery did not suffer from a lack of adequate housing. The structures they lived in, having been created for whites, were well made, built with a concern for privacy. As the black population grew and more houses were built, the privacy gave way to closeness, but in the beginning there was at least one window a person could look through without seeing his neighbor's chimney.

14

When there were enough of them to support the effort, they built a church in the field across the road from Norman Fillis's house. White people marveled at the speed with which it was constructed (it was completed in six months, and was white, like the courthouse), and they shook their heads when they discovered that the pastor, Melinda Mclain, was a woman. Eventually they grew used to her, and by the time she began dying her hair peacock blue, they were so respectful of the size of her bank account and the bloc of votes she controlled that they pretended not to notice.

There was so much that wasn't in 1948. Zacharias had not demonstrated his gentleness. The beautiful gray-eyed girl was still in North Carolina; she'd neither fallen in love with Gerald Fletcher nor lost her hand. The naked man with flowers decorating his penis had yet to invade Abigal Fletcher's kitchen, and patricide was a word only English teachers knew.

There was no black barber in Montgomery in 1948. No beautician, no black undertaker. Women did one another's hair and the children's; the men traveled four miles to the black barbershop in South Fallsburgh, where they sat around a potbellied stove, drank soda pop, and swapped tales. But while hair grew on the heads of men and boys, and stubbornly outlasted the straightening effects of hot combs, not a black person died. In itself, this last fact is not exceptional. Christopher Silas was the oldest black person in town; he was eighty-two in 1948. The black people in Montgomery back then seldom smoked or drank, since most belonged to a church that forbade it. They didn't have television, although they listened to "Inner Sanctum" and the "Lone Ranger" on the radio. Men and women alike wore long underwear in the winter and kept something on their heads until July. A cautious people, who found it difficult to experiment with anything so different as another brand of tuna fish, they had succeeded in avoiding all but the most minor of accidents. The illnesses that afflicted them were ordinary; the children endured mumps and measles and chicken pox, the adults their periodic colds, the old folks the rheumatism and diminished memory which are to be expected. That none of them had died by 1948 was not strange. What was strange was how so many of them began dying in 1949. This rash of deaths could only mean the presence of evil in their midst, Pastor Mclain said, and the black church-going people began to point a collective finger toward the racetrack. Pastor Mclain's instincts told her that the track had nothing to do with it, but just to be on the safe side of the Lord's wrath, she strengthened the dress code for women, banning open-toed shoes and short-sleeved dresses. She had everyone go on a thirty-day fast, during which they ingested only soda crackers and orange juice. In case she'd missed anything, she called in an evangelist from South Carolina, who ran a two-week revival meeting so intense it left everybody limp.

What no one knew except the perpetrator and Norman Fillis was that the first black person who went to meet his Maker was not counted among the deceased, and that he had been sent along his way by the hand of a murderer in 1948. The murderer wasn't telling, not for the obvious reasons, but because she'd forgotten. Norman Fillis's reasons for keeping quiet were more complicated. In his unassuming way, he'd lost his mind.

CHAPTER 3

Norman lived in a large house that had been converted into a three-family dwelling; in 1947, his in-laws occupied the two apartments. Set some 120 feet back from Little Pond Road, directly across from the church and diagonally across from the house Hosea would leave unfinished, the building was distinguished by the magnificent pair of oak trees that grew at the front edge of the property and formed an arch under which the sidewalk passed.

Norman was thirty-eight in 1947, a tall, fair-skinned man with remarkably intense eyes, and a shy, engaging smile. Married to Claire, a woman who always seemed to be pulling her dress down from where it had bunched at her ample hips, he had produced three children, all of whom, without the least effort on their part, managed to disappoint him.

Norman was conscientious about his family and faithful to his God, but in neither relationship was there any passion. This he reserved for trees, all kinds of which but one he loved beyond description. He loved most the huge oaks and towering evergreens, saplings thinner than his arm, the maples that grew sunlight and fire in the fall. Driven by the human need to believe in things greater than himself, Norman felt that trees were a symbol of divinity. A practicing Christian since 1930, he still found the question of the Godhead incomprehensible. He did not allow this to shake him; he was well aware that faith was the belief in things unseen, not understood. But it helped to be able to see, and he could see trees. Moreover,

17

they had been here before him, would remain after he was gone, and were finite enough to comprehend. It was not a question of heresy for Norman; he used trees to prove the existence of God.

By extension, for they were the creatures which lived where trees chose to congregate, he had an affection for wild animals. For him, an interlude of recreation was to sit for an hour in the wood and feed squirrels and chipmunks from the palm of his hand. In time, bigger game came to trust him, the porcupine and woodchuck. He lugged blocks of salt to the stream where deer drank in winter, and the six feeding stations in his back yard permanently disrupted the migratory patterns of several species of birds.

By most definitions, Norman was ordinary. Two events occurred in 1948 that irrevocably changed him. One was his discovery of the properties of fire. The other was the discovery of the shape of his head.

Six inches of snow had fallen the night before. As Norman walked to work this February morning, the world seemed created from blue sky and sparkling powder, soiled only by the elevated storage tanks that stalked the landscape like prehistoric beasts. On the hill across from the tanks, like black girls in silver dresses, stood the motionless, snow-covered trees. Charged with excitement, dying to strut and preen, but knowing that movement would shatter their perfection, they called out to him: "Look at us. See how beautiful we are."

A car was coming from behind him, slowed; Lee Madison offered a ride. Norman said no, thank you, and watched as Lee drove on. The car's movement made him aware of his own, and he stopped for what he thought was a moment and allowed the stillness to swallow him. Five minutes later, with the distorted perception of a man suffering from jet lag, knowing he'd lost something, but not remembering what, he began to walk.

He could see as he approached the curve of the hill an intensification of light. Still, when he reached the curve, he was not prepared for the explosion. The hill had blunted the sun's impact; now the slope precipitously fell away and the world was shards of blue and white and silver bathed in gold. The beauty gave him an ache in his groin.

At first he thought the brilliant light was at fault. But by the time he passed the freight house, where heavily bundled men were removing lumber from boxcars, he was not sure what caused the impression that something smooth, but heavy, was sitting on his head. It felt as if he were balancing a paperweight, a rectangular piece of glass that weighed about a pound. He turned his head to one side in an abrupt gesture, then forward in a violent nod. The weight stayed in the same place, defying gravity; his hat fell off. He ran a hand across his head and bent to retrieve his hat.

When he got to school, he went straight to the boiler room and added coal to the furnace. Then he sat down on a milk crate, opened a Thermos of coffee, and thought about the weight. It seemed to be about three inches by five inches and about an inch thick. It was not unbearable. What did it mean? He took a sip of coffee and began to pray, less for relief from the burden than for an answer to the mystery. The prayer made him feel better, but the mystery remained. Sighing, he went to check the furnace. When he opened the door, he was met by a blast of heat, and he stepped back, then bent to look inside. The fire was blue and yellow and red, festive, raging. Norman had been looking inside this furnace for twelve years; today the fire struck him as beautiful. He thought: The flames

19

are dancing colored teeth in the black mouth of the furnace. The thought touched him like an unexpected gift. When he closed the furnace, he discovered the symmetry of gray flecks in the cast-iron door. Looking around the room, he found the indolent angle at which the broom leaned against the wall, the mop like an abandoned woman near the sink. There was a taste of pomegranate in his mouth, fading; he sucked at it, and opened the furnace again. The taste grew stronger, flooded his mouth with saliva and sweetness. Fire has taste, he thought, interested. He looked around the room again, the details of which sharpened and leaped at him. "Fire," he said, "makes me see." Excited now, he repeated himself. "It makes me see." That this in no way affected the weight on his head did not, at that moment, matter.

Like a man with a new car who uses it sparingly, to preserve, not the car, but the quality of his excitement, Norman did not play with fire any more that day at school. He did his job with the expression of a man with a pocketful of found money; from time to time he patted his pocket to see if it was still there. He never paused to consider to whom it had belonged. That he had found it did not necessarily mean that it had been lost. He knew, with a certainty so quiet even deer couldn't detect it, that it was his all along, that someone, or something, had placed it in his path for him to claim.

At home, after dinner, he began to experiment. In the kitchen he struck several matches and held them at varying lengths from his face. Then, one by one, registering the impact, he lit the four burners on top of the range. Finally, he got down on his knees and lit the oven, turned the flame to broil, and peered into the stove's belly. The larger the flame, the sweeter the taste—the greater the change in his vision. Yet there was something appealing about the smaller fires; in their diminished power was a soothing touch. For five minutes he stared into the oven, longer than he'd looked at fire this close up in all his life. He began to feel an irritation, a jangling of overstimulated nerves. As he leaned back, frowning, Claire came into the kitchen.

"What you doing with the stove on?"

He tiptoed along the edge of lying, telling the truth, but smiling a sickly grin as he did so. "Looking at fire."

Claire, who'd gotten what she came for, left, shaking her head. "You the *strangest* man."

In his easy chair, across from his children, who were huddled around the radio listening to "Amos 'n' Andy," Norman pretended to read the newspaper. The weight sat uncomfortably on his head, but he wouldn't think of it. He preferred to consider the effect on his nervous system of his sustained looking into fire. Was it the nature of the flame that caused this, or was length of time the factor? Was there a fire soft enough, yet strong enough, into which he could look forever, maintaining the intensity of taste and seeing, or was this mystery—like that of sex— simply too powerful to be endured for extended periods of time? What about bonfires after they had burned down to just before the embers? Brush fires? What would a torch do, a stave of wood wrapped in kerosene-soaked rags carried across an open field in pitch-black darkness? There leaped into his imagination a series of images, fragmented, yet connected, all of them with such stunning clarity as to suggest an experience recently his own. A snatch of song, the clank of metal. FIRE. A stake, a black man burning, stains redder than flame where his thighs met, a baying hound, the scream of a woman—above it all the moon, full, like a white man's mocking eye. He, Norman, who hid there as witness, was discovered, and now behind him in violent pursuit, shouting "Run, nigger," came the men who demanded nothing less from him than his life. He could not outrun them; the realization came to burn like sickness at his asshole. When he felt their breath hot and sour on his neck, he gave one mighty leap and began to fly, soaring toward the moon, that eye, once mocking, now wide in disbelief.

Then the disturbing images were gone, or, rather, Norman dismissed them. As lifelike as the experience had been, it was clear that it was not his own. He knew that lynching had gone on a long time ago in the South, but that didn't happen any more. And he'd never seen one. A little annoyed that the images had taken him away from his research, yet wondering what it would be like to fly, he returned to his inventory, only to discover that he'd nearly exhausted the possibilities. Campfires. House fires. He remembered candles.

He shuffled into the kitchen, took down the box of five-inch candles from above the sink, and lit one with a trembling hand. The flame around the tiny wick burst into perfect being, soft, illuminating. He held the candle the length of his outstretched arm from his face, brought it closer, and found himself dangerously close to crying. He felt like Christopher Columbus; he saw the face of his first love, Carrie, the scarlet ribbon in her hair. Candlelight. He wanted to be alone with it in a dark place, the door closed against intrusion. He carried the box into the bathroom, locked the door, and began to draw a bath. Then he arranged the candles around the room: on the sink, the top of the toilet, the edges of the tub. Ceremoniously, he undressed, folding each item of clothing carefully and laying it on the floor near the door. When he was naked, he lit the candles, turned the light off, and eased himself into the steaming water. He shut the faucet and leaned back against the cold porcelain surface, the riot of pomegranate in his mouth, his eyes alive with seeing, the tiny flames throwing their shadows across the walls, the tub, the

22

water. What peace. He watched as his penis, limp between his legs, stiffened, rose cautiously to bob above his thighs. He could see the profusion of blood vessels and nerve endings beneath its skin.

"Daddy?"

He didn't answer.

"Daddy, I got to go to the bathroom."

It was George, his youngest. If he didn't answer, maybe he would go away.

"I got to go *bad*."

"Go upstairs to your Aunt Lilly."

"I got to go bad, Daddy."

"What I say?"

He closed his eyes, sank into the water. He began to dream of a full moon and a black man burning. He began to fly. . . .

"Norman!" She was banging on the door, rattling the doorknob. The water was tepid. The candles had burned halfway down their lengths.

"What?"

"I need to use the bathroom."

"*I'm* in the bathroom."

"You been in there half an hour."

"Go upstairs."

"I'm a woman grown, man, in her own house. I ain't going to nobody else's bathroom. Open this door."

He dug both hands into his head, squeezed until it hurt. He was outraged, feeling like a ten-year-old rather than a man who had rights and the power to exercise them. This surprised him; rage of any kind had never been his style, and he was stunned when it refused, despite his bidding, to go on about its business.

"You hear me?"

"*Just a minute.*"

Rage swaggered on the street corner of his mind.

"What you gonna do, man?" Norman put a headlock on him, wrestled him to the pavement. Growling, he stepped from the tub, wrapped a towel around his waist. He turned on the light and blew out all the candles. Then he opened the door. Claire was scowling, arms folded, bent slightly from the waist.

"What you doing in here? What's burning?" She pushed past him. "What these candles for? You trying to set the house on fire? You got another house we can live in?"

He didn't answer. Rage writhed beneath him, playing the dozens on his manhood. Norman strained to hold him down, to preserve what was left of his inner peace. But though he managed to contain the rage, peace vanished with his ability to see the bones of Claire's skull, whiter than snow or heat, delicate, the mass of mouse-colored brain tissue swimming in its juice.

"Edison do all that inventing for nothing? You got to try to burn the house down?"

"Go on to the bathroom, Claire."

"I will. Soon as you get out of here." Her jaw was thrown at him, the hand on her ample hip threatened to knock him out. If he could disappear, fly away . . . He stepped into the hallway and closed the door. Shivering in the darkness, he stood there listening to her pee.

"And you need to get a haircut," Claire called. "Hair growing down the back of your neck like an African."

The weight on his head drove him into the floor. He imagined it transferred to Claire's head, and he above her, pushing with both hands, squeezing her into the toilet. Her legs and torso making a vee, forcing her buttocks down the narrow curved canal, deeper, now only the crown of her head showing, an inverse birthing, the triumphant flush. In the wake of Claire's departure grew a tree, tall, lean, cool, with leaves larger than his hand.

Rage shook him. "Let me up, man. Come on, let's *do* something. Kick the door down. *Smack* the bitch."

Norman began to pray.

This day marked the beginning of Norman's seeing the world. In time his vision became a burden in the way that blindness is a burden. There is not much difference between seeing everything and seeing nothing.

Since there was no one to instruct him otherwise, Norman thought of all of this as magical. The acquisition of his sight might have been achieved through magic, but the world he suddenly began to see had always been there. Blades of grass had forever grown in the fluted shapes he marveled at, flowers had always had secrets at their hearts, and insects their mystery. He was not the first to wonder at the darting, angular flight of swallows or the taste of fire. But even if he had known that there were others before him who had discovered the gift of sight, this would not have diminished his joy. That is one of the nice things about discovery. Another is that discovery is down to earth; it is not particular about where you make it. Norman made his first discovery in a boiler room. The next was in a barbershop.

CHAPTER
4

February, with uncharacteristic kindness, had turned
warm. Had he been less cautious, the midget who owned
Clean Cut Freedom Barbershop would have extinguished
the fire in the potbellied stove. Instead, he cracked the
door of the shop to let in air. Norman, wearing the weight
on his head, sat nearest the door, listening to the drip of
melting snow.

Besides the midget and Norman, three other men occupied the shop: U. L. Washington (U for Ulysses, L for
Lincoln), Lee Madison, and the Professor, a tall, dark,
pock-faced man, dishwasher at one of the hotels, dressed,
as usual, all in black. The Professor, a man in his late
fifties, was for real; he'd been a schoolteacher in Mississippi twenty-five years ago. Something had happened that
he wouldn't talk about, and he had departed that section of
the country and the classroom. Whatever it was, folks decided, must have been pretty bad. They measured this by
two things: the color of the clothes he wore, as if to mark
a perpetual mourning, and the tenacity with which he
attempted to drink himself to death. Today he was sober,
as he was every third Saturday in the month when he
came to South Fallsburgh to get his hair cut. Everyone
knew that foolishness wasn't allowed in Freedom Barbershop. On the floor near the back door was a bottle of
lye with a skull and bones on it that fairly screamed a
warning. For the hard of hearing, the midget kept a
double-barreled shotgun in his closet.

Norman searched the patterns in the worn yellow

linoleum, trying to find there an image that would hold his attention and keep him from staring into the stove. He'd spent the morning in his tub, surrounded by candles, and he didn't think he could take any more stimulation for a while. But except for a hole in the linoleum near the barber chair, the almost perfect circle of which resembled a gasping fish or an infant's sucking mouth, the floor was singularly without interest. He raised his eyes to the mirror that covered most of one wall, saw the rows of hair tonic and talcum. Above these was the image of the midget, who, standing on a box so he could reach, carefully curled a razor around U. L.'s lathered ear.

The Professor chewed a half-smoked, unlit cigar. Lee Madison, one hand wrapped around an empty soda bottle, was leaning forward, nodding enthusiastically as the midget described the current weather, assigning to it the characteristics of a cunning, low-down, just-won't-do-right woman, who, in the middle of a winter marked by ice and barren landscape, a cold so bitter it bred loneliness like garbage bred flies, would appear lush and brown and fertile, whispering that you should take your clothes off and lie down beside her, meeting your hesitation with the most lascivious promises of warmth and carnal delight.

"And if you fool enough to take them snuggies off," the midget said, referring to the long woolen underwear all of them wore, "and crawl on in the sack with Missy Weather, well, that's all she wrote. You got a icicle for a ding-a-ling and a behind won't thaw till June. Course, by that time they done throwed six feet of God's earth in your face. By then you's pushing up daisies."

"Ain't it the truth," Lee said, and recollected how, due to the exact same circumstances, the croup had eaten up his granddaddy's cousin back in 1926.

"Did you hear where they decided to build the track?" the Professor asked.

"Devil's work," U. L. said.

"They say it'll mean jobs and so forth."

The midget had responded carefully. He, like the Professor, was not a practicing Christian, but because he owned a business Christians frequented, he was respectful.

"Jobs?" U. L. snorted. "What it profit a man to gain the world, but lose his soul? Gambling's sin, brother. Says so in big black letters right up on the sign in church. Course it's kind of hard to read from a racetrack. Or a gin mill."

"Well, *brother*," the midget said, "we all serves the Lord in our own way. Ain't no need for you to try to change me. Nobody's perfect. Was so, wouldn't need the Lord. Now ain't that right?"

And he smiled and held the razor in such a way that the light reflected from it shone in U. L.'s eyes. It might have been possible to miss the warning in the midget's tone, but the one in his smile was incandescent. The air was tense until the Professor said, "As I was saying. They ain't using Golden's farm. They building it over near Honeybear Road."

Norman, who'd been dreaming of flying, looked up. "Ain't nothing but trees there."

"Why they change their mind?" Lee asked.

"Decided Golden's wasn't big enough. Track'll be sitting right on top of town."

U. L. said something, but Norman wasn't listening. He had heard, of course, the arguments supporting the track, and he was familiar with those, theological and secular, that opposed it. He had not, really, cared one way or the other. Whether it was built or not would have nothing to do with what he, or most anybody else, wanted. But why didn't they build it someplace that would not mean the destruction of trees? And what about the animals? Their homes would be destroyed, their food and water and safety. An observer of animals, Norman understood that they knew instinctively what to do when things happened according to season or cycle. But the unexpected bred two reactions only: the desire to flee, or a sickening inability to move from the spot where danger had found them. Either would result in destruction, especially to the young. Norman closed his eyes and saw them crushed beneath steel-toed boots, beneath the military treads of tractors. It would be a massacre. And who would commemorate them? Who would bury the dead?

But he knew in the next instant that neither commemoration nor burial would be necessary. Not for the animals; the trees were another story. He could not see any way he could prevent their destruction. He could, however, warn the animals. How, he did not know, yet he vowed to himself that he would find a way.

Relieved, he looked up and saw that the Professor, eyes narrowed, was watching him. Their eyes met, connected. Norman felt a force; had he known the word, he would have called it fusion. His body flooded with warmth and the feeling that he and the man dressed in black were united, one flesh, one mind. Then the Professor looked away, and the warmth came not from union, but from the stove, and he was by himself again.

For anyone but a man who had discovered the properties of fire, the power and intensity of that moment would have been frightening. Norman knew, however, that there was an explanation, which would either come to him or would not. Nothing he did or did not do would change the time or the appointed place if there was to be a revelation. That is why, in the presence of all that mystery, he could pick up a magazine from a pile on the chair next to him and, with all the casualness of a man waiting his turn in a barbershop, begin idly leafing through its pages.

None of the faces in the magazine was black. Norman seldom saw white people who looked like these: impeccably groomed, self-assured, universally smiling. He wondered where they lived. Probably in California; they all had tans.

U. L. got out of the chair, said his good-byes, and left, a righteous huff in the slant of his shoulders. Lee sat down and took his glasses off; the midget wrapped a collar of white tissue around his neck. The shop was quiet. The Professor, unlit cigar rolling in one corner of his mouth, was staring at his boots, the toes of which were covered with mud. Outside, a car went past, its chains clattering. It was warm, and the silence not uncomfortable, and Norman turned the pages of his magazine.

A Dutchboy with his finger pointed. A strange machine called a "television." An article that discussed the possibility that one day man would walk on the moon. Norman smiled. He turned another page and came upon a photograph of one of the most beautiful things he'd ever seen, a wooden head, hairless, in profile. The skull was elongated, like the skull of a newborn, the one visible eye wide, as if life had no secrets. Full lips, a hole in the earlobe. The head looked very old; the paint was chipped, areas of mottled white showed through. It reminded Norman a little of his youngest son when he'd been a baby—the large round nose, the reddish skin. Except that this figure's mouth was closed in contentment; George, who'd been colicky, had cried all the time. And though he'd been a handsome infant, George could not compare with this head's beauty.

Curious, Norman read the words at the left of the photograph:

As a work of art the painted wooden figure
shown at the right stands out among the whole

30

contents of Tutankhamun's tomb. It illustrates one of the most picturesque ancient Egyptian accounts of the initial creation: it represents the infant sun god at the moment of birth, emerging from a blue lotus that grew in a pool left by the receding waters of the primordial ocean. The features are unmistakably those of Tutankhamun, and the shape of the elongated skull is very reminiscent of the Amarna princesses who may have been his half-sisters. By having the model in his tomb, Tutankhamun, through the process of imitative magic, would have an instrument that would enable him to be reborn as the sun god every day.

Many of the words he couldn't understand, but he got the gist of the passage. He turned pages and saw items of gold and ivory, statues inlaid with stones, which even his inexperienced eye told him were priceless. There were other images of the king; one, a magnificent gold mask, looked straight at him with a calm seen only on the faces of those who possessed great power. But it was the first photograph that arrested him, and he turned to it again.

"Anybody ever hear of King Tuta . . . Tutak . . . ?"

"King Tut," the Professor answered. "The boy king. Short for Tutankhamun. Reigned 1,300 years before the birth of Christ. Husband to Ankhsenpaaten, daughter of Nefertiti."

"Nefer . . . who?"

"Nefertiti. Black queen of extraordinary beauty and intelligence."

"Where's Egypt?"

"Asia," Lee said.

"Ain't not," the midget snorted. "It's someplace near Africa."

"It *is* Africa."

"Go way from here."

"Egypt," the Professor insisted, "is in Africa."

"Then how come they ain't colored?" the midget demanded.

"They are. Different shades is all, just like us."

"They swing on trees there, too?"

The Professor shook his head, less in denial than in exasperation. "Quiet as it's kept, Lee, folks in Africa don't swing on trees. They been too busy building empires."

"Empires?"

"If I'm lying, I'm flying," the Professor said. "Believe it or no."

Norman was aware that he was descended from an African people, but the knowledge generated no more interest than the fact that he was related to Adam and Eve. Being African was not something the black people he knew referred to with regularity or pride. For him, Africa existed not as a vast continent staggering in its history and diversity, but as a country of jungles and black savages, who, in their Godlessness, dined on human flesh. Because of this perception he'd never seriously entertained questions of his origins. This was, after all, 1948, before Alex Haley had fired the curiosity of the world, and when the search for roots in America was the province of inbred New England families and genealogists who toiled in sunless rooms. Family trees were the only variety Norman had no interest in.

But now the question of where he'd come from glowed like a neon sign in his brain, and he sat like a man who'd seen yet another vision, staring at the glorious likeness of the infant king. Could he, Norman, descended from Africans, be related to such beauty? And if he was, how could this connection be determined, through what process could he learn the truth?

The voice spoke to him in a frequency so rapid he

felt needles in his ears. *I know*, it said. There was a pause, a modulation. The erect hairs along his arms collapsed back against his skin.

Talk to me, the voice said.

Norman wanted to say, "How do I find out where I comes from?" but other words, unbidden, filled his head. *I have dreams*, he said.

What kind?

Of flying. A burning colored man. And when I looks at fire, I sees things.

What do you see now?

Norman looked up. The Professor, legs crossed, pulled a book of matches from his jacket pocket and lit his cigar. In the glow of the match flame were revealed the once broken cheekbone, healed, but a bone scar as jagged as a permanent bolt of lightning, a circle of rope burn around his neck, beneath the matted pubic hair the bruises, discolored still.

How? Norman asked.

A lynch mob.

But you live.

I was saved by a man who could fly.

Norman collided with his dream. He wanted to say, "Can I fly?" but again the words were different. *How do I find out where I comes from?*

You'll discover the way. There is someone you must protect. Someone to pass on to what you will know.

Something snapped. The Professor stubbed out what remained of his cigar. Lee climbed out of the chair, brushing hair from his shoulders, and Norman, in a daze, took his place.

"See you in church in the morning," Lee said as he left, and Norman nodded, the muscle of his mind fixed in a warm, moist grip around the exchange with the Professor. He had a mission. Someone to protect, to pass on his knowledge to.

33

"How you want it?" the midget asked, wrapping the sheet around him. "Sides close? Half off the top?"

The inspiration set him to trembling. For a moment he couldn't get the words out; then they came with a rush. "Take it all off."

The midget peered at him. "You talk to your wife about this?"

"All of it."

"You the boss."

Norman closed his eyes. As his hair went, he felt the weight on his head diminish, until it was gone. Excitement sat like emptiness in his stomach, primed the pump of his heart. When the midget had wiped the shaving cream from his skull, he tapped Norman on the shoulder. "Okay, sport, you can open your eyes now."

Norman looked into the mirror. At first he was struck by the difference in color. His skull was lighter than the rest of him, almost white. He ran a tentative hand across the surface and rejoiced. So smooth, like the skin of infants, like the insides of Claire's thighs, dusted with talcum, on their wedding night. He turned to profile and found in the mirror the shape that he'd fallen in love with. He stared, and whispered, "It's beautiful."

The midget grunted. "It's different. What you think, Professor?"

"Distinguished."

"The weight's gone."

"Well," the midget said, gesturing to the clots of hair on the floor, "you had a headful."

Norman slipped from the chair, paid, and stood admiring himself in the mirror. Then he turned to look at the Professor, who moved toward the chair, on his face nothing but the most ordinary smile. Their eyes met, without recognition, without force.

Norman put his hat on, covering all that beauty, and

shrugged into his coat. "Good day, gentlemen," he said, formally, and they, looking at him as if to say "Doesn't he take the cake?" mimicked his mood, responding, "Good day." They watched as he squared his shoulders and stepped into the improbable weather, carrying his head like a precious gift.

CHAPTER
5

An almanac from the period says that on a certain Sunday evening in March 1948, the moon was seventeen hours past its fullness, the clouds were cirrostratus, and a wind from the northwest blew at eleven miles an hour with gusts up to twenty-two. The weather that had turned warm in February had lingered except for one three-day period of plummeting mercury and a heavy rain that had turned freakishly to snow. That was a week ago, and now, with daily temperatures flirting with seventy, what patches of snow had not melted lay like sores festering on a sleeping earth.

It was the conviction of weathermen that no more snow would fall that season, that there would be an early and temperate spring, and, with an accuracy uncommon to that profession, this proved to be the case. Based upon that prediction, the crews had moved some of the machinery to the doorstep of the forest, which, in the morning, they would begin to clear.

Though the wind and clouds at times decreased its wattage, there was moonlight enough for Norman to see from the hill all that lay below him: the patches of snow, the watchman's trailer with a light in the window, and the forest, a mass of huddled shadows, like beseiged villagers braced for the final assault. To the left of the trailer, stretching into the night like the ranks of an invading army, sat the trucks and bulldozers, a solitary crane. In the morning they would begin to cut the trees. Norman felt the grief rise in his throat; involuntarily, he moaned.

But he pushed past the grief, for there was nothing he could do to save the trees. The animals, however, must not be allowed to die.

Now that he was here, had fashioned an excuse for Claire ("I'm going for a walk. Don't wait up for me"), his task loomed before him with an immensity that shook his self-belief. His stomach turned over; perspiration visited the surface of his skin. Then, so radiant he could feel its heat, the words "It will come to you; you will know," flashed like a comet across the dark screen of his mind.

He looked out over the scene and gathered himself, muscles clenched, breath held like a man about to scream, or to leap from a precipice. Then he hurled his silent voice into the forest, not in words, but in images like those found in the canvases of revolutionary Russian painters: giant men with tools dripping blood, machines drunk and insensible with their opportunity to destroy. He created the joyful sounds of birds around a pool clearer than any window; deer lay at its edges watching their reflections in the water. He drenched this scene with a sunlight so rare it could have been a standard for currency; served, with a sweep of his hand, bees and butterflies, the last of which moved with the grace and abandonment of children. Then, with the unerring instinct of an artist, he moved away from excess, fashioned, using only sand and rock and tree stump, a wasteland writhing beneath the medallion of a stark and murderous sun.

And he felt it when the animals heard him. Felt the dilation of the owl's eyes, the uncoiling of the snake, the ear of the doe cocking. Felt them as they moved to awaken those still sleeping, the tap at the rock, the scratch at the bowels of the tree, the cold, moist nose nuzzled into the brush. The birds fluttered from their branches, squirrels crept from knotholes, from beneath the mossy stones slithered the earthworms and the slugs.

There were the young, sleep in their eyes. There the wounded, and those sick with disease, and those afflicted by nothing more than the accumulation of age. Females swollen with litter moved with a cautious, lumbering gait. From limb nest and thicket nest, from the hollows of trees, the sure of hand and mouth gathered the eggs, brown, blue, and white, speckled, tranquil in their curving. To transport the sick and the old, and for the unhatched eggs, stretchers of branch and leaf were hastily constructed. The six chipmunks who'd been sent to sweep the area returned, prodding before them the grumbling groundhog, who insisted he had two weeks left to sleep.

And when they were ready, the owl, because of her night vision, signaled the way, and they began to move. One line of two ranks, which, despite the suddenness of formation, despite the young and unborn and infirm, was orderly, so disciplined it would have warmed a general's heart.

Norman did not wait for the evacuation to be complete. He began the walk back home, exhilarated, but so exhausted his feet dragged. If only he could fly, he'd be home in a minute. With a feeling he hadn't experienced since he'd discovered the shape of his head, the thought came to him: Suppose he could fly. How did he know he couldn't, since he'd never tried? Summoning all that remained of his strength, he broke into a run. When he'd built up a full head of steam, he leaped and began flapping his arms. A second later, laughing at himself, he came back down to earth.

When he reached the oil storage tanks on Freight House Drive, he moved at a forty-five-degree angle behind the company offices toward the narrow path that provided a shortcut to Little Pond Road. Impassable in the dead of winter, when snow choked and hid it from view, the moonlit trail sliced in half the mile he would have had to walk. The path ended at the rear of Hosea's house; from there he was no more than one hundred yards from his front door.

As he approached, he could see through the leafless branches the lights in Hosea's living room. Moving with the ease and silence of a man who is at home in the woods, he went past the last trees and came to a tangle of blueberry bushes, which grew as high as his head. There he stopped, alert, cautious. A shape was moving in the shadows of Hosea's yard; Norman's instincts told him it was human. Someone was breathing with exertion; he heard a thump, a slicing of dirt with something metal, the whisper made by a shower of soil. Carefully, he edged closer, sent his right eye curving around the bush. There, in the imperfect moonlight, was Meredith, paused for the moment, leaning against a shovel, the blade of which was plunged into the earth. With a singleness of purpose Norman could almost smell, she began to dig again. She was in the dress she'd worn to church that evening, a long, dark-green woolen affair with white cuffs and collar. The wind gusted and gathered the skirt tight against her thighs. Her hair was pulled back from her face, tied with a ribbon the color of her dress. On her feet were black patent-leather slippers.

Puzzled, Norman knelt there in the darkness. What did she plan to do with that hole, take something out of it or put something in? He looked around the yard. A wheelbarrow lay on its side, across from it a child's abandoned doll, its pink plastic nakedness lewd in the milky light. His eyes roamed the earth and caught something in the shadow cast by Meredith's body. He squinted, trying to make it out. When she moved a little, he saw that the object was a small red rubber ball. Her movement also revealed the entirety of the mound of earth she'd created, and he saw, protruding from behind it, what looked like the corner of a blanket.

None of it answered his questions. He scratched the

itch that had attacked the small of his back, changed his position slightly to ease the growing aches in his thighs. Meredith, the hole finished, laid her shovel down, moved around the mound of earth, and bent. When she stood, Norman saw that she held the blanket in her arms, or, rather, she cradled whatever it was that the blanket wrapped. She knelt before the hole, held the burden for a long moment. Then she placed it in the hole. As she did so, a corner of the blanket fell away, and Norman saw what it had hidden.

Startled, he stood, his head crashing against the bush. There was no suddenness in Meredith's motion, nor fear, not even curiosity, just the slow, measured turning of her head. Their eyes met someplace between them in the moonlight, joined with a sound like that of a bolt being thrown to barricade a door. Then she stood, picked up the shovel, and began to fill the hole. In the arc of her shoulders was an indifference to the presence of a witness. Even if she'd cared, there was no way for her to know what was assaulting Norman's punch-drunk mind: *this* might be his sign, she the person he was to protect and eventually pass on to his knowledge. Certainly she needed protection, a woman with seven children, abandoned by her husband, and who now had a secret, the divulging of which would mean her certain doom. Was Meredith the chosen one? His mind spun with the clicks of weights falling into the cylinders of a combination lock; he tugged at the door, but the safe where the answer was kept would not open.

She was finished now, tamping the earth with shoes unsuitable for the task, and then she was turning, heading across the yard into the house. He heard the door slam. For a little while he stood there, looking from the house to the filled-in hole and back to the unfinished house again. Remembering what he'd just seen, he started across the yard.

40

When he reached the side of the house where the parlor window was, he saw that the shade was undrawn. Bending from the waist, he looked into the worn and melancholy room. Meredith stood there, her back to the window, naked. She began to pace the room, arms folded across her breasts, on her face an expression of deepest disbelief. Norman knew that she knew he stood there, but she never so much as glanced in his direction. He left her that way, went home and crawled into bed next to the snoring Claire. For a long while he lay sleepless, his mind suffused with images of Meredith. Not the Meredith in the yard burying her secret, but the one through the window. She was beautiful. He imagined her body in candlelight and tried to ignore what was happening between his legs. He wondered what their eyes would say to one another the next time they met.

But by the morning, Meredith had forgotten everything about this night, except for Hosea's leaving that second time.

PART TWO
1949–1959

CHAPTER
6

When the trees were uprooted and the ground scraped into evenness by the blades of tractors, they began to build the racetrack over near Honeybear Road. For a little while the absence of animals created a stir, but soon everyone's attention was riveted by the intricacies of construction and the startling recognition that black people had begun to die.

At the first funeral, Lee Madison's, the young undertaker brought in from Poughkeepsie spent the entire afternoon glaring, his lips poked out. Lee had walked into the path of an iron shovel swinging from a crane. The impact had broken his spine and smashed most of the bones in his face. Made dizzy by the body's condition (this was his third assignment; the first two had died in their sleep), Moses Duewright had gone to work, stumbling in the process upon a skill he'd not known he possessed. On shaky terms with the craftsman in him, he'd discovered the artist. He was pouting because his feelings were hurt; not a single person had acknowledged his masterpiece. No one had said how good Lee looked, how lifelike, as if he were sleeping.

To top it off, these Montgomery Negroes did not know the first thing about going to a funeral. Crying was moderate, restrained, the way white people cried. There were not enough flowers. The piano player kept missing her cues. Dressed in a black, meant-to-be-floor-length gown that barely covered her shins, the soloist neglected to break down and sob in the middle, and her singing, while not without pathos, did not move people to consider their own untimely deaths. The ushers, whose responsibility it was to supervise the flow of viewers past the casket, found themselves befuddled by a traffic jam. As a result, they were out of position when the widow collapsed, and her children, in the confusion caused by their mother's grief, were left alone. Finally, Pastor Mclain, who was usually sure of herself, went off in three directions before she staggered into a suitable text, and there was that awful moment at the end when she realized she had been less than commemorative and much too brief. Only the weather was right: a cutting wind of the kind that has made March famous, a glowering day that matched Moses Duewright's face.

This awkwardness was, in retrospect, understandable. Black people in Montgomery had not had any recent experience with mourning. Later they realized that they had approached the occasion unprepared, convinced that they, of all people, knew how to act when death dropped by—which was to prepare his supper, bring him up to date on births and marriages, and pour a last cup of Maxwell House before they handed him his hat. But it had been so long between visits that they had forgotten the food death liked to eat, how many sugars he took in his coffee, and what he cared to talk about. Shocked, dismayed, they went to work, rummaged in the cluttered drawers and closets of their memories, dusted off the recollections of the old folks. Letters were posted to relatives in the South. The president of the Missionary Club sent away to Arizona for free literature on funeral protocol, and when it arrived she held in her finished basement a series of seminars called "Deceased Conduct." The last seminar was a role-playing session, the highlight of which was her husband, who played the corpse. As a result, by the time Louisa Bannister passed, the proper behavior at funerals was established. The undertaker was praised until his face ached with smiling, and his hand was shaken until his fingers throbbed. The woman who sang Louisa's favorite song ("Nearer, My God to Thee") was dressed in white of appropriate length, in her hair a red carnation plucked from the wealth of floral arrangements that banked the casket and fired the church with scent. For weeks people talked about her performance—how her knees kept buckling with sorrow until it seemed that all that kept her upright was the sound of her own sweet song. A respectable number of women screamed "Jesus, oh, sweet Jesus, take me, Jesus," and several, with a grace that did not go unremarked, swooned neatly into the ushers' arms. Even the men participated; they moaned and hid their faces in snow-white handkerchiefs.

Afterward, all the talk of sadness had to do with how Louisa, who loved a good time as much as anyone, had not been there to see it. Everybody had enjoyed it so, that they all began to look to death's next visit, having forgotten in the ecstacy of mourning why death had looked them up—that, whether it was hanging out at the race-track or just above their heads, evil had come to town.

Two years and two months after they destroyed the trees, the racetrack was officially opened. All the stores were closed along Broadway, and Montgomery was dressed in banners. Playing off-key military music, the high-school band led the parade from the courthouse to the track, where, in the blazing sun, people circled the temporary platform constructed on the infield for the dignitaries. As was usual to such events, the proceedings were much too long, and Norman wandered off with most of the crowd to marvel at the premises: the grandstands that could sit 15,000, the staggering array of urinals, and the stables, cleaner than some folk's kitchens, in which the magnificent horses lived. As Norman had suspected, there was not a trace of evil about the place; evil was as nonexistent as trees. If anything, the complex made him think of a hospital, so neat and antiseptic he was afraid to touch anything. After everyone was chased out of the stables (it was feeding time for the horses), he began to be bored. He hung around long enough for the free lemonade and the two gifts everyone was given (a miniature American flag and a ball-point pen embossed with the words "Montgomery Raceway"). Then he headed home.

For Norman, the two years had not been uneventful. His daughter had "become a woman," and he had found himself preoccupied for a season with the motives of every male under seventy-five. To fill the vacancy left by Hosea, the church had made him a deacon. At work he had set a record for most consecutive days without sick leave, for which he received a certificate from the Board of Education. Although the disturbing details of the burning black man had disappeared, he still dreamed of flying. Trusting his instincts, which told him flying was related to jumping, he had thought the matter through, determining that flight was the activity that lived in the space beyond his ability to jump. Once he discovered that limit, he had merely to surpass it and he'd be airborne.

So he had, for the past two years, been practicing his leaps. Forty-one years old in 1950, a man who'd never been much of an athlete, he could, with a running start, cover eighteen feet, an achievement he looked upon with pride.

These activities would have provided a full life for most men, but for Norman they were only a beginning. Christopher Silas, Montgomery's oldest black citizen, passed in September. In July, U. L. Washington's twelve-year-old, Jonah, drowned in the pond behind Gerald Fletcher's house. Sam "Big Boy" Richardson choked to death on a fishbone the following May. Norman had all those funerals to attend. In addition, there were his sessions of staring into fire. There, too, he experimented with limits. Sometimes he looked so long that his vision became painful, sharp enough to slice flesh, and he would retreat, exhausted, pale, and starving, as if he'd been involved in a debauch, the sweet taste of which remained in his mouth for hours. The person he was to protect, however, was yet a mystery. Although Meredith still left the light burning and the shade undrawn, so that he could watch her naked, the identifying sign for which he waited had failed to come.

In the fall of 1948, Norman had begun to suffer periods of unexplained fear and foreboding, which only prolonged communion with fire would dispel. He might have worried more about this had it not been for the puzzling nature of what happened to him next. With a frequency that knew no rhythm, he began to come upon the answers to things, the process of which had nothing to do with fire. He would find these answers everywhere: in the silhouettes of tree limbs against the sky, in the ribbed pattern of a sparrow's wing. He would look and *know*, not in words, but in feelings. Since he was accustomed to truth being revealed in feelings, he was not troubled by the absence of words. What troubled him was that the answers had nothing to do with trees, or sky, or sparrows' wings. Neither were they responses to any questions he had asked. One answer he felt translated finally to "They throw titties over their shoulders." Another was "It's the mind." Simplicity marked them all; one emphatically stated, "Yes." It was disconcerting. There he was, a man in the enviable position of having the answers and not a decent question to his name.

Not without resources, he sought to create his own

49

questions, ones whose gravity he felt suitable to the weight of his revelations. Why am I here? he asked. Why is this happening to me? These questions came hurtling back at him, intact, from whatever wall they'd bounced off. He would catch them, turn them in his hand, and feel anxiety thicken.

Claire found herself living with a man who was not only off in a cloud most of the time, but also losing his sweet disposition. He'd become jumpy and short with her and the kids. The sound of his name was enough to give him a start; a dropped pot in the kitchen would send him bolting to investigate.

"Norman," she'd say, "what's wrong?"

Mouth open, shirttail pulled from his waist, he would stare at her, then turn away, muttering "Nothing."

How long Claire would have endured this had it not been for Soapsuds is anybody's guess. Soapsuds was fifteen, tall and gorgeous and smart, with a voice like Ronald Colman's. He'd gotten his name as a child when he'd begun repeating curses, the sounds of which he found beautiful. His mother learned of this when a stranger behind her in the check-out line rubbed the child's head and asked in a gruff, but kind, voice, "What you know, boy?"

The child told him in a voice that carried to the produce section. "Mother fucker, son of a bitch, bastard, shit. Alligator pussy."

Edna, a small, cat-eyed woman with marvelous breasts, was one of a few black people in Montgomery who did not belong to the church, but she did have her values. Leaving her groceries to a baffled check-out girl, she dragged the child home, where she poured half a cup of Tide in his mouth and followed it with water. Choking, the detergent scalding his throat and vocal cords and permanently deepening his voice, the child panicked and dashed from the house, his mother in hot pursuit. He'd gone through half the streets in town, foam bubbling from his lips, before she caught him. This experience, traumatizing as it had been, had not cured the boy's fascination. It simply socialized him; he knew now not to use that beautiful language in the presence of adults.

His combination of good looks and foul mouth made Soapsuds irresistible to many of the girls in Montgomery, one of whom was Norman's daughter. When Claire returned from shopping one day to find her alone with Soapsuds in the bedroom, and Norman, in the bathtub surrounded by candles, not aware of their presence, she exploded. Fortunately, nothing irreversible had occurred; Claire made the girl strip and examined her. But what *might* have happened! The thought made her light-headed. Soapsuds ought to be taken off the streets, put away. But Claire did not so much as speak about the episode to either of Soapsuds' parents. First, she was intimidated by Soapsuds' mother's eyes and the thrust of her breasts, conditions that had probably produced in the child his unnatural tendencies. Second, she didn't know sign language. Soapsuds' father, Jack, was a deaf-mute who made his living by being the best handyman around. Frustrated, Claire slapped her daughter until her palms smoked. "If I catch Soapsuds hanging around here again, I'll . . ." She could not think of anything to say except that she would kill him, and the leniency of that punishment scarcely fit the crime. Apoplectic, she screamed at Norman, accused him of not caring. How could he have left his guard down? Shepherds had lost entire flocks for such laxity; thieves had emptied decent people's homes. . . .

When she'd calmed down, she began to consider more rationally her husband's behavior. Something was obviously wrong with him. With a suddenness that made her breath catch, it came to her. *Evil.* Norman had sinned. He had sinned and not confessed. It was guilt that had caused this change in him.

51

That night, in bed, she suggested that he talk to Pastor Mclain.

"For what?" He resented the intrusion; he was sliding down the slope of sleep.

"Honey, you ain't been yourself lately. It ain't like you not to know what's going on in your own house with your own daughter. Not the way you used to worry bout her."

Instantly, he was wide awake, suspicious. She seldom called him anything but his given name. To deflect her, he grunted, a noncommittal sound he hoped she would interpret as consent.

"Norman?"

Oh, dear, Norman thought, and rolled his eyes. Neither promising nor refusing, he said, "That might be a good idea."

Satisfied, Claire laid a maternal hand on his shoulder. She turned away, wondering what his sin was. Maybe it was something he did during all that time he spent in the bathroom. A delicious shiver set her belly to shaking, then she experienced inadequacy and regret. Didn't he get enough? She did, but men, she knew, had larger appetites. She recalled, with a clarity sharper than desire, when they'd first been married, and how it seemed that not a day had passed without some touching. That was a nice memory; it made her warm inside. Lord knows she didn't want to be no stumbling block, she didn't want to be the cause of her helpmate sinning. She did a quick computation in her head, decided it was safe, and rolled over. Norman, one short step ahead of her, pretended to be asleep.

Three days later, when Norman still hadn't gone to see the pastor, Claire went in his place. Delicately avoiding the exact nature of her suspicions, she sketched out the change in Norman, and asked the minister if she would speak to him. Pastor Mclain, alarmed at the frequency with which black people were dying, acted with dispatch. That is why, on a Monday night in August 1949, Norman, not without apprehension, sat across from her in her house.

"Brother," she said, "let us pray." Both slid to their knees. Prayer, as always, made Norman feel better. After a decent interval, he looked over his shoulder. The pastor still had her eyes closed. Norman repeated his prayer. Then, to pass the time, he considered the spacious room. Like most living rooms he'd been in, this had a couch, at which he knelt, two chairs and a coffee table. The light came from two bronze lamps in the shape of giant sea horses; the shades had roses in the pattern. It was a tasteful, modern room, which, he guessed, was to be expected from a woman who dyed her hair blue, but it suffered from an abundance of doilies and bric-a-brac, most of the latter in the image of cats. There was a portrait of the Saviour on one wall, his expression as enigmatic as the cats', and there were two large reproductions of the Last Supper, each by a different hand. These hung opposite one another, as if, beyond the inspiration they provided, they kept the room in constant balance.

Norman looked again at his praying pastor. She could pray, he knew, for hours. Once, she'd gone at it from sundown to sunup, stopped to eat, and continued into evening. That was when the doctors said she couldn't conceive, and she'd taken her longing for a child to the Lord. Tonight, asleep in this house, was a four-year-old boy, whom she'd named after Jesus. Ever since then, her prayer had been characterized by length; she was convinced that the Lord was susceptible to persistence.

Norman fidgeted; his knees, traumatized by the stress

of daily leaping, began to ache. Uncomfortable and bored, he considered dreaming of flying, but then he heard the pastor's crisp "Amen." He had barely settled into his seat when she asked if he had anything to confess, the tone of her voice indicating that he ought to. Norman did a quick, superficial audit, and found that, as he'd expected, his life was an open book.

"You sure?"

For a moment he suspected she'd gotten scent of his experiments with fire, but he relaxed. There was no sin in this. He turned his eyes to the ceiling and racked his brain. Try as he might, he couldn't think of anything.

"You're a deacon now. We depend on you to set an example."

"I tries my best."

"Hmph," the pastor said, and looked at him. Norman looked back for the count of a heartbeat, then dropped his eyes.

"You know I don't set no rules about my people's hair style. But Sister Claire says you been different since you got yours cut."

Reflexively, Norman stroked his skull. Having been asked nothing, however, he said nothing.

"What made you cut it off?"

He didn't remember. He knew it had something to do with beauty and something to do with weight. The easiest answer had to do with weight, and he said, "It was heavy."

The pastor did not hide her exasperation. Lest he be left vulnerable to further inquiry, Norman hastened to let her know he appreciated her concern. "I'm going to pray more, and I ask for you to pray more for me."

Mollified by this response, Pastor Mclain dismissed him.

It was not until he had left that he remembered the gravity of what he'd seen Meredith doing in her backyard.

He considered heading back to the pastor's house, but he was already halfway home and it was hot and dark and all that praying had made him hungry. Despite his discomfort, he took the time to stop at Meredith's window, where, in movement that was almost blinding, she used her fingers to open the glistening gap between her legs.

When autumn lit the trees, it occurred to Norman that his anxiety came from not yet knowing whom he was to protect and pass on his knowledge to. He experienced a growing alarm that this person was in danger. After a twelve-month absence, the dream of the burning black man came again, and he learned the next day that the Professor, drunk, had fallen asleep with a lighted cigar and incinerated himself. As winter shriveled the earth, the dream haunted him nightly, driving him down into water that was black but had no wetness. He would awaken wrapped in sweat, moaning, and Claire would question and implore and offer her body, which he did not want. Despite the prayers of the church (Pastor Mclain had instructed from the pulpit that everyone pray for him), his distraction mushroomed. Once, he snapped out of a reverie to find that he'd walked two miles past the school. On another, lamentable, occasion he poured floor wax instead of detergent into his pail and scrubbed down the teachers' lavatories, then faced, without understanding, their indignant cries that the toilet seats had stuck to their bottoms. He turned the furnace up too high one day; on another, the children had to be sent home because he'd failed to order coal. The principal, a secret alcoholic who was hanging on until retirement, called him in for a rambling consultation. Teachers looked at him askance; children tittered when he passed in the hallways. He dealt with these calamities as best he could, repairing the damage when it was possible, reacting with equal parts of stoicism and repentance when it was not. He sensed that people were beginning to get serious when they said he was crazy and ought to be put away. Panicked, summoning a strength that left him exhausted every evening, he bore down and made it through the winter.

He was living with the terror of a man alone in the wilderness clinging to a cliff. In the spring, just when he thought he couldn't hold on, that he *wanted* to fall, he got his sign. It was Saturday. Claire was out visiting the sick. His oldest boy was at the ESSO station, where he pumped gas on weekends; his youngest was at a friend's. Outside, a steady rain was falling. Norman, after checking to make sure his daughter was alone, wandered into the kitchen and pulled a chair to the rain-streaked window. He was sitting there watching the monotonous weather when, to relieve the ache in his neck, he turned to his left. A wind had sprung up, tangling the hair of the girlish trees that grew at the edge of his property. He was watching this activity with mild interest, considering how his passion for trees had been replaced by that for fire, when he realized that the rain had stopped. He looked to his right. There, with a persistence that brought to mind the adversity of Noah, fell the driving rain. Norman blinked. Before him, in a line so straight he could have laid a foundation by it, the rain both stopped and started. Since childhood he'd been fascinated by the notion that, subsequent to God's giving the rainbow sign, the rain any human witnessed had to begin and end somewhere. Now, on this afternoon in May, his heart leaped. It was the first answer he'd come upon in the past twelve months for which he knew the question, and he figured that his change had come.

In July, drunk from a night's orgy of staring into flame, he went in the morning to swim in the pond behind the Fletchers' house. More swamp than pond, the water had been declared off-limits after Jonah Washington drowned there, and now, except for the frogs, the darting insects, and a snake or two, Norman was guaranteed his privacy. He didn't recall his decision to visit the Fletchers, or realize that he'd failed to put his clothes on. When he came to himself, he was dripping water all over Abigal Fletcher's kitchen floor, and was butt naked except for the lilies that had wrapped around his penis. Abigal, who was peeling apples for a pie, surged to her feet, one hand going to her mouth. Resisting the urge to check out the lovely flowers, she looked him straight in the eye. "Norman Fillis, *shame* on you. You sit down and hide yourself."

Norman, awe-struck, obeyed. Abigal went to the phone and called Claire, her husband, and Pastor Mclain, in that order. Norman knew he was in big trouble, but he didn't care. He was mesmerized by the child who clung to his mother's skirt, in his right eye, beautiful against the white, a dark-brown circular marking. There were other marks; what looked like welts only recently healed scarred the boy's arms. But these had no interest for Norman. It was the circle in the eye that held him rapt.

He's the one, Norman shouted, but not out loud.

CHAPTER
7

Gerald Fletcher's mark, a congenital mole, is not unknown to medical science. Its erratic tendency to visit the eyes of black newborns is well documented, if not explained. Still, the mark is sufficiently rare; Gerald would meet only one other person who had it. This meeting took place in the winter of his seventh year, in Brooklyn, at his aunt Clara's house. He'd never been to Aunt Clara's, or, for that matter, to Brooklyn. For what reason his father was taking him now his mother wouldn't say. But she did warn him not to ask his father. "He'll tell you when he's ready," she said.

They left Montgomery late that afternoon. All during the trip Gerald snuck glances at his father's face, lit now by the distant fire of a setting sun, now by the dashboard lights. He was looking for the anger. His father had a violent temper, which, when it erupted, always seemed directed at him. He would beat Gerald with a belt that made the boy's skin blossom with welts. As a result, Gerald lived in terror of his father and believed that for some unexplained and awful reason his father did not love him. Tonight, uncharacteristically, he felt a tentative safety. Tonight anger was absent from his father's face, and those terrible hands, without which there could be no beating, were curved around the steering wheel.

Neither spoke until they reached New Jersey, when the night sky bloomed suddenly like a vast inferno above the black horizon. Gerald, his heart in his mouth, asked what was burning.

"Lights. New York City." His father did not speak again until he reached his sister's street and stood, shoulders hunched, on the sidewalk. "Feels like snow," he said.

All the buildings were, to Gerald, indistinguishable, yet his father unhesitantly entered one. They climbed and knocked. Clara, a scarlet ribbon in her hair, opened the door.

"Lord, you growed!" She bent to kiss the boy. Smelling sweet, she straightened and faced her brother. "So you came?"

"I'm here, ain't I?"

She looked, it seemed to Gerald, not *at* his father, but *for* him. "You're here all right. But why?"

"Is *he* here?"

"In the back."

"What . . . does he look like?"

"If you didn't know, you'd never think it. But I asked you a question. Why'd you come?"

"It ain't your concern."

"It *is* my concern."

"I didn't drive two hours to stand here in the hall having a fool conversation."

"Oh. Excuse me. I clean forgot my manners. *Do* come in."

Inside, there was a party going on. Men and women leaned against the walls of a corridor that disappeared abruptly around a corner. These people were sinners. They wore rings and bracelets and smoked cigarettes. Yet they were laughing and touching like folks did after church in Montgomery. It puzzled Gerald that this common ground existed; he wanted to ask his father about it, but he'd learned that his father did not like to answer questions. He turned the corner; the hall widened into a living room. There, in a soft blue light, people were dancing. The women wore lipstick and the men who held them

59

had their eyes closed. Like the laughing and touching, the music reminded Gerald of church. Confused, sensing his father's escalating disapproval, he watched the dancers but a moment, then looked toward the room's far corner, where a man in a gray suit perched majestically on a stool beneath a spotlight. His black, wing-tipped shoes hung by their heels on the bottom rung. Sitting on the floor, a delighted circle of men and women gazed up at him. The man glanced across the room and saw Gerald and his father. Impolitely, Gerald thought, the man stared; even when the group turned to follow his eyes, he refused to drop them. But he did nod and hold a hand up, beckoning the newcomers to enter the circle, which was, unmistakably, his. In that gesture was something that suggested that this man had power over Gerald's father, and, instantly, Gerald liked him. Still, he reached for his father's hand as they slid between the dancing bodies. The hand was slick with sweat; the fingers fluttered. When they reached the opening that moving bodies made, his father stopped. Startled, Gerald froze. "Go on," his father said, and pushed him forward.

Everyone was looking at him. Wearing their eyes like a coat too heavy, its hem too long, the boy moved closer. The man was old, not ancient, but older than his father. He was smiling. There was love in his smile and an intensity that deepened the lines in his face. He pulled the boy to a chest fragrant with mint and tobacco, squeezed him, held him at arm's length. Then he said to Gerald's father, "He's a fine boy. Got the mark in his eye. Thought I remembered that. Look, boy, see mine?" He pointed to his right eye, where Gerald saw a mark identical to his own.

"What mark is that, J. D.?" a pretty woman said, smiling. "The mark of the Devil?"

"Never you mind whose mark it is." J. D. laughed.

"Just know it's special." He winked at Gerald and spoke to the man who stood rigid and glowering at the circle's edge. "I know this ain't your kind of company, but go on and relax as best you can. Must be something here besides liquor for a man to drink. Leave the boy with me for a spell."

He picked Gerald up and set him on his lap. As he did so, a short, explosive grunt parted his lips, and he tensed, as if the effort had rudely rearranged something deep inside him. Then he recovered, kissed Gerald on the forehead, and said, "Did I ever tell you all bout Marilee Maplestone?"

They assured him he hadn't.

"Well, her husband got sent to Italy in 1943. . . . Ya'll Negroes knows where Italy is, don't you?"

"We know." They laughed. "Now tell the story."

And he did. For as long as Gerald sat on his lap, he told stories, none of which the boy understood, but all of which he knew were wonderful. He could tell this from the rhythms of the man's voice, which, had he not been so excited, would have lulled him to sleep. He could tell it from the laughing everywhere around him, and the kisses the man from time to time left on his cheek, and from the hands that stroked him, hands so gentle they could never have formed fists. Gerald felt safe; safety made him bold. In the space left at the end of a story, he said, "Will you come live with me?"

The question darkened the man's eyes. "Son, I can't. But if I could live with anybody, it would be with you. Do you believe that?"

"Yes," Gerald said, and blinked back tears of disappointment. Now everyone around him was sad. A man in a blue suit hid his face in huge black hands; a woman grasped one of his thick fingers. Gerald was frightened. It was his fault, and he knew he should say he was sorry.

But his father loomed again at the circle's edge, and he did not want to confess to misbehavior in his presence.

"We got to go," his father announced. "Got a long drive ahead."

"I know," the man said. "But I wish you could stay longer just the same." He hugged Gerald. "You be good, hear?" and slid the boy from his lap. Gerald felt him tense again, as though something inside him was hurting. "I thank you for coming," the man said to Gerald's father. "I'd have understood if you didn't."

"I wanted you to see the boy."

"I'm grateful."

"I'm . . . I'm sorry this had to happen."

The man shrugged and smiled. "Quiet as it's kept, it happens in the best of families."

The boy's father seemed to consider this. "Well . . ." He licked his lips and his right hand jerked at his side. "Good-bye."

"Good-bye. Take care of yourself."

At the door, Clara, her ribbon undone, kissed Gerald. Then she said to her brother, "You did a good thing by coming. It meant a lot to him."

"I did what was right."

"Still," she repeated, "you did a good thing. Get home safe. Love to Abigal."

They went down steps, Gerald's hand tight in his father's. When they reached the sidewalk, he asked a question. "Daddy, who was that man?"

"*What?* He didn't tell you?" It was not his father's voice. This was a howl of pain and rage, demented. Instinctively, Gerald reached for the free hand. "Tell me what, Daddy?"

But his father was scowling back at the building out of which they'd come, as if he'd left something, a scarf perhaps, or his wallet. In a voice that began matter-offactly and ended in disbelief, he said again, "He didn't tell you."

"What, Daddy?"

"Get in the car," his father barked.

They were in the car, it was cold, the motor roared into life. His father laughed the way he sometimes laughed when there was nothing funny, an awful sound more frightening than one of rage. He began drumming his hands against the steering wheel, *boom, boom, boom.* "He didn't tell you." Gerald was terrified. His father was angry, and his hands were free. He and his father were alone, and his father was angry and his hands were free. But he had to know.

"Who was he, Daddy?"

His father was still. For a long moment he stared through the windshield, as if the parked cars and huddled buildings had hypnotized him with their squalor. In a voice that made the boy think "dead," he whispered, "That man is my father."

Gerald didn't understand. "Like you're *my* father?"

"*I* take care of you."

"Why didn't he tell me? Was I bad? Was I bad and he didn't tell me?"

His father snorted. "Nobody's that bad. Not even you."

"Daddy, why?"

"Because he never took responsibility for anything in his life, that's why. Not even for telling you who he was." He made a sound that was close to laughing. "He probably figured somebody else would do it. All his life, whenever there was something had to be done, he figured somebody else would do it. . . ." His voice, ponderous, slid beneath the engine's growl, resurfaced. "Do you know why all those people were up there?"

Gerald shook his head.

"For *him*. Because he's dying."

"No," Gerald said.

"And because he's always been so different, and charming, and *free*, he's having his funeral *before* he dies. So he can enjoy it, he says. That's what they're doing up there, all his drinking buddies and loose women; they're going to his funeral." His voice was faster now, rising. "They all think he's so terrific. Well, he ain't terrific. He's *trifling*."

He slammed the car into gear.

"I don't want him to die," Gerald cried. "Don't let him die. Let him come live with us."

"Shut up! You're just like him. I'll break your neck you say that again. You hear me?"

Oh, God, Gerald pleaded. Why didn't he tell me? Please don't let him die.

His father was driving like a madman, honking the horn, tailgating. Mercifully, traffic thinned. They crossed a bridge, the grid of which made the tires sing. Lights sparkled on the black surface of the water; a long flatboat sat motionless in the middle. Now the streets grew shabbier; abandoned buildings disfigured the landscape. Through the thick snow, which had suddenly, insistently, begun to fall, Gerald saw shadows on the sidewalk. His father swung to the curb, parked the car.

"Get out."

Doors were locked. He was taken in a grip that crushed his hand, yanked down the street. Steam hissed and billowed from a hole in the ground; a stray cat on yellow haunches fought with snowflakes. In the distance, Gerald heard a siren sob.

"You looking? You see?" His father was pointing to the shadows. They were men, all of them dressed in rags, unshaven, unclean. This one fused a bottle to his mouth, passed it on. Gerald smelled something rotten and something burned.

"These are men who refused to take responsibility," his father said, his voice harsh, driving. "This is their home. It's called the Bowery. It's where you'll end up if you're trifling." He was shouting. Several men camped around a fire in a garbage can turned in his direction. One called out, asking if he could spare some change.

"Look."

In the doorway of a building without eyes, illuminated by a streetlight, sprawled a black man, his head cradled in the lap of another sleeping figure, this one younger, with clotted blond hair. Vomit not yet dried covered the black's man mouth and chin, dripped onto his filthy coat.

"You want to end up like this?" His father pushed him forward, and the stench drove into the boy's throat. "You want to smell like that? This man didn't take responsibility. Touch him. I want you to remember. I said *touch him.*"

He gripped Gerald's hand and placed it on the black man's leg. The pants were wet with what he hoped was not vomit; head pounding, dizzy with terror, he felt the bone beneath the sliding flesh. The man groaned, opened one bloodshot eye to fix his tormentor in a baleful stare. Then the eye widened and he called out in a voice as clear and melodious as a church bell, "Hey, Idaho. *Idaho.* Scope this, will ya? Freaking kid's got three eyes."

Gerald began to scream. The sound laced the night, going on and on and on until his father slapped him. All the commotion roused the sleeping Idaho, who, in a flat, Midwestern drawl, wondered when in hell a body was supposed to get some rest.

CHAPTER
8

There were only two things of any importance that Gerald never shared with Iceman, and one was about what happened that night. Iceman was his best friend, a plump, plum-colored boy whose eyeglasses were always sliding down his nose. This tended to make him look finky, but he wasn't. Iceman's father, Ezra Poole, was one of the first black men in Montgomery to own his business, The Restoration Company, the crew of which went into offices to clean at the end of the day. As a result of this enterprise, the Poole family was relatively well off: they got a new car every three years, had all their living-room furniture covered with the best of plastic, and owned no fewer than three TVs. To Gerald, these last possessions were impressive. His father refused to buy a television, insisting that it fostered idleness. Instead, he sent his son to the library, where, grudgingly, Gerald fell in love with books.

In the beginning of his life, Iceman was known as Zack, short for Zacharias, a child of fiendish curiosity and imitative gifts. At the age of five he could mimic the amusing waddle of an overweight woman and the way a particularly graceless man "shouted" in church. He could borrow voices, capture the vacancy of Norman Fillis's face when he was dreaming, and reproduce, unerringly, the angle of the hand Ruth Potts wore perpetually on her hip. To such a child, television was a gold mine; it expanded his world and, consequently, the possibilities of imitation.

Inspired above all by Western movies, Zack received

one Christmas a cowboy suit replete with boots and matched cap pistols. When his parents flatly refused to buy him a horse, he raided the rolls of snow fencing stockpiled behind the town barn and made his own. These animals were meticulously wrought. Zack made manes from cloth, which he tore into fringes. The reins were braided string. Leather saddles were cut with razor blades from discarded belts. At one time he had a stable consisting of a roan, a white stallion, and a pinto one could almost hear whinnying.

Their noise was deafening, but a shot from Zack's guns could not cause even an arm wound. He had to depend upon the poor ability of his playmates to provide the anguished, poetic deaths he saw on Channel 3. His playmates did not like to die; they would take a bullet through the heart, fall, and jump right up, insisting it was now their turn to do the killing. Zack tried to instruct by example: when *he* was shot, he'd pirouette, stagger, and take five seconds to fall, and he'd lie holding his breath, refusing to move or open his eyes until he was tickled. But nobody except Zack ever learned to die with grace, although everyone mastered the technique of killing.

Even though their bullets could not take life, each of Zack's guns was a multipurpose instrument, heavy and hard enough to enable him to drive nails and to knock his younger brother unconscious by hitting him over the head with the butt in a barroom brawl. For this error in judgment, Zack was whipped. A lawman in a white hat, but without real rustlers to bring to justice, Zack hanged from a tree a kitten convicted of stealing the last horse from a widow. This resulted in another whipping. Gerald was envious of Zack's whippings for two reasons: their lack of frequency and their lack of severity; they consisted of his being laid across a lap and having his bottom smacked five or six times with the palm of an open hand. They never lasted longer, Zack's behind being, his father said, only slightly softer than his head.

In fairness to Zack, it should be said that he didn't expect either incident to result in permanency. After he'd hit his brother, he bent, tapped him on the shoulder, and commanded him to wake, but it was not until six hours later, in a hospital bed, that he did so, asking for chocolate ice cream and complaining of blurred vision in his left eye, which would remain forever. When he cut down the cat, Zack prodded at the furry body, fully expecting it to get up and go running off, presumably to hunt for mice. When it didn't, when he understood what his action had resulted in, he broke down and sobbed.

That day marked the beginning of Zack's gentleness, of his abhorrence of pain and suffering and violence, and death in any guise. No longer did he make fun of people. He stopped watching cowboy movies. He would not take the life of a fly or a mosquito, and went out of his way to remove earthworms from sidewalks where some dumb, unthinking human would have crushed them beneath his feet. When he discovered its relationship to living things, he refused to eat any meat. Most remarkable, he grew up to become honest. While other adolescent boys devised elaborate and disastrous schemes to impress the girls with their affection, Zack would walk over to one and say, "I like your eyes and the way your hair curls on the back of your neck." He confronted, with a frequency alarming to adults, any of their perceptions and beliefs that made no sense to him. Once, he threw Sunday school into an uproar by bringing in an encyclopedia to prove that the membrane at the back of the creature's throat would not have allowed the whale to swallow Jonah. Told he was made in God's image, he suggested that God was colored and wore glasses. He got away with all of this because his intransigence was marked by deference and a simple, incandescent love. Yet, there were consequences, for his openness provided adults with a glimpse of what children were really like on the inside: tough and smart and capable. To defend themselves against a loss of power, adults closed the little people off, denied access to what they knew, and came up with stricter rules to keep children "in their place." In spiteful acknowledgment of Zack's honesty and the weight he'd caused to fall, kids his age said he didn't know how to keep his business out of the street; he wasn't cool. Sarcastically, they called him Iceman. Gerald thought it was a lot better than *his* nickname, which was Trips, short for Triple, which came from Three Eyes. Gerald's nickname didn't last. Zack's stuck because Zack liked it and made it his own. He did it without fanfare, the same way that he loved his best friend, for whom he created a plan designed to diminish Gerald's suffering.

It took nothing more than the clump of his father's foot on the porch to set off in Gerald a trembling only a little less violent than his father's disposition, only a little less brutal than the arc of the whistling black belt held in his father's hand falling with a crack across the flayed skin of his naked back. There were three wishes that Gerald daily resurrected: that he would not die and go to Hell, that he would not die a virgin, and that his father would encounter a most mean and ignominious death. Having been raised in the church, believing its doctrine (now because he did, now because he was terrified not to—disbelief being the most mortal of sins), he was aware of the contradiction in his wishes. Yet it was a measure of their strength that this was no deterrent to his longing. Even when he awoke in the middle of the night and went to his window to look, in the white moonlight, for the

Second Coming, even as he scanned the earth that would burst and give up its dead, as he listened for the whirring locusts that would, once the anointed were whisked to Heaven, descend to eat his flesh, and he trembled, saying, "Lord, not yet," even then Gerald wished his father dead.

He spent hours planning ways to murder his father, imagining his hands around his father's throat, driving a knife between his ribs, slicing away the tool that caused his mother to cry out in the bedroom. He planted explosive devices under the car hood, put glass in his food, hired a killer. These fantasies filled him with power; he would imagine his mother and himself together, free of the tyrant. He would grow up and be rich and famous, a doctor, maybe, a lawyer, or an engineer.

And in a rhythm as predictable as the one that brought light in the morning and darkness at night, at the height of his sense of power, he would somehow manage to inspire his father's wrath: he had not hung up his clothes the right way, or had not hung them up at all; he'd neglected to take out the garbage; he'd failed math or talked in Sunday school; he'd looked at his father the wrong way, or there was insolence in his decision not to look. And then would come the beatings, which seemed, especially when compared to Iceman's, interminable. Apologies and promises to do better (even when he'd done no wrong, even when he'd done his best) had no effect on beating time. Neither did screams or trickles of blood where the welted tissue of skin gave way, or silence (because to cry out meant spending energy better focused on containing pain). His father stopped when his mother appeared, unspeaking, in the doorway, having endured it as long as she could. If she didn't come, as sometimes— for what reasons, Gerald couldn't fathom—she did not, his father would continue until he'd grown exhausted, until the muscles in the arm that hurled the belt cried out "Enough. It's finished."

70

CHAPTER 9

Alexander Fletcher, Gerald's father, was born in Denmark, South Carolina, a little town about thirty-five miles northeast of the Georgia border. He was a bright child, for whom only the briefest opportunity for schooling had been provided. Instead, he was hired out in 1927 to a carpenter, who, over the next seven years, taught Alexander the trade. He also taught him to read, something the teacher in the one-room school had not. A fair-skinned woman from Cleveland whose breeding was indicated by her ability to faint (popular belief was that Negroes couldn't), she thought black children were stupid and was efficiently fulfilling her expectations that all but the lightest would fail.

By the time Alexander realized that education might have helped him in life, he figured it was too late. He was married and the father of two children, born in such rapid succession that he awoke one morning, to a chorus of crying, to wonder what had hit him. He lay with his eyes closed, fingering the ache that marked his existence. Life had dealt him a hand from the bottom of the deck, had given birth to him in a backward Southern town, had made him poor and black, and had assigned to him a father who had deserted him. This last, unhappy, event occurred in 1934. A year later, Alexander, his mother, and his sister moved to New York City.

He was fifteen in 1935; Clara, his sister, was nine. A master carpenter, with a letter in longhand to prove it, he set out to find work, only to discover, myth notwithstanding, that New York was not the Promised Land. Times were hard, and he was an uppity black boy, and the union was sensitive to this. In the fall, his mother took to her bed with an undetermined illness whose symptom was failing strength, and the income she'd earned as a house-worker ended. Through a series of odd jobs for Harlem landlords, Alexander managed to provide for the family through the winter, but in the spring his mother died. At her grave he scattered rose petals and cursed his father. It was not until he was back in the grim apartment, holding his bewildered sister, that he broke his vow not to show grief. His sobbing frightened the child in a way that death had not, and she began to cry. Alexander comforted her and made a promise. "Forever," he said. "I'll take care of you. Forever."

For five years he bounced from odd job to odd job. When he could find no work, he stole. For a time he ran numbers and bootleg whiskey. Then the war began. The woman who cared for his sister after school agreed to take the girl in, and he swaggered off to sign up for the fight-ing. To his dismay, he failed the physical. Flatfooted, shoulders slumped into immobility, he took the A train back to Harlem. Two months later, he got a job in a muni-tions plant in New Jersey. There, with a bitterness he did not attempt to conceal, he machined rifle shells for men who were man enough to fight.

His bitterness grew. It was evident in his relation-ships with men and women alike; although the acting out took different forms, it sprang from the same sources: his disappointment in his father, and his sense that because of a raw deal his life was slated for failure. Men described him as "having a chip on his shoulder." They were scorn-ful of the way he carried himself, aloof and distant, like a white man with a million dollars, they said, when he didn't have a pot to piss in. Displaying a cattiness that rivaled that of certain women, these men called him Alexander the Great behind his back, and saw a demented quality in his instant and consuming anger, and in his willingness to use his fists at the merest hint of slight. Someone had once angrily suggested that Alexander take his penchant for battling into the boxing ring, and he had endured a brief, unspectacular career as a prize fighter. His lack of success was due to an inability to counter-punch effectively, and to his discovery that he could not hurt another man unless it was in anger.

Women, however, found him irresistible. A sharp dresser, he loved what good life there was for black men in the forties, and knew his way around the clubs and after-hours joints that populated Harlem. When he had the money, he would go downtown to the Copa or Bird-land and spend extravagantly. More than his style, how-ever, women were drawn to the explosiveness that quiv-ered just beneath his skin. They interpreted the vacancy in his gaze as innocence, and fairly trembled at the pros-pect of harnessing and directing all that power. The truth was that Alexander did not like women; the vacancy in his eyes was simply a result of his not being afraid of them, as so many men, he'd discovered, were. His only use for women was in the legitimacy of his manhood they pro-vided when on his arm—that and what satisfaction he could extract from them between the sheets. His love-making was marked by a violence only slightly more con-tained than the mayhem of a race riot and an intensity of purpose that all but the most perceptive women mis-characterized as passion.

Abigal was perceptive. She'd been born in Louisiana in 1921, in the back room of a shanty in a place called Horn a Plenty, a town so small, so stagnant, that proof of its existence has yet to grace a map. Sent to live with her aunt in Harlem in 1934, she had, in the next nine years, completed high schoool and been hired as a secretary for a black insurance firm. Through it all, she waited for someone to come along whom she could take care of and protect. The waiting was not defined by any purpose; she did not know what she was waiting for until she met Alexander.

In the silence left after the first time they made love, Abigal, driven breathless by his hammering, had looked behind the emptiness in his eyes and begun, with hands that had so recently been clenched, to stroke his back. "There's so much anger in you," she said. "So much sad." What she didn't say was that she'd seen the fear behind the emptiness, a pool of it, glistening, deeper than the sea. Alexander, whose custom it was to get up, get dressed, and take his leave, lay there beneath the pressure of her hands and let her soothe the anger from him. It was as close to peace as he'd been in a long time, and he was so grateful for the respite that he married her. "For your hands," he said. "I married you for your hands."

Immediately, they had a child, whom they named Gerald. Abigal, who had grown accustomed to leaving for work every morning, now found herself confined by the walls of a three-room apartment, and the baffling mystery of a newborn. By the time she'd solved the mystery, she discovered that she was pregnant again. Still, when she looked back, those first two were the best years; Alexander had kept her going with the quality of his dream, which was, simply, that he would one day make a living at his trade. When it became apparent that he would not, with any speed, accomplish this, since he was kept out of the union, his frustration began to sharpen. Abigal, while she could blunt his rage, could not control it; it seemed that her magic hands had lost their touch. One day she knew that he'd begun seeing other women. Mother of one child, another on its way, she held her peace. Whether she did not confront him because she sensed he had no other outlet for his frustrations, or whether she was afraid that if confronted he would leave, Abigal herself did not know. She only knew that she could not go on this way much longer; something had to happen.

One afternoon in July 1947, Alexander stopped on the corner of 125th Street and Lenox Avenue to get his shoes shined, not because they needed it, but because he was coming from another woman and wanted to delay facing his wife. His attention held by the crowd on the southwest corner, where in a singsong voice a black man mourned Ethiopia's fate, he'd felt the tap at the sole of his shoe, the universal signal that he'd been taken care of. He got down from the chair, found a quarter in his pocket, and looked into his father's face. All the power went out of Alexander; the world fell away, leaving the sharp scent of polish, a roaring outside the silence he stood in. The word "you, you, you" began to stutter in his brain. His father regarded him with eyes that said he'd known all along whose shoes he'd been shining, and it had come to this, hadn't it?

"Hello, son."

"Don't call me 'son,'" Alexander bleated. "Don't never call me 'son.'"

His father looked at him. He might have been reading the marquee of a movie house, or deciding what shirt, in the morning, he would wear.

"My mother's *dead*."

"I know."

"You know? That all you can say?"

His father glanced at the sky, at the sidewalk, across the street to where the black man ranted, as if his vision were a hat he was looking for a hook to hang it on. "There's some things," he said slowly, "I don't expect for you to understand. Never. But just cause you don't understand, don't mean there ain't no reason."

"You can't even look at me. *Killer*."

"Have it your way," his father said, and shrugged. Then, perhaps just to show that he could, he looked at his son. "The shine's on me."

Something in Alexander had begun to throb in a place that no longer existed, like the missing leg throbs stupidly in the head of the amputee. "I don't want *nothing* from you," he screamed. He flung the quarter into his father's face. He wanted him to make a move, just one move, and he would drive the bastard into the sidewalk. But his father's eyes refused to be touched. He put a slender, graceful hand to his bruised lip, then bent to retrieve the quarter. Like a man who trusted no one, he studied the coin, bit it, and nodded, as if to say, even if it was Alexander's, it was good cash money.

From then on, Alexander avoided that corner. He did not see his father again until the night of his funeral.

Alexander told Abigal about the meeting when he got home, relieved that he had something to talk about. She didn't tell him that she knew his father was in New York, or that right after the birth of Gerald she'd been introduced to him. Alexander's sister, Clara, who had found her own place when her brother got married, had brought her father by to see his grandson. After that, he'd come two other times to see the child; then he disappeared.

That night after supper, Alexander picked oxtail meat from between his teeth and watched his firstborn. He had never admitted to anyone that there was something about the boy he didn't like. Now, he knew what had troubled him. He stared glumly at the mark in his son's right eye. It was exactly like his father's.

In the fall of 1947, the second child, a baby girl, died of pneumonia. Abigal, battered by grief, blaming herself, cried that she couldn't stand living in a place that still smelled of her baby. Alexander, not unkindly, said she would have to endure it; they couldn't afford to move. Thinking that another child would stop up the hole of her sorrow, Abigal set about trying to conceive. Nothing happened. She took to sitting at the window all day long watching the varied, exciting lives of people passing in the street, rising only to care for Gerald, pull the house together before her husband got home, and fashion dinner. Finally, she began devouring romantic dime-store novels, finding in the charmed, privileged lives of the characters an avenue of escape.

The third thing that happened in 1947 was that Alexander met a musician in a bar on 136th Street and Lenox Avenue. The musician, a drummer who'd just done a gig upstate, had heard that folks in Montgomery were planning to build a racetrack. Knowing that this meant opportunities for jobs New York City had not provided, Alexander scraped together whatever he could and moved in March 1948. To his astonishment, he immediately found work as a carpenter with Jackson Smalls Ltd., a contracting outfit. The company lent him the down payment for a house on Little Pond Road, a quarter mile from the church and across the street from the town barn. A year after they arrived in Montgomery, Abigal joined the church. Alexander, in a move that forever cemented his wife's faith, joined a year and a half later. That meant, of course, no more women on the side. In truth, Alexander was relieved that this was over. He was tired of the joyless couplings, of the guilt, the self-recriminations, and his conviction that Abigal, despite her silence, knew about and looked down upon his weakness. Besides, his boy had just turned four, and was big enough to be properly punished. It was strange, Alexander thought, how traits got passed on. Already he could see the grandfather in the child. First, the mark in his eye. Then, the weak character and a tendency to lie at the drop of a hat. All of this had to be beaten out of the child, for the child's good, or he would grow up to be a failure. With a severity that stunned his wife, he set about preventing this from occurring. Only once did Abigal protest, and he sent her to read again the warning no less a source than the Bible provided: Spare the rod and spoil the child. Perhaps drawn to the attractive logic that the rod unceasingly employed would produce perfection in her issue, certainly believing that the child would survive, Abigal retreated, appearing at the door when she could no longer stand the screaming, choosing to ignore the joy receding from her husband's face as he put his belt back on.

CHAPTER
10

Gerald was ten years old before he mustered the courage to ask his mother why his father beat him so often and so long. His mother said it was because his father loved him, and because he wanted Gerald to grow up to be somebody. She did not look at him when she said this.

Like all children, he had questions that, because he was afraid of his father, he shared only with his mother. Recently, she had begun failing to come through for him, saying helplessly that the questions he asked only God knew the answers to. Gerald did not think his questions that spectacular: Where do rivers come from? How many grains of sand were there in the world? What was there before God? His mother should have heard some of Iceman's questions, the last of which, "Did Jesus Christ have a girl friend?," even Iceman was afraid to ask.

But of all Gerald's questions, the ones that occupied him most were why his father beat him, and why his father did not love the son he'd brought into the world. One thing became clear. Gerald would never have the power to kill his father. His father was too mighty, too smart. "You've been up to something," he'd say, out of the blue, and Gerald, to his everlasting astonishment, would discover that he had been. To discover otherwise, he learned, would be to call his father a liar.

Gerald thought his father Godlike in his ability to know what Gerald had done wrong before Gerald knew it. That explained why, at the height of his fantasies of murder, his father would strike him down, the outcome being that these fantasies no longer consoled him. Deprived of this release, Gerald created another; he began to contemplate his own death. Death by automobile or death by sickness; it did not matter. Only that he was finished, stock-still as he lay in the flickering shadow of the undertaker's parlor, as he was lowered into the earth, a solitary rose prefiguring his descent. His heart swelled when he witnessed this last event, for there, beating his fists against the earth with a terrible insistency, writhed his father. He was grieving for the departed son he'd unforgivingly abused. Now there could be no forgiveness, for death had stopped up Gerald's ears and taken his understanding. His father was left to wander the earth crazed with his loss and guilt, and his father would live to be a hundred.

Equally satisfying was the prospect of suicide. Perhaps he would swallow poison. In the hour before he gave up the ghost, in the midst of his agony, he would compose a letter in which he chronicled his father's crimes. There would be no anger in this letter, and it would be written in language that signaled a great, poetic gift.

He never wrote the letter. He would imagine it as he lay in bed in his darkened room. The night was desolate and he was devastatingly alone, and it was all so sad and beautiful that he wept.

Norman suffered. He knew about the beatings: when they happened, how long, and for what purported reason. The birds who fed in his yard sang of it; trees swayed in the wind, lowering their eyes when they sighed of it. Norman didn't, frankly, know what to do. He'd considered interfering in some fashion; perhaps he could take Alexander to the side and speak to him man to man. "Listen," he'd say. "Your child been chosen to carry on my knowledge. I'd like him to be in shape to carry it." This gave him pause, but he decided against it. If a man beat his wife, you stayed out of it for fear that both would turn on you; it was the same way, probably, with a child. Besides, Norman had to watch his step. He knew that if he did anything out of the ordinary, he'd be sent back to the asylum.

The asylum really wasn't such a bad place. His first stay had resulted from his visit to Abigal's kitchen the day he'd discovered Gerald. He'd been driven to Midstown in a white ambulance whose siren had given him a toothache. Although the attendants had strapped him down when there was no reason to do so, this was their only unthoughtful act during the trip, and he'd disembarked to find himself in front of a brick building that looked reassuringly like a school. It was more than reassuring—it was downright pretty. The grass stretched like a copy of the courthouse lawn back home. Flowers edged the bright white sidewalks. Above it all a washed-out sky curved like a secondhand canopy, through the hole of which a swollen sun drenched the windows with gold.

Inside, he was given a bed in a room full of men. One was snatching imaginary flies out of the air and popping them into his mouth, after which he would groan in ecstasy and smack his lips. There was a red-headed man trying to get both feet into one slipper, and a good-looking brown-skinned boy who walked backward everywhere he went, eyes careful, both hands protecting his behind. For a while Norman was interested; these were the first crazy people he'd come in contact with, but soon he grew used to them. None was a bother. Several he played checkers with.

The bed was comfortable; the food was good. On two occasions, a woman doctor who was addicted to saying "um" asked a lot of questions about his mother. Norman thought she was trying to play the dozens and was amused at her lack of inventiveness. The next time they met she placed several cards on the desk between them and asked Norman to tell her what he saw.

"Scribblin."

"Really. What's that?"

He held his finger up and drew nonsense on the air. "Scribblin."

When he saw how disappointed she was, he considered telling what he saw in the pattern of peeling paint on the ceiling (a woman with male genitalia, a canary sitting on a water buffalo), but instinct made him cautious. She said that it was very nice talking to him and she would see him in a month. But it was six weeks before he saw her again.

In the meantime, things had fallen into place like clockwork. His major concerns upon hospitalization had been the lack of opportunity to commune with fire and to practice his jumps. Both concerns proved to be without basis. The asylum had a gym which was seldom used; there he could jump to his heart's content. The occupational therapist assigned him to help in the kitchen, and he spent mornings peeling carrots and potatoes and throwing them into a black pot big enough to boil a man in. In the kitchen he was close to fire, and it was easy to find an excuse to wander over to the stoves. He could not, of course, look into the flames for the extended periods he'd grown accustomed to, but he discovered that the imposition of discipline had a favorable result: it toned down his imagination, left it focused, trim, and fit. The drug they daily gave him created joy and warmth and a sense of floating that was almost as good as flight. He began to enjoy this life without responsibility and called it freedom.

Then he began to dream, or, rather, he began to remember that he dreamed. The first time, he awoke into a gray dawn, not recalling the dream's contents, but admonishing his pounding heart and aware of the knot above his groin that was only now dissolving. Immediately, he thought of Gerald. Maybe the boy needed him. For a moment he regretted that it was Gerald who'd been chosen. Why couldn't he have been given someone who was less problematic? Someone who had a reasonable father? Then he knew that his dream had nothing to do with the boy, and he spent the whole day in a state, trying to figure what was wrong.

The next dream he remembered in its entirety. Meredith, her naked body oiled, opened her thighs and whispered, "Come here, Norman. Look what I got for you." He awoke, regarded the tent in his pajamas. He seldom got this way. He thought it must be the food, the easy life, and all that exercise.

For three nights Meredith returned to taunt his sleep, leaving him ragged and edgy in the morning. Whenever Norman came near, the brown boy who walked backward would moan and stand with his back to the wall. Norman was embarrassed. "I don't go for boys," he finally barked, but the boy kept moaning.

On the fourth night, Norman dreamed of Claire. Not the Claire who'd let her hips spread, but Claire, his bride. Sweet, shy Claire, whose girlish, downcast eyes had failed to prepare him for the woman she was in bed. The things she'd *said* to him. Norman came out of that dream talking —"Oh, dear." He stared at the pole reaching skyward from his loins; the seam in his pajamas was beginning to give. For a moment he considered taking matters into his hand, but that undertaking was for convicts and desperate boys. Besides, there were rumored consequences of the activity; the one he feared most was the effect upon his vision. No, none of that. He would have to get out of here.

He looked for the answer in fire and found it. The only way he would be allowed to go home was if he changed his behavior. To do this he had to prevent them from controlling him. Reluctantly, he stopped taking his medication, held the capsule beneath his tongue until the attendant walked away, then threw it in the wastebasket. He'd been letting his beard go; now he asked for and received a daily shave. When he was told one day that he would visit the doctor the next morning, he went to the hospital barbershop and got an oil treatment for his scalp. Determined to make a good impression, he washed his pajamas with starch and bribed the attendant to find him an iron. He went to the shower, scrubbed until his skin protested, and did his nails. In the morning, when he walked into the doctor's office, he was so clean he shone. He had never been a bad-looking man; now his body was fit and muscular from jumping, and his eyes, now that he was off the drug, were clear, full of what the doctor did not want to believe was passion. This and the fact that she'd always had a thing for baldheaded men had her reprimanding herself for what she was thinking. But she was too good a psychiatrist not to reinforce his obviously good feelings about himself.

"You look terrific, Mr. Fillis."

"Thank you." He sat and crossed his legs.

"How've you been?"

"Fine."

"Um." She studied him. "What are you thinking?"

"I'd sure like to go home."

"You know you've been ill." She smiled.

"Yes. But I'm better." He smiled back, dazzling, seductive.

"Oh . . . What brought *this* about?"

"Well, I *wanted* to get better. And now"—he smiled again—"I am."

"Um." The doctor leafed through his folder. "You've been on medication."

"I don't take them no more."

She looked up, eyes narrowed. "Excuse me?"

"I ain't taken them pills for three weeks now."

"Mr. Fillis, if you don't co-operate, how can we help you get better?"

"But I *am* better."

"Um." She pushed three cards toward him. They were the same size as the cards she'd shown him last time, but while those had been without character, these were dark, angry, the most depressing scribbles Norman had ever seen. "Tell me what you see in this one."

"I see flowers," he lied. "Sunshine. A little girl playing."

"Um. What about these dark patches?"

"Rain," he said. "Rain's coming."

"What do you think about the rain?"

"The little girl'll get wet. But it'll make the flowers grow."

The doctor sat back in her chair, regarded him above a pyramid of fingers. "Have you thought about your mother since we last met?"

"She's dead."

"How old were you when she died?"

"Fifteen."

"How did you feel?"

"At first I cried a lot. Then it got better."

"What do you remember about her?"

"She was nice. She used to hug me and all and make me hot cocoa."

"Well." The doctor was very cheery. "This has been a very productive session."

"Can I go home?"

"Um." She frowned. "I must meet with the other members of the group. I'll be sure to bring up your request."

Norman stood, thrust his hand out. Confused, the doctor banged her knee against the desk as she rose. Norman held her hand like he would have held a robin's egg. He brushed her knuckles with the flat of his thumb. "I likes your dress," he said. "It sure becomes you."

To her dismay, the doctor blushed. "Why, thank you, Mr. Fillis. And good day to you."

"Good day to you, too," Norman said.

Six weeks later he was on his way home. Claire, bless her heart, had prepared his favorite meal: smothered pork chops, rice, and black-eyed peas. But before he ate, he sent the kids outside and took his wife to bed, where, in a fashion the church might have frowned upon, he set her on fire, inspiring in her ample frame moves she'd forgotten that she knew.

Norman had amassed over eighty days of sick leave, so he'd been paid for the time he spent in the asylum. He fully expected to go immediately back to work, but the Board of Education dragged its heels, pointing to Norman's aberrant behavior and his proximity to children. The alcoholic principal, a man enlightened by his own disease, got himself together and in the last assertive act of his career, had his chief custodian put back on the job. That is why Norman, hanging at the edge of the playground where the garbage bin was kept, was there the day Gerald fell off the slide. Gerald was at the top of the ladder, standing up (which was forbidden). There was a line of children behind him, impatiently shouting. Someone pushed, and Norman heard a teacher cry out and watched the boy fall twelve feet to the asphalt pavement. Fortunately, nothing serious resulted. Gerald spent the night in the hospital, where a nurse grumbled to her supervisor about the scars on the boy's back. In the morning, the supervisor told the social worker, who decided to send a note to the family's pastor. Before she wrote the note, she advised the chief administrator, who praised her judgment in coming to him. Melinda Mclain's church donated a sizable check every year to the hospital. He wasn't going to jeopardize that to save some pickanniny's hide. When the social worker protested, she was fired.

That was in the spring of 1951. Norman had the ground beneath the slides and swings covered with rubber matting, an idea for which he received a twenty-dollar bonus. By concentrating on not dreaming in public places, he made it through the summer without incident, but in the fall he went to buy shoes at Spiegal and Sons on Broadway, where they were having their annual Columbus Day sale. He had removed his old shoes and reached for the new when his mind seized the opportunity to go off on its own. When he finally tracked it down, he found himself standing in the middle of the store dressed only in his undershirt, a gray suede Oxford in his hand. "Oh, dear," Norman said. They ushered him back to the asylum, where he stayed for six months, during which time the alcoholic principal retired. With no one to go to bat for him, Norman was placed on disability. Since everyone except the Board of Education knew he was harmless, he had his run of Montgomery; when he got outrageous, they simply sent him back to Midstown for a spell. With so much time on his hands, Norman was free to keep an eye on Gerald. Gerald paid no more attention to him than he would have to a stray dog. Once, with Iceman, he'd made fun of Norman, and Iceman had rebuked him so sharply that the retort stung for days. Norman was glad that Gerald had Iceman. Iceman was smart and tough and would have been the perfect one to pass his knowledge to. He wondered why Iceman hadn't been chosen, and when the fire told him, he was sorry he'd wanted to know.

So Norman lived: communing with fire, practicing his leaps, dreaming of flight. The spaces in his days left him opportunity to explore, and one afternoon he wandered into the courthouse Hall of Records, where he learned that the house he lived in had been built by a man who was murdered in 1899. By the time he'd gone through all the records and knew who owned what and who was married to whom, he'd developed a taste for research that led him to the library. There, over the years, he painstakingly read every book he could find about colored people and Africa, discovering questions for all those answers that had plagued him in 1949. Sometimes, for an evening's recreation, he visited Meredith's window, where he began to notice that her breasts were sagging, and the gap between her legs no longer glistened. Like the memory of poverty to a man who's hit the number, his desire for Claire faded, as did the confusion about what to do every time the birds brought news of Gerald's beatings. Even when they told of the permanent scar the child would have on his back from the belt buckle's gouging of his flesh, even then Norman held his peace. The boy had to devise some survival skills for himself. It was part of growing up, of getting ready for the day Norman would reveal to him that he was chosen.

CHAPTER
11

Gerald's sister, Delight, fell out of her carriage in May 1957. Abigal had only recently stopped pinching herself when considering the child. For five years after the death of her daughter in 1947, she had tried to conceive; for the next three years she'd made love without expectation, resigned to the thought that nothing more than pleasure would come of it. She felt cheated. Never again would her waist thicken or her tongue crave the density of ice. She would not cry, "Oh, *feel*, Alexander, it's moving." When she discovered she was pregnant, she was ecstatic. Half her days she spent giggling at herself in mirrors; at night she dreamed of powdering satin rumps. She let all her dresses out and practiced sleeping on her back.

Delight's impending arrival was marked with all the ceremony customarily reserved for firstborns. Alexander was so pleased with himself that he walked around with his chest thrust out, and allowed four weeks to pass without remembering to beat his son. During this period he handcrafted a cradle and painted the extra bedroom blue, a decision that cost him another two days' toil when the baby turned out to be a girl.

Everyone agreed that the Fletchers had named the child right. Eleven months old at the time of the accident, Delight had been distinguished by an absence of crying that for a time concerned Abigal, it being a well-known fact that retarded children did not know enough to cry. But Delight was one of those children who are born content. At her birthing, the doctor had to smack her three times before he could hurt her feelings. Anybody could make her burst into giggling, even Hattie Silas, Christopher's widow, who was ninety-one, half blind, and toothless. But if Delight reacted to everyone with favor, it seemed to Gerald that she loved him most of all. Even in her mother's arms she would reach for her brother, enjoying nothing so much as to pull his ears or stick a finger in his nose. In light of this, the fact that Gerald had contributed to her accident was punishment enough. But his father did not understand this.

Abigal had gone shopping, leaving Gerald to babysit. As a result, he'd had to reschedule his meeting with Iceman. That day he and Iceman were to discuss strategies for dealing with Gerald's father, the possibility of murder having been dismissed and that of suicide not yet implemented. It was Iceman who insisted that this meeting be held. Although he knew from Gerald about the beatings, he had never witnessed one until the previous week. Gerald had been caught talking in school again, and his teacher had sent a terse note home. Iceman and he were in the living room playing checkers when Alexander stormed in, the note in one hand, the belt in the other. Horrified, unable at first to abandon his friend, then, in the presence of such brutality unable to stay, Iceman had slunk home, using the Lord's name in vain. Wise enough to know that he could expect no assistance from adults in Montgomery, he resolved to come up with a solution himself.

So the meeting was established, and then delayed by Gerald's responsibility. It did not occur to either boy that they could have met in Gerald's front yard, rather than in the woods behind the town barn; each was too fond of ritual. So Gerald fretted, wondering when his mother would return, and what plan Iceman had come up with. It was a lazy morning, blue sky and bright sun, hot, but pleasant. Behind the house a cardinal was singing its tiny heart out. The carriage in which Delight slept was parked on the concrete sidewalk, and Gerald glanced at it from where he lay on the lawn, and closed his eyes. He was never able to reconstruct the sequence after that point. Perhaps he'd fallen asleep; when he looked, Delight was standing, her balance precarious as she gurgled at him, fists held above her head. Then she was tumbling, head-first, and Gerald, on his haunches now, dove, trying with his hands to break the fall. Her head hit the pavement with a crack that activated a siren in his head and enveloped him in heat. Flat on the ground, his hands inches from her nose, he looked at her still and crumpled body, at the blood streaming from her head. It was only an instant between the shock of her fall and her screaming, but in that moment he'd been certain she was dead. Dizzy with relief, he struggled to his feet, picked her up, and was trying to assess the damage when his father's white Buick rolled up. What Gerald felt then was what condemned men feel in the instant before the trigger is pulled, the switch thrown, the pellet dropped into acid. The fact that his mother, arms laden with packages, sat beside his father was no more comfort than the droning of the priest's last benediction. Abigal dropped her packages, bolted from the car, and ran toward them. Wordlessly, she reached for the child; wordlessly, Gerald gave her up. Left empty now, hearing bird song and a smack on the sidewalk, wrapped suddenly in a cool, soft mist, he looked toward the car. Alexander sat with his head bowed; both hands gripped the dashboard. For a moment Gerald thought he would not get out, that he would head back to work, without lunch, without speaking. The door opened. His father swung from his seat, leaving the car door gaping, stalked toward him. Delight had stopped screaming; his mother took her into the house.

91

He was alone.

"What happened?"

Incoherent with fear, Gerald began to speak of bird song and sunlight . . . perhaps he'd been sleeping . . . her fists raised like a warrior's . . . His father, understanding it perfectly, unleashed his belt. Terror flooded Gerald, receded; when it returned, it was capped with defiance. Always, he'd stood and taken his punishment, in the beginning too afraid to run, later much too proud. Now he knew he wasn't going to take this beating. He didn't deserve it; it was an accident. He turned and ran. Alexander, in his astonishment, froze, then leaped in silent pursuit. Gerald had made it around the corner of the house when his foot caught in the coil of new clothesline his father had been promising to string. He tried to kick his way out of the trap, but his father was upon him, the force of his first blow driving the boy to the ground. "Run from me, will you?" Alexander grunted. "Trifling Negro." The belt fell—not the leather, the buckle. Gerald closed his eyes and lay there, curling his body into the smallest possible target. This beating, he knew, would last forever. This one he would not live through.

He had lived. Not through any strength of his own, but because Abigal had come to remind her husband that he'd not eaten lunch and had to get back to work. When Gerald had gone to discover that the extent of Delight's injury was a nasty bump (which eventually faded and left her flawless), he went to the bathroom to assess his own condition. The welts on his arms he gingerly smeared with Vaseline. His back presented a problem. He couldn't reach the hole beneath his right shoulder where the buckle had literally eaten his flesh. The blood had stuck to his shirt, took skin with it when he pulled it away. As he looked at his back in the mirror, his stomach turned and a wave of heat and dizziness drove him, terrified, to his knees. "Ma!" he screamed. "Ma. Help me." Abigal came into the bathroom. "I got dizzy," he said. He looked helplessly at her and vomited. She moved back as he retched, then pulled him to his feet and guided him into her bedroom. "Lay down," she said. "I'll be right back." The room turned. When she came back she washed his face with a warm cloth, gripped his shoulder. He winced. Gently, she turned him around, peeled his undershirt. He screamed. She gasped at the wound and closed her eyes. "It'll be all right," she said. He wouldn't look at her. She bathed and bandaged his back, put her lips to his forehead. "You got a little fever. Go lay down a while."

He didn't. He called Iceman. "Let's meet."

"You all right?"

"Let's meet."

"Okay, when?"

"Right now. Same place."

"Five minutes," Iceman said. "You all right?"

Three minutes later, fighting dizziness, Gerald sat in the middle of the small clearing he and his friend used as a hideout.

Iceman burst into the opening. "Jesus," he whispered. "What happened to you?"

To his own amazement, Gerald began to sob. Iceman knelt, gathered him in his arms. He began to rock him.

"Iceman, why don't he love me?"

"I don't know. But *I* love you. You know I love you, don't you?"

Gerald, sniffling, was appalled.

"*Don't you?*"

"You know guys don't love each other."

"I can love anybody I want," Iceman said. "And I love you. You love me, too, don't you?"

93

Iceman was rocking him. The dizziness welled, subsided. "Yes," Gerald said. "I love you."

"Then nobody can hurt us. As long as we love each other, nobody can hurt us. Not on the inside. They might hurt us on the outside, like your father hurts you, but they can't touch us on the inside."

"You sure?"

"Do a bear shit in the woods?"

Gerald smiled against his friend's chest, but inside, the storm was building. "Ice!"

"Yeah?"

"I'm gonna cry again."

"Go on," Iceman said. "I got you covered."

When the crying had spent itself, Gerald wiped his face and nose on his undershirt.

"How you feeling?"

"I keep getting dizzy and I'm hot and cold. But mostly just my back hurts."

"Lemme see." He pulled Gerald's shirt up and with hands gentler than Abigal's removed enough of the bandage to enable him to see. He didn't say anything, but neither did he close his eyes. He covered the mangled flesh and kissed Gerald on the back. Then he put his arms around him. They sat, Gerald light-headed and feverish, the print of a kiss on his back below the wound. He held on to Iceman until his head cleared. He was better now. He was going to make it. This time. But there would be another. And another. Despair battered him.

"Ice, what am I going to do? I can't take it any more."

"I got it all figured out."

"You do?"

"Yup."

"Well, tell me."

"You're going to join the church." Iceman smiled. "You're going to get saved."

"You're crazy."

"Unh-unh. Smart. Join the church and your father will *have* to treat you better. You'll be . . . what do they call it? The Lord's annointed."

"But you don't believe in that."

Iceman's glasses had slipped down his nose again. "No. But you do."

"I'm scared not to."

"Ain't no difference."

Gerald thought about it. Ever since he'd been old enough to understand, his mother had urged him to accept Christ as his personal Savior, to bow down before the altar and pray until his heart cracked and opened, whereupon the Spirit could enter. He'd been baptized at the age of five: dressed in soft white baptismal garments and immersed in the galvanized tub that sat shrouded by curtains behind the pulpit. This preparatory step taken without his consent, he'd never taken the next. It was not that he was unmoved by religion. He loved the singing and the clapping of hands, the whirling dances that occurred when members of the church were brushed by God's hand and made "happy." He liked the way the shafts of sunlight came through the windows on Sunday morning, looking, Iceman said, like the broad blades of angel swords. But the sermons, replete with images of death and desolation, of hellfire that waited for the ungodly as surely as night waited for the day, fired him with fear and confusion: how could a God who was merciful devise such unfair and fiendish punishment? Fear might have driven him to the altar by the time he was ten had he not been too stubborn to embrace a God who had allowed his grandfather to die. That was the first time he had really prayed for something besides his father's death, and God had not interceded. One night the phone had rung, and in the morning his father had left to go to the burial. Now Alexander had been made a deacon in the church, and had authority. Gerald did not want anything to do with a religion that exalted his father. His fear remained, but he refused to pray. He began to be scornful, took to heart the dictum that said everybody talking about Heaven wasn't going there. Several of them he knew; they were in the congregation. He discovered the sins they were guilty of (self-righteousness and self-pride, small-mindedness and cruelty) on the large white sign hanging on the pulpit, on which were printed most of the sins any creative human being could conceive of. At the bottom of the sign was the legend: *The Wages of Sin is Death.* He did not remember when he'd recognized the alarming lack of agreement between that sentence's subject and verb, but he could never enter the church without noting it and feeling superior. He always expected to be struck down for this vanity. But he couldn't control it, and his relationship to his father's religion continued to be characterized by his bouncing between one pole of terror and one pole of scorn.

Now Iceman had suggested a possibility that just might work. Those who were in the church had vowed to follow a code of conduct, one tenet of which was that each was the other's servant and must be treated with love and deep respect. Once a year they participated in a ceremony to reaffirm this vow: they washed one another's feet— male knelt before male, female before female. Would his father kneel before Gerald? Could he beat somone whose feet he'd bathed?

"It might work. But I'm scared."

"Of what?"

"To get up in front of all those people. To walk to the altar by myself."

"Is that all?" Iceman said. "Forget it. I'll go with you."

And he did. The next Sunday, after the sermon, Pastor Mclain made the "altar call," in which she asked if any in their midst were prepared to accept Christ. Iceman tapped him on the arm. In a move that would forever fix his memory in Gerald's pounding heart, Iceman stood first. As they walked the blood-red runner to the altar, Gerald did not know that the amazed whispering had nothing to do with him, but with the fact that God had succeeded in bringing Iceman to his knees. That close behind followed the boy with three eyes was of interest only to Alexander (who felt suddenly exhausted) and Abigal (whose eyes were shining), and to Norman, who, home from the asylum, wondered at this unexpected turn of events.

The church lifted its collective voice in song, and Gerald began silently to pray. He knew that his heart must be repentant, that he must feel sorrow for all the sins that he'd committed. He began to enumerate them. Sorrow for what he did to himself with his hands. Sorrow for stealing candy from the five-and-ten. Sorrow for wishing he was dead. When he tried to feel sorry for having wished for his father's death, it took him fifteen minutes to acquire what even he would have characterized as imperfect conviction.

But now, everywhere around him, there was singing and the chanting of hallelujah. The singing was beautiful, the voices called out encouragement, the bodies pressed against him smelled of perfume and Ivory soap, and formed a barrier between him and his father. Now, in the space behind his tightly shut eyes, yawned the black, bottomless chasm beyond which stretched the corridor defined by bright light and clamoring silence. The chasm was his intelligence and disbelief. The corridor was the path of righteousness, the way to grace and perfect immunity. No one in this company would revile him while he walked there, none would lay a hand on him in anger; he would be exalted, chosen, elect. He had merely to take the step across the chasm, which meant dispelling his fear that without his intelligence he was nothing, that the silence in the corridor was that of creatures struck dumb by the brilliance of its light. But what had his intelligence done for him lately? Wasn't it better to be safe? The voices called out to him, insisted he could make it if only he believed. The God that dispensed to the converted new feet and eyes and hands would give him a new mind. The voices cajoled and caressed him. It was so nice to be a part of this, the object of everyone's attention and concern. He believed, stepped trembling across the dark and empty space. He was in the corridor now, the light illuminated and warmed the surface of his skin, the silence gave way to sweetest music. He was well on his way to getting religion when he thought about Iceman and wondered how he was doing. He half opened one eye, only to discover that Iceman, having kept to the letter of his promise, had left him at the altar.

CHAPTER
12

Gerald dropped from the rolls of the annointed six months later, not because his conversion had not succeeded in containing his father's wrath, but because Gerald could not keep his hands off himself. He knew that this failure resulted in sin; not only had he endured his mother's repeated warnings of blindness and insanity, but also he had read it on the sign in church. There, between gluttony and fornication, groaned the word "self-love." If this feverish clutching of himself were that, given its frequency, he had literally swept himself off his feet. Dazed by his obsession, fearing that he had been afflicted by calamity no one else suffered, he screwed up his courage and asked Iceman.

"Do you do it?"

"Do what?"

Unable to say it, Gerald pointed.

"Oh, *that*." Iceman grinned. "Not much. Only every chance I get."

Although Gerald laughed with his friend, the revelation did little to ease his mind. Iceman was different. He got away with things other kids would never dream of. For all Gerald knew, God had adopted the same lenient attitude toward Iceman that everybody else had.

That exchange with Iceman had occurred before his conversion. Now was a different story, for Gerald was, by everyone's acknowledgment, changed, and he was expected to have the strength to resist temptation. For six months he valiantly did so, during which time he was plagued by what to do with his hands. For obvious reasons, he couldn't keep them in his pockets. Even limp at his sides they had an annoying habit of straying toward the center of his body. He tried walking with them clasped behind his back, but his father threatened to beat him for acting "mannish." Finally he took to going around with his hands on top of his head. This worked when he was awake, but at night in bed with the lewd sheets caressing him, his hands, like homing pigeons, zeroed in between his thighs. He would find them there in the morning.

It seemed that he'd been obsessed by sex forever, that as far back as he could remember he'd been marked by heat and tumescence. Recently, after school and on Saturdays, he'd begun visiting the town barn across the street. There was nothing about machinery or tools that interested him, but he liked the easiness that flowed among the men, this and their curiously vulgar references to women. Most of all he liked the pinups on the walls, in which the women bared their breasts and curved hips, vulvas artfully concealed by a thigh or two coy hands. In a few the legs were opened, but an airbrush had removed the mystery, replacing it with the disappointing lack of hair and definition he found in his sister's dolls.

One day, in the room where the men took their coffee breaks and ate their lunch, he discovered beneath a pile of *Field and Stream* and *American Mechanics*, a half-dozen or more serious girlie magazines, the insides of which instantly made him crazy. He had finally found a suitable focus for his dreaming, better than pinups or women in the Sears catalogue, better than his mother in a full slip, better than Wanda, his baby-sitter until he was ten. Wanda was a sixteen-year-old who had allowed him to fondle her breasts until he was exhausted, but who had always caught and held his desperate hands when they tried to plunge between her legs. He began to love the women in these magazines because they had the ability to match his fantasies. In their smiles and eyes and bodies was the message that they would deny him nothing, would, finally, be more than happy to make him a man.

The existence of these women was the second thing that Gerald did not share with Iceman. It was not until he was married and looking back that he realized that he had stumbled upon the possessiveness and exclusivity that characterize matters of the heart. His discovery of these women marked the beginning of what adults called "growing up." That he did not tell Iceman is an indication of how important the women were to him. That he stole three of the magazines and neglected to throw them away when he got religion are two others.

On the day that Gerald formally left the church (it was called "backsliding"), Emmeline Robinson had dropped by with her five children, the oldest of whom, Dorothy, was a thirteen-year-old with the hips of a woman. The mothers had gone out (there was a sale someplace), leaving the children in Dorothy's and Gerald's care. Things developed. Dorothy began to tease him, called him Three Eyes. When he chased her to teach her a lesson, she led him twice around the house, back inside, and upstairs to his room. He had not understood what she was doing until she'd closed the door and stood with her back to it, her eyes brilliant with cunning, her smile daring him to take advantage. His response was to grab her in a headlock. She bit his leg. Wrestling, they fell on the bed, where, in a moment, deception ended, she panting as he explored the marsh between her legs, he terrified at the opportunity that was spread before him.

"Go on," she said. "Do it."

He couldn't. Though his heart galloped and his

mouth was dry, the only thing hard was the knot in his throat. What he really wanted was for her to allow him to look "down there," for while part of his fear was theological, part was good old-fashioned terror of the unknown. But he was afraid to ask; she might laugh and call him weird. To distract her he began rotating his fingers again, which only sharpened her insistence that he get on about the business currently at hand. It was with delirious relief that he heard the car turn into the driveway. Both jumped up. Dorothy, retrieving her panties and smoothing her skirt, leaped from the room, dashed down the steps, and was sitting on the couch reading a Sunday-school book when the women walked in. Upstairs, Gerald was looking disbelievingly at his transformation. He couldn't stand it. While it was possible that he would go crazy if he touched himself, he was certain to go crazy if he didn't.

He wandered downstairs just to let his mother see him. Dorothy smiled and winked and licked her lips in a motion that boiled his blood. Like an addict going for his overdue fix, he went back to his room and opened the closet. There, hidden in his winter boots, were his magazines, his women. He took one without looking and went down the hall to the bathroom. Inside, he locked the door, sniffed his fingers, and sat on the toilet. Turning the pages of the magazine with one hand, holding with the other a living hammer hard enough to drive nails into granite, he and the women whispered to one another. Groaning, he beat his body into submission, in the process, tumbling from grace.

When it was clear that he had fallen, his mother looked at him with a sadness that seared him with shame. The expression in his father's eyes was devastating: it said that once again Gerald had confirmed his worthlessness. Gerald stopped resisting. His father was right. He was no good, a failure, and would always be until Alexander loved him.

There was no one to talk about it with except Iceman, who insisted he was not worthless—he was valuable and unique. Reassured in Iceman's presence, when away from him Gerald lacked the courage to believe his friend. Living in his father's house had made him timid and confused. At times, the only things he felt sure of were his hatred and fear of Alexander, this and the shattering hunger for his father's love. Then he would exhaust himself trying to discover the means to earn this love, for it had become the ticket by which he could enter the community of his peers. He did not think of it precisely in these terms, but he knew he was an outsider, different. He did not possess the ability to pretend self-confidence or toughness as other boys did, and his imagination failed at playing the dozens. It was impossible for him to look anybody but Iceman in the eye, and he spoke to adults in a whisper that eventually infuriated them because they figured anybody as smart as he was ought to have the sense to speak up. As an athlete he was mediocre, not because he had no skill, but because he was afraid to take chances. So he would never go for the extra base on the ball hit into the gap, and when he had the open jump shot in a close contest, he would invariably pass it up. The last one chosen in pick-up games, he was the first to be picked on by the current bully. Most fights he avoided by guile; if he could not, he took a thrashing, for getting beat up was somehow less terrifying than fighting back. He felt alone, different, the one spoiled apple in the barrel. He longed to belong to someone or something. There was only Iceman.

CHAPTER
13

So many things began to happen in 1960. It was as if Montgomery had held its collective breath all through the lame-duck year of '59, waiting for the new decade to let it out. Then the force and heat of the exhalation howled like a whirlwind through the town, bending things freakishly before it. By the time 1961 lay limp with sweat, exhausted, but satisfied that it had made a name for itself, grownups were locking doors to their bedrooms and hiding knives in places children couldn't find.

Not that nothing happened in 1959. Andre Fillis, Norman's firstborn, was promoted by the army to staff sergeant. Meredith's oldest daughter, Rachel, was arrested when she began underselling the other prostitutes out at the racetrack. Soapsuds took his doctorate in linguistics from Howard University; his dissertation was titled "Profane Etymologies." In the spring, Iceman discovered in *Look* aspects of a certain Eastern philosophy; he was currently trying to figure out how to walk through fire and lie upon a bed of nails. This caused a falling-out between Iceman and Gerald, Gerald's position being that Iceman had gone off the deep end. Iceman was furious. "I ain't never said nothing about what you believe in. Virgin Mary and miracles and shit. What the fuck's the matter with you?"

Angry, and hurt, Gerald walked away. For two days he nursed his pain, avoiding Iceman, who approached him once, but backed off when Gerald refused to speak. When loneliness forced him to consider it without self-pity, Gerald realized that Iceman was right. He went to look for him, found him behind his house constructing a flat bed.

"Hey."

Iceman looked up, pushed his glasses off his nose, "Hey back at you."

"I'm sorry."

Iceman didn't even think about it. "I forgive you," he said. "Hand me that board over there. Please."

Gerald had his thirteenth birthday that August. It was not special to him, mainly because Iceman had been sent for two weeks to a relative in Tennessee and wasn't around to help him celebrate. Alexander, before he went to work, congratulated him for having made it to thirteen, As was her custom, his mother asked him how it felt to be a year older. She baked a cake, the candle on which Delight blew out before he had a chance to, ensuring that his wish for his father's death would not be granted. For presents he received a new bathrobe, a belt, and three books, which he'd already read.

Fifteen minutes after he'd eaten his cake, he was bored. He realized he should have gone to the golf course, where he'd recently begun to caddy, but he'd thought taking the day off on his birthday was the adult thing to do. Now it was too late; assignments at the golf course were on a first-come, first-served basis, and most of the caddies arrived around seven in the morning. With nothing to do and no one to do it with, he filled his pockets with smooth, flat stones and went down to the forbidden pond. When he'd thrown all the stones into the water, he tried unsuccessfully to catch a frog. Then he wandered across the road to the town barn. But the men were in a foul mood today, cursing and waving their hands about a denied pay increase, and he decided to go exploring in the woods behind the barn, the end of which he and Iceman had looked for but never found.

It was gratifying to think of the forest as having no end. It was a beautiful wood with a variety of splendid trees, the most evident of which was evergreen. In many spots the trees were thick enough to block the sky, but here and there they thinned to let in sunlight. There was a stream, where, if you sat perfectly still, you could watch the animals tiptoe up to drink, or to lick the salt Norman laid out for them in winter.

So Gerald walked, his mind flitting, now to Iceman in a place called Tennessee, now to the bright streak of a startled blue jay, now to the woman he'd yet to possess. He was involved in creating this being, made up of parts of females he'd found in magazines, when he felt something on the trail behind him. He turned, but there was nothing. For a whole minute he was motionless, studying the branches and brush the way Iceman had taught him, looking for movement that spoke of living things. Nothing moved. This could only mean that there was an animal hiding in fear, or a human who, for whatever reason, did not choose to be detected.

"Iceman?"

But he could see nothing, and now, as the minute wound down, he no longer *felt* that anything was there. He continued walking.

This time the sound was unmistakable, a sharp crack as a foot fell across a fallen branch. Gerald whirled. There, some twenty yards behind him, in a white long-sleeved shirt, white pants, and sneakers, stood Norman. It was not the first time Gerald had seen him in these woods; he and Iceman had often crossed his path. Depending upon his mood, he would speak or not, but he never stopped or bothered them. So Gerald wasn't afraid, only a little annoyed that Norman had interrupted the creation of his dream woman's breasts.

"Go on about your business, Norman Fillis," he hollered. "Go on."

But when he turned again, Norman was still behind him, the twenty-yard gap reduced to ten.

"I said go *on!*" Gerald bent, picked up a small stick, and threw it. Norman dodged the missile and stood with his hands behind his back, patient, as if he had the rest of his life to accomplish his mission.

What the heck, Gerald decided. If he wanted to follow, let him. He continued walking, but it wasn't the same. Somehow the presence of Norman had taken out of the afternoon what little fun there was. When he got to the ravine, which was twenty feet wide and forty down to the jagged rocks that littered its bottom, he decided to turn and go home, rather than walk to the spot where he could jump across. He turned, and found Norman standing close enough to touch. Suddenly, Gerald was afraid.

"Don't be scared," Norman said gently. "Ain't no reason."

"Why don't you leave me alone, Norman? I got no time to be messin with you."

"Do you know what you scared of?"

"Who says I'm scared?"

"Not me," Norman said, "not your father, but death. Ain't no reason to be scared, Gerald. Death ain't dying. It's just a passing stage. I'm here to tell you."

"What you talking about?"

"You the chosen one."

Now he was really frightened. "Chosen? For what?"

"To be the one I pass my knowledge to. You're chosen. Special."

Gerald took a step back, but in that direction lay the ravine, the rocks at the bottom.

"Easy," Norman said. "You ever knowed me to hurt someone?"

"What you want?"

"To talk. Will you listen?"

"I ain't got all day. My mama . . ."

"Don't need all day. Will you listen?"

Here he was, on his thirteenth birthday, in the middle of nowhere with a madman. Like most of those Gerald had read about, this one wanted to talk. Well, at least he'd have something to tell Iceman when he returned from Tennessee.

"Sit down," Norman said. Gerald moved away from the edge of the rocky place, sat with his back against a tree. For the next half hour, the madman held him spellbound.

In the olden days, Norman said, colored people used to fly. At the very beginning of the world they developed tremendous control of their bodies. This control came from the only place it could have—the mind—and was yet apparent in the grace with which colored people moved, in their walk and dance, and in their athletic ability.

Did Gerald know about slavery? Not how his schoolbooks painted the picture, which made you ashamed, but what it was really like, how it had lacerated the soul and made you angry just to think about it. In the teeth of this oppression, colored people had artfully pretended to have no mind, or at least not enough to shake a stick at. This deception was necessary, for it allowed the physical self to survive.

Then he said the strangest thing in that strangest afternoon: there can be no survival without deception.

But while they practiced deception, Norman con-

108

tinued, they did not preach it. As a result, the children grew up mistaking mask for matter, never wondering at where the marvelous grace in their bodies came from, never questioning its possibilities. So they only danced, when they could have flown.

"They never made the connection. Read about Moses partin the Red Sea, Jesus walkin on the water, clapped hands when the Hebrew boys stroll out the fiery furnace. Looked at pictures of Asia man walking through flame or lying like feathers cross a bed of nails ["Iceman!" Gerald thought] and never *once* made a connection. Think of it! It's so simple a little baby could understand. How'd we know what was in Edison's mind before we could turn it on? *The only way the mind can be made manifest is through the physical.* See what I'm sayin?"

White people, Norman said, knew this, but kept it hidden for fear the skies would be full of flying black folks. They created the myth of the dumb athlete and made the achievement of physical excellence a second-class act. "But the body can't do but two things the mind don't tell it to. That's blink and breathe."

Then he changed course, without pause or transition. The things white folks claimed they discovered, he said, black folks knew from jump street. "We knew the earth wasn't no center of the universe. That's why we worshiped the sun. We *respected* the earth—only a fool don't respect the place he live in—but the sun was number one. We knew why apples fall down, stead of up, that certain plants could heal. *Shoot*. Naming something don't mean you discovered it.

"But all of that was child's play, really. The tough stuff they ain't no closer to than China is from Timbuktu. Ask em why Nassau women down in Florida, no more than four feet high, got titties they can throw over their shoulders and muscles like a man. Ask em why there's a

109

river in Georgia, the bottom half muddy, the top like chalk, and why the muddy flows *up*stream and the chalky down, and why they comes together but *does not mix*."

Then he paused, and said calmly, "You didn't know that, did you?"

"No," Gerald said, his brain soft with visions. "I didn't."

"Boy," Norman exulted, "I got so much to tell you. Watch!" He snapped his fingers, and the air was suddenly thick with birds, their wings slapping against the breeze-less day. They lighted on his shaven head, on his arms and shoulders, hovered at his thighs, kept coming until he was dark bird feathers in the shape of man. Then he shouted, and they lifted into the magic air, circled, disappeared.

"Jesus," Gerald whispered.

"That ain't nothing. I can fly. Not well as I want to, but I can." He took two steps and poised at the edge of the ravine.

"No," Gerald cried. "You can't. . . ." But Norman was leaping, soaring like some aged and improbably attired ballet dancer, coming down lightly on sneakered feet on the distant other side. Turning, he called, "Come on. You can do it."

Gerald looked at Norman, then he looked down at the jagged rocks. There was a river inside him trying to flow both ways. Everything was in twos: one voice saying, "Fool, don't be a fool," the other screaming that he should try it, even though the distance was nearly twice as far as he'd ever jumped, and the rocks down forty feet below would smash his body if he fell. In a soothing, seductive tone, Norman called again. Gerald let the voice caress him, begin to dissolve his doubt. Inexplicably, he looked above. The sky was empty, blue, impassive. "Fly, boy," Norman whispered. "Fly." The river flowed one way. Gerald was calm now, strong, certain. He'd stepped to the edge of the ravine and gathered his body, when, in the distance, way off in the middle of Montgomery, the fire alarm went off, sobbing of destruction caused by flame. Startled, he teetered, nearly lost his balance; fear enveloped him in heat. He remembered what he'd been taught in Sunday school: demons were housed in the bodies of madmen, these demons were disciples of the Devil, who had many voices, any one of which could be tuned to the ear of one Satan wished destroyed. Trembling, he looked down at the rocks. He'd come so close to jumping. So close. He took another look at Norman's crumbling face and turned to run back home, in his ears as he fled the madman's anguished wail of disappointment.

When Gerald told Iceman about that afternoon, Iceman didn't think it was funny. "You stay away from him," he said, and drove a nail into his bed of torture.

Gerald looked at the menacing contraption. Here with Iceman, his adventure didn't seem so dangerous. "Oh, he wouldn't hurt me. I'm his chosen one. I'm special."

"You're special to me, too. You want to jump, jump where I can see you."

"Why? If I fall, I won't die. Norman said so."

Iceman scowled at him. "*That ain't funny.*"

"I'm only kidding. Ease up."

"Don't let that bird thing fool you. You feed em enough, they come."

"I know. . . . He talked about lying on nails like you want to."

"He read it in a book."

"What about what he said about slavery?"

"I don't like to think about that."

"Me neither . . ." A robin swooped onto the eave of Iceman's house. Gerald watched it watch him. "Ice, you ever wish you was white?"

Iceman looked away. "Do you?"

"Sometimes. Not *white* white, just . . . you know."

"I used to," Iceman said. "When I was littler. I didn't want fat lips, or nappy hair. I wanted to be able to toss hair out of my eyes, like the white boys, you know?" Both were grinning. "But the church helped me."

"The church?"

"Yeah. I'm made in God's image, so . . ."

"So God's colored and wears glasses." Gerald laughed.

They felt they had come too close to something and each backed away from the silence that surrounded it.

"He really jumped?" Iceman asked. "I mean he jumped *over* it? Standing start?"

"Yup."

"Must be some kind of world record."

"Wonder what the record is?"

"Come on." Iceman took him inside to his room, where he looked it up in *World Record Holders*.

"Twenty-five feet."

"Let me see. . . . Ice, that's the running broad jump. Look, world record *standing* jump. Eighteen feet. Holy Moses, how you figure that?"

"Maybe they don't let niggers jump for that record."

"Could be."

"Still," Iceman said in a small distant voice, "it's a long way, ain't it?"

"Yup."

"Who knows?" He shrugged and looked out the window. "Maybe the sucker *can* fly."

"Yeah. And maybe my father'll stop beating me. Maybe we'll be rich and famous and live forever."

He said it jokingly, and he expected Iceman to laugh. But he didn't. He pushed his glasses back up on his nose and looked his best friend straight in the eye.

"Maybe we will," he said.

112

PART THREE
1960-1961

CHAPTER
14

Nobody realized they'd been holding their breath all through 1959. It was as if the decade of the sixties had sent vibrations of the slaughter and beauty that were to mark it, the frequency of which arrested everybody's respiratory system. Twenty years later, folks in Montgomery could look back and see they weren't the only ones acting like they had the hiccoughs. People were holding their breath everywhere—in Vietnam and Kenya, in Harlem and Cuba, in Dallas and Watts and Mississippi. Even the man in the moon had stopped breathing, aware that soon his dark side would be revealed, and everyone would know what he was made of.

The year 1960 started off without any real distinction. Iceman gave up nails for the New Year and developed a passion for Navajo Indians that lasted five months. In February, Ruth Potts gave birth to a baby boy. Pastor Mclain announced that her second cousin was moving to town, but didn't say her cousin's husband was a drunk. As it did every year, spring swept into Montgomery at the last minute, breathless, apologizing for having once again mislaid her calendar. Hard on the lady's heels, as cool as she was flustered, came Hosea Malone, bringing with him a trunkload of dope, a fat white woman, and all those earthworms.

The night before the morning Hosea left the first time, he had made extraordinary love to Meredith, a prolonged, passionate handling of her body that created in her a sense of confusion. As the mother of seven children, she did not consider herself inexperienced; she had sent away for a marriage manual after the birth of her first child, and had, over the next several years, introduced her husband to the information she'd discovered there. She had done this incrementally, the way a woman bent on marriage secretly slips the potion into her reluctant lover's food, sensing that too much too soon would threaten her man and her scheming.

In 1948, black folks in Montgomery did not think of sex as an art form susceptible to the kind of improvisation they demonstrated in their music, in the way they wore hats and walked and named things. But had anyone had the inclination to frame the question "Is your husband a good lover?," Meredith would have paused and answered, "Yes." Then, having already violated the boundaries of good taste, she would have smiled and said, "Thanks to me."

This night was permanently to rearrange her vision. Had the possibility of Hosea's leaving ever occurred to her (how could it? Did fire quench thirst? Did a hog have any business with a holiday?), she might have been suspicious, and therefore prepared for the devastation that would come with the dawn. But she could think of no reason for this marvelous thing that was happening to her except that Hosea, in his own way, was attempting to apologize for having slapped her. For Meredith, being slapped once by her husband in all those years was no big thing, and she lay back, stopped thinking, and gave herself to the wonder.

Years later, the memory of that night would reveal itself to her only as the most fleeting and unsubstantiated déjà vu, the feeling disconnected from image—not memory, but memory of memory. Before that, she had grown fond of recalling the night in segments. A morning spent cleaning houses for the succession of white women she worked for would be devoted to awe that he'd gotten up and turned the light on. On afternoons when the weather permitted her to walk the mile from town, she'd pretend to spend the taxi money she'd saved on remembering his hands, how they'd held her breasts, as if weighing them or testing for ripeness, then moved across her body ("Turn over," he'd said), lingered, as if memorizing her flesh, as if memory lived not in his brain, but in his fingertips.

She was now, husbandless, parent to six children, a woman still young and attractive, but shouldering a burden no man in his right mind would leap to assume. In the beginning, the memory of that night allowed Meredith to hide from her condition. She submerged her bitterness in its splendor, so that when she thought to blame Hosea it was not to accuse him of a foul and cowardly abandonment, but of taking from her that feeling. Eventually she came to make the connection between his leaving and his disappointment over his deformed son, and she discovered her hatred of the child. But there was nothing she could do about that except to pray that the Lord would change her heart. The child was gone; Hosea had taken it. Besides, remembering Hosea was another full-time job; she did not have the energy to think about the child. He was gone, so she forgot it.

In time, the night possessed her. She would find herself sitting in church, enveloped by the pounding music, the rhythmic clapping of hands, and she would remember, not the Saviour Who had died for her, but Hosea's thrusting that both created and filled her emptiness. Then she would pray a prayer so simple it never occurred to her that it might be inappropriate: "Oh, Lord, oh, Lord. I need it." "It" became the word that could plunge her into frenzy, cause the ache in her groin, the itch between her thighs, make her juices flow. Hosea had given it, and he

117

had taken it away. Would she ever find it again? She couldn't live without it.

She prayed for deliverance until the Lord, as was His disconcerting habit, gave her what she asked for. He did not grant her request for a lover; never again did a man lower himself between the sweet columns of her thighs. Instead, He erased the night's memory, took her understanding of desire. What was left had no name but confusion. She did not know why sometimes she couldn't bear the weight of fabric on her breasts, or why her belly was hot to the touch, or for what movement her limbs were trembling. She sought relief by pacing late at night naked in her living room, the shades undrawn.

Twelve years later, nine after the death of this understanding, Hosea came knocking at her door. His head was bare, his hair cut short and glistening. It was April. A layer of water covered the earth. Montgomery was alive with earthworms. On the streets and sidewalks, in the yards, they were everywhere, curved like the limp penises of drunken men. When Meredith saw who it was, she didn't allow it to register all at once. The sunlight negotiated a path through the earthworms, came halfway up the porch, and licked at the heels of his wine-colored shoes. She'd been washing dishes; she dried her hands on her apron, pushed hair back from her face. Then, in a movement that seemed as familiar to her as peeling carrots, she began to chew the ends of her hair. It was she who spoke first, slightly muffled because of the hair in her mouth.

"You back?"

She was smitten at once by the stupidity of this question, but if he shared the feeling, she couldn't read it on his face. His face was, understandably, older—not aged, matured. The mustache was a line of obsidian above his lips. He didn't speak, but his fingers moved as if they were caressing a hat's brim. A bird in the yard began to sing; Meredith found herself listening as if it would, in the next instant, tell her how to act.

"You looking fine," he said.

He was lying, and she knew it. She was skinny. Her breasts sagged and her skin had lost its tautness. She had on the ugliest housedress she owned, the blue one with the pattern of orange softballs. She was chewing the ends of her hair. But the sound of his voice was the first real thing that had happened to her in the last two minutes, and she was grateful. So grateful that she smiled, opened the screen door, asked him in. When he walked by, he brushed against her, and she felt on her bare arm the caress of silk, of which his suit was made. He stood in the middle of the parlor floor, out of place in that room; he was too grand, too fancy. She snuck a glance at his eyes, but his face was turned, throwing into sharp relief the curve of tendon in his neck. Something moved in Meredith, although later, when Hosea left that third time, she would not remember it as movement. It would linger as the smell of green things, as the sound a foot makes when it's pulled free from the sucking mud. Her heart was beating with the cadence of bird song, and a mysterious moistness pooled between her thighs. She didn't recognize the feeling, so she ignored it.

"You want some coffee?"

"Nope."

"Sit down?"

He sat, carefully, on the couch, avoiding the hole where white stuffing showed through. Just as carefully, Meredith sat across from him. "So," she said, her voice bright and breathless ("stupid," she thought), "what brings you this way?"

"I comes to live."

"Here? In Montgomery?"

"That's right."

He had found something fascinating in the room's filth and clutter, in the bare walls that needed painting, in the motto above the kitchen door, which spelled in bright-red letters: GOD BLESS OUR HOME. Now he studied the dime-store reproduction of the white Christ in its plastic frame on the end table. Meredith found herself oppressed by the silence. In her mind there was everything to talk about and there was nothing. She could ask him where he'd been all these years and how he'd gotten those clothes, finer than any she'd seen even on a white man, but she didn't want to pry. She could accuse him of desertion, but that would be saying the obvious, and she, already agonizingly aware of how terrible she looked, did not want to compound it with stupidity. She could have talked to him about the night before he left the second time, but she didn't remember it. She wanted to ask what made the tendon curve in his neck. But she couldn't even ask that question. There was a space around him like a cage of glass, a sign that said, "Don't ask me."

"How the children?"

"Oh, fine. All grown up. Rachel moved to Lantic City. Angela's married, living in Poughkeepsie. Susan Ann and Joyce got an apartment together. The rest in school."

"The boy. How he turn out?"

Meredith fell back against her chair as if she'd been smacked. She remembered that she'd forgotten the boy. Hosea was looking at her out of gray eyes startling in their lack of intensity. She wasn't sure what was more upsetting, his eyes or the fact that she'd forgotten.

"Hosea, Jr. dead."

"Oh? How long?"

"Right after you left the second time."

"From what?"

"Just stop breathing."

"He suffer?"

"Went in his sleep. The Lord is good."

"Why?"

She smiled brightly. "Why what?"

"Why is the Lord so good?"

She couldn't answer; she didn't know. She thought the gray in his eyes was suddenly deeper, the color of his suit. He grunted, stood. "I got to be going."

Meredith surged to her feet. "Already?"

"You got the money?"

She nodded. It had come the first week of every month for twelve years, like clockwork.

"Tell the girls their daddy'll be by to see em."

His back was turned. Just like that he was leaving, with nothing settled or explained. She hadn't even had the nerve to ask what made the tendon curve in his neck.

"When you coming back, Hose-ee?"

"Later."

"Tonight?"

He was gone, in a car wider than her living room. She did not know how long she stood there as if nailed to the floor, clinging to the memory of his neck. When she finally came out of her trance, she had the sense that she'd dreamed this encounter, although she knew she hadn't. His odor remained, a rich green-smelling after-shave, twined with the sound of his name. And there was the word he'd spoken that wrapped her in a cloud, quickened her.

"Later."

All day she moved as if she were blind, bumping into things. That night she made the girls go to bed early, scrubbed the house from sink to porch steps, and changed the linen. She turned the porch light on, so he could see

121

and avoid the earthworms. Then she bathed, washed her hair, and crawled into bed, where she lay naked. There, without certainty, fingering the unfamiliar wet between her thighs, she waited, thinking of gray eyes and a length of tendon. Finally, she fell asleep with the light on, still not understanding that when Hosea returned he would bring with him knowledge of what she'd done.

CHAPTER
15

Pastor Mclain had appointed a welcoming committee to greet her cousin. She recommended that this group, chaired by Abigal Fletcher, spread its itinerary over the period of a week, with staggered daily visits. If it were typed and sent ahead, the woman could plan her day and not have to get up off her knees while she was scrubbing the bathroom to greet unexpected visitors. Planning would also prevent her from being overwhelmed by guests the first few days and then left with the loneliness of an unfamiliar house during the next. In the meantime, the pastor said, everybody should pray for deliverance from these earthworms.

As the head of the welcoming committee, Abigal was the first to visit the new family. Early that Saturday morning she baked an apple pie, picked a bouquet of wildflowers, and took down her last jar of homemade strawberry preserves she'd been saving for the right occasion. A few minutes after noon, she set out on her mission, taking Delight and Gerald with her, since she'd been told that the new family had a daughter around Gerald's age.

The new couple, Percy and Gertrude Moore, had moved into the house next door to Pastor Mclain. The pastor lived in what was once a "white" part of town; there were still white families on her street. Across from her was a parcel of brush-studded undeveloped land, which, it had been rumored since the racetrack was completed, might be the site of a housing complex. This rumor had driven up the value of real estate in the area, and provided the pastor with an unexpected windfall.

Back in 1945, when she'd bought the house she currently lived in, the appalled white families on either side had immediately moved out. The pastor could not decide whether their flight had been caused by the color of her hair or the color of her skin, but she didn't waste a lot of time trying to come up with the answer. Instead, she bought both houses, selling one at a considerable profit when the rumor drove the price up. The second, she kept, against her deacon board's best judgment, occasionally renting it out. It was this house that the Moores had moved into.

It was a small, neat house, white, with green shutters, and someone had, as recently as this morning, swept the sidewalk. Ridges of worm flesh tangled in the defeated grass on either side, and worm secretions dried on the pavement like the script of a foreign tongue. Gertrude Moore, on the lookout for the past half hour, stepped onto the porch, her eyes squinting against the sun. She was tall, with a dark, pinched face. Her head was tied in a red kerchief, and her apron was purple. "My name Gertrude Moore," she said, "but everybody call me Gert." Gerald's mother smiled and said that nobody called her Abby, but Gert could.

Boxes littered the living room, and the atmosphere was redolent of disinfectant. Scrupulously clean, Gert was washing down everything—walls, ceilings, windows—with Lysol. You couldn't be too careful, she said. You didn't know what kinds of habits or sicknesses people who'd lived there had had. Besides, the Bible said cleanliness was next to Godliness. Abigal, still smiling, agreed. Gert thanked her for the gifts, buried her face in the flowers. In the kitchen, where she placed the bouquet in a jelly jar of water, the women chatted like old friends. When asked, Gert dropped her eyes and said that her husband was off "familiarizing" himself with the town—she meant he was out determining which bar would be most conducive to getting drunk in. From then on she looked at Abigal's throat when she talked, a habit so discomfiting that Abigal gargled with Listerine when she got home.

When Gert said what fine-looking children Gerald and Delight were, Abigal said, "Didn't I hear you had a daughter?"

"She went to the store to get some soap powder. Be back directly. Would you like some lemonade?" she asked Gerald's throat.

He said no, thank you, and went out into the back.

In the adjacent yard, penned in by a chain link fence, Jesus Mclain was trying to keep a soccer ball bouncing from foot to foot without letting it touch the ground. He was being as spectacularly unsuccessful as he was over-weight and arrogant. When he saw Gerald watching, he sneered and turned his back.

"Hey, scum bag," Gerald said.

"Yo mama wears army boots."

Jesus was the only person Gerald could hold his own with in the dozens. "Yo mama *is* an army boot."

"Yo mama chew glass."

"Yo mama's yo daddy."

"Yo mama suck worms."

"*Jesus*," Melinda Mclain called. "Come inside." She stuck a blue head festive with pink rollers through the back door. "And *you*," she said to Gerald, "stop messing with Jesus. Else I'll tell your daddy. You know what *he'll* do for you."

Gerald turned away, calling Jesus out of his name.

That the boy was overweight and arrogant could be blamed on his mother. Forty-one years old when she birthed him, Melinda Mclain called him her gift from Jesus, thus his name. Any gift from the Lord must be cared for; her way of caring was to isolate him from other children and continually to stuff food into his face. His arrogance came from his recognition of his mother's exalted position, and from being told that he was superior to the average colored child. Fiercely protective of her issue, his mother perpetually sounded a warning: "Don't mess with Jesus," words that soon became part of Montgomery's vocabulary. "Don't mess with Jesus," one man might say to another instead of "Good-bye" or "See you later." "You'd be better off messing with Jesus," a tired parent might say to a misbehaving child.

Jesus' whole name was Jesus Marcellus Mclain. In the late 1960s he went to Harvard (he was arrogant, but exceptionally bright), where in his first semester he passed for a Spaniard and called himself what sounded like Hey, Zeus. When people began referring to him as Zeus, he dropped his first name and introduced himself as Marc. Growing up slimmed him down, and he decided that he was handsome and should be a lady's man. He was aided in this deception by the shortage of young men that plagued America (they were all in Canada, or Vietnam, or dead) and by the fact that this was the season when black men of all persuasions found themselves pursued by white America's daughters. To these, he told his name, and insisted that they use it when alone with him. He would casually mention to his voyeuristic classmates whom he was seeing and when. This was how he got his reputation as a great lover. "Oh, Jesus," the girls cried out for three years. "Do it to me. *Yes*, Jesus." He was not above tape-recording the sessions.

There had been much flak about Melinda Mclain naming her son after the Lord. White folks thought it was funny. On the day of his birth, the local newsman on the radio began the six o'clock report with: "Today Jesus was born in Montgomery," an offense for which Melinda

126

Mclain had him fired. Church folks were a different matter. The naming was in poor taste, they said. Civilized people who spoke American should know better. Others said that whenever the child was summoned, the caller would be involved in blasphemy.

Pastor Mclain taught a Bible class on the subject. She made no mention of taste, simply dressed in the sky-blue chiffon dress that went so well with her hair, put on her Chinese alligator slippers, and strutted into the pulpit with a Blackgama mink draped casually over her shoulders. This was the dispensation of Christ, she said. The law given to the Israelites was superseded. Although Jesus was God, the Spirit, He was also Son, the flesh, human like all of them, and she went into a twenty-minute lecture on the Trinity that confused some people to the point of shaking their belief. Even the confused, however, were clear about who was boss.

Gerald was watching two intertwined earthworms when a voice behind him drawled, "Hello." He turned and stood staring, holding desperately to the last meaningful thought that had visited his head, which was: how do earthworms make love?

The second thing he noticed was her left arm. She carried it in front of her, held waist high, like a weapon or a portable barrier. From shoulder to elbow the limb was healthy, the skin smooth and pecan-colored, but from elbow to wrist the flesh turned angry, skin the color and texture of a pomegranate. Where the hand should have been was nothing.

He stared. The arm was held for the purpose of staring, invited you to discover its absence of hair, the corrugated surface that looked as if it had been boiled and scraped and boiled again. He had no way of knowing that women looked and experienced a hot flush of relief, or that old men found themselves entertaining images of tall gals in spike heels, and didn't know where the images came from. He knew what boys felt: irrational fear and a perverse longing to touch.

Of course he didn't want to stare. He was trained to turn away from others' deformities, to pretend they didn't exist. Oh, I'm sorry, I didn't notice you were missing a leg. Forgive me, I didn't see your prosthesis, your harelip, the hole in your face where your nose used to be. Guiltily, he looked up from all that ugliness, back into the most startling, breath-taking beauty he'd ever seen.

"Cat got your tongue?"

She had the thickest Southern accent. He shook his head. She smiled and flowed toward him.

"I made a bet with myself that I'd fall in love with the first boy come to visit." She stopped in front of him, her head to one side. "Think I will?"

He shrugged. She smelled of lilacs.

"I'm missing a hand. An accident. You obviously can't talk."

"I can talk," he croaked, and cleared his throat.

"Praise the Lord, the boy can talk. What's your name?"

"Gerald." Her eyes were light brown, or gray; were they changing color? Where had she gotten that face?

"How'd you get those scars on your arms?"

"I fell."

"Fell? Look like beating scars to me. Who beats you? Your mama or your daddy?"

"My father."

128

"My mama say I'm getting too grown for beating. My daddy never hit me. What you do to get beatings?"

"Nothing."

"Your daddy beat you for nothing? You don't *never* do nothing?"

"Sometimes."

"What?"

He shrugged.

"I bet *I* know what you do sometime. Don't you?"

"What?"

She smiled; he regained his balance. "What's *your* name?"

"Josephine. Josephine Elizabeth Moore. Formerly of Beacon, North Carolina." She made it sound like a question. "You see *Gone With the Wind*?"

He shook his head.

"Want to touch my arm?"

"No!"

"That's funny. How old are you?"

"Fourteen . . . in August."

"I'm fifteen last month."

He nodded.

"What do earthworms remind you of?"

"I don't know."

"Ain't you got no imagination? You believe in God, don't you?"

He nodded.

"Good. People don't believe in God ain't got no imagination. I couldn't love a boy didn't believe in God."

"I've got a spot in my eye."

"Do? Let's see. Ain't that peculiar. You got a girl friend?"

"No."

When she said that she had a boyfriend, Gerald grew weak with jealousy. She said he was an older man, twenty-

129

five; his name was Blue, short for Blueberry, a name she'd given to commemorate the color of his skin. She liked giving the names of colors to things; already she had named Gerald "Yellow," for the way the sun had lit his eyes the first time she saw him.

"You like it?"

She could have called him anything. She said why didn't they sit down on the porch steps, the grass was full of worms.

"Well, what you think?"

"About what?"

"Me, silly."

He felt poised on the edge of a high place; he leaped. "You're beautiful."

"I *do* declare," she said. "You say the sweetest things. I might fall in love with you after all. Want to kiss me?"

His heart thundered. "Yes."

"Touch my arm first."

He brushed it with his fingertips. It was soft. Her lips were soft. Her mouth tasted of peppermint. Then she pulled away. Her eyes, which had been laughing, mocking, now narrowed, grew grave. She touched a scar on his arm. Her finger was curious, sad.

"Hurt?"

"No."

"He beat you bad, don't he?"

"He don't love me," Gerald blurted. The unfairness of it brought tears to his eyes, and he looked away, dismayed that he was crying in front of a girl, a stranger. "You're lucky," he said. "You're lucky your daddy loves you."

"Well, that don't mean he always treat me right."

He wiped his face on his shirt. "He doesn't?"

Her eyes darkened and she took a deep breath. "Let's don't talk about daddies," she whispered. "Kiss me again."

Her tongue thrust at his teeth, wedged them open,

130

licked his gums and the roof of his mouth. "Gerald," his
mother called. "*You*, Gerald. Time to go."

He staggered into the house. He heard his mother
say, "Look like the children gets along."

"Good," Gert replied. "Josey needs a friend. She's
kind of moody sometimes."

On the way home Gerald marveled that the world
had been scrubbed clean for his return trip. When his
mother, something more than pity in her voice, said,
"Ain't it a shame for such a pretty child to be like that?"
he didn't answer. He was committing to memory the date:
Saturday, May 20, 1960. He thought he just might be in
love.

CHAPTER
16

A steady rain had fallen through the night, and when Montgomery woke on the morning of May 21st, it was to discover a landscape free of worms. Iceman, who'd worn himself out trying to keep the sidewalks clear, looked out his window and went back to sleep for two days.

The earthworms had wreaked havoc in people's personal lives. Having lost interest in fishing, men slouched around the house on weekends, criticizing the texture of corn bread and the quantity of starch in their shirts. Soon, more wives than was statistically probable were rolling over at night complaining of headaches. In the presence of their irritable elders, children grew skittish and subdued. They were being slapped more than usual, refused second helpings of dessert, and forced to eat kale and okra.

Even after the creatures had disappeared, reminders of their visit remained for months, principally in the nightmares of those afraid of snakes. More than one child refused to eat spaghetti. Folks who'd walked funny, who'd taken tiny steps and kept their eyes glued to the ground, gradually lengthened their strides, discovering the good taste of sunshine in their mouths and that the aches in their necks were not permanent. Only the philosophical and Pastor Mclain occupied themselves with questions of why and where the worms had come from. Nobody cared why and where they'd gone.

◆ ◆ ◆

Since the academic year was winding down, Gertrude Moore had considered keeping her daughter out of school until September. But she finally decided that whenever Josephine enrolled there would be a period of adjustment, so she went ahead and sent her for the remaining month. Although a year older than Gerald, Josephine was placed a year behind him. The guidance counselor explained to Gertrude that colored schools in the South were generally two years slower, and for the child's well-being she should be placed in a nonpressure situation. When the records were sent from North Carolina, the counselor said, she would re-evaluate in September.

So Josephine became a fifteen-year-old seventh grader. The reaction of her classmates was predictable. Twelve- and thirteen-year-olds make fun of what they consider to be different, and Josephine was illuminated by difference. She was older and larger. She was beautiful, stunningly so. Her drawl was so pronounced that someone suggested she use it for glue in art class, where they were making a wall-sized collage. And there was her arm without a hand, which she refused to cover or to allow to occupy any but center stage of her presence.

Gerald had walked her home after church on Sunday and had promised to meet her on Monday for lunch. They ate their sandwiches on the steps of the main entrance to the auditorium. The steps were usually covered with students when the weather was nice, but today, since Iceman had not come to school (or to church; he was still sleeping), Gerald and Josephine sat alone. Everybody else milled in small groups on the grass, or congregated across the street, where they held their hands over their mouths, laughing.

"I declare," Josephine said. "These is the rudest peoples I ever met. Who they mamas?"

"Don't pay them any mind."

"How I'm *not* going to pay em no mind?"

133

"Want to go inside?"

He took her hand and opened one of the four heavy auditorium doors. The door needed oiling; it cried as it closed. Inside the foyer she leaned against him, breathing hard.

"We'll hide in the cloakroom."

The room was dark and smelled of dust. He locked the door. Empty coatracks lined the walls. He put a finger to her lips as the outside door squealed; someone suppressed a giggle. Footsteps slapped into the auditorium, returned, clumped back outside.

"See?" He could barely make out her features.

"You're so nice." She lifted her face. He kissed her. Then he opened his mouth and her tongue slipped past his dry lips. She withdrew, he entered; for the first time in his life his tongue was in a girl's mouth. She sucked it, then broke for air. As he held her head against his chest he was trembling, not so much from arousal as from wonder at the tenderness he'd just experienced. He had another ally against his father, against life. Iceman on one side of him, Josephine on the other. It never occurred to him that only his flanks were protected. The bell rang. Wordlessly, they parted, headed back to class.

Every eighth-grade boy, black and white, was smitten by Josephine's beauty, but none would say so. Instead, they teased Gerald unmercifully. First, he was hanging out with a seventh grader: "cradle robbing," they called it. When they found out that Josephine was older than they were, they said she was stupid, a crippled retard who talked funny. By the time three o'clock rolled around, the new riddle was alive in the halls: what's brown, has five eyes and three hands? Why didn't Gerald trade in one of his eyes for a hand for Josephine? The girls, relieved that Josephine would pose no threat, expressed their relief in invective. Her dress was too long. She hadn't rolled her bobbysocks the right way, and her brand-new sneakers were not only unfashionably clean, but also the wrong kind. Had she gotten them from John's Bargain Store, or had a monkey made them in North Carolina?

Through all that afternoon, Josephine kept her head up, having learned long ago that the best way to deal with what she was feeling was to hide it. She made herself concentrate on her schoolwork, knowing that at three o'clock Gerald would be there to walk her home. As they left the jeering school and hurried through streets only recently recovered from earthworms, she chatted and reached for his hand, which, when she found it, was limp. This and the fact that he had not spoken or really looked at her slammed her into a silence that lasted until they reached her house. Then she said that the people in school did not act very Christian. "You know what color they are? Green. Pea-soup green."

He nodded.

"You all right?"

"Yeah."

"Come inside. Mama made chocolate cake."

"I got to get home." He returned her books. She regarded him, her eyes uncertain. Then her arm rose from her waist to her chest.

"See you tomorrow?"

"We go," he said flatly, "to the same school."

This caused her eyes to narrow. "Walk me home?"

"I guess so. Look, I got to go."

"*Kiss* me."

He looked at her mother's house, at Pastor Mclain's, at the sidewalk. "Unh-unh. Not here."

"You shamed?"

"I don't want to kiss you out here," he said angrily. "We'll get in trouble. I'll see you tomorrow."

"What," she said deliberately, "about yesterday?"

135

On the way home from church they had discussed the disappearance of earthworms and their discovery of one another, Josephine taking seriously his suggestion that the two events were linked. In the fifteen-minute walk that they stretched to thirty, he had found himself both fascinated and puzzled. She seemed older than he, yet younger. She would not comment on what she'd meant about her father not always treating her right. This condition, he thought, would give them something in common, but when he insisted that she tell, she laughed unconvincingly and said that her father was stingy, that in all her life he'd only once bought her a doll. She wanted him to talk about *his* father, and when he'd told her something of the beatings and the absence of love (it was hard to talk about; he didn't understand why it shamed him), she said she knew what it was like to be missing something you needed. He told her about Norman and being chosen, laughing when he said it, but she responded that it was clear to her that he was special. When she said that, he'd wanted to touch her mutilated arm.

"What *about* yesterday?"

When she would not honor that evasion with speech, he said, "Yesterday's got nothing to do with it. I just don't want to get in trouble."

"You know I ain't talking bout no kissing me."

She was talking about his betrayal. She was talking about the hope he'd given her and the fact that he, of everyone her age she'd ever met, had not treated her like a freak. That and the loneliness in his eyes were all it had taken for her to fall in love with him (she had not fallen; she had flown), and now he was taking that away. He was seeing her now through other people's eyes, and the only thing that kept her from hating him was the crushing sadness she felt, and the concentration it took to keep from crying. She wondered what he would say if she told him this, but she refused to beg. So she stood, blinking rapidly to stem the tears, and he said, "I got to be going."

She leaned forward, as if she were about to speak or attack him. Then she straightened. "Okay."

He walked away, feeling miserable. He'd gone about ten steps when she called, "Gerald?"

He turned. "What?"

"Nothing."

All the way home his shame was a taunting companion. Everything he'd been taught about responsibility, about doing what was right regardless of how people reacted, repeated itself mockingly in his ears. The way Josephine had been treated was sickening, and he should have stood up for her, but he couldn't take being the focus of everyone's derision. He'd rather be yelled at in anger than laughed at in scorn. He had to live in that school. What was he supposed to do? He'd thought he'd found a buffer in Josephine, but his being with her made him more vulnerable, more of an outsider. And he wanted to belong.

When he got home, his mother asked why he was late.

"I walked Josephine Moore home."

"That's nice."

Nice? He wandered upstairs, sprawled across his bed. What was he going to do? His palms began to sweat. Maybe he could get sick, stay home tomorrow. But tomorrow he had an algebra test. Whenever he said he was sick during the school year, his father asked him if he had a test; if he did, he had to go if he was able to walk. The one time he'd lied, Alexander had gone to school, and Gerald had paid for it with his flesh. He looked bleakly through the window where an afternoon sun benevolently beat. It was warm, springtime; he felt like December. Rolling from his bed, his stomach hollow, a sour taste in his mouth, he went downstairs and told his mother he was going to Iceman's.

Iceman was in his bedroom, wrapped in a white sheet, sitting on the floor in the lotus position. The radio was tuned to the one station in Montgomery that played classical music. Books, a basketball, and a model racing car were scattered across the bed. Iceman had given up Navajo Indians to fall in love with Martin Luther King, and, by extension, Mahatma Gandhi. These were the books in his room; on some of the covers was the brown, round face of King, on others the ascetic Gandhi. In their midst was a copy of the New Testament opened to the Book of Luke.

Having hated violence since he'd killed the cat, Iceman had discovered in passive resistance a means for confronting it, a tactic that, if properly employed, was infinitely more powerful. King had taught him new respect for Jesus, who, Iceman insisted, was a revolutionary, the ultimate human symbol of the nonviolent philosophy. Ultimate because he had given his life, in the process changing the course of history; human because he was imperfect, had resorted to violence to drive the moneylenders from the temple. It didn't make sense to Gerald, but he didn't say anything. He remembered the last time he'd expressed doubt about one of Iceman's passions.

When he'd sat on the floor and told his friend about his day, Iceman said, "Forgive em. They don't know any better."

"Easy for you to say."

"You know those kids. Ignore em long enough and they'll leave you alone."

"*You*, they might leave alone. Me, they'll hound to death."

"You deal with your father. You can't deal with this?"

138

"I don't see what my father's got to do with anything."

Iceman pushed his glasses back up his nose. "You like this girl, don't you?"

"Yes."

"You like her a lot."

"Yes."

"You're my friend," Iceman said, "and I love you. You'll do what's right."

"How do you know what's right?"

"You feel it. Want to borrow one of my books?"

"Nah."

"Play some basketball?"

"I got an algebra test tomorrow."

"My mama says she is one pretty child," Iceman said.

Gerald looked at him. Iceman was tossing the basketball from one hand to the other. He was a weird sight in his sheet and glasses, surrounded by books, the mournful music in the background. But he was solid, he was good people, Gerald's main man.

"She is," he said.

At dinner that night, Alexander unwittingly solved Gerald's dilemma. On his way home from work he'd seen Percy Moore, Josephine's father, staggering along Broadway, drunk as a skunk. The man was trifling and had already given the Moore family a bad reputation. Alexander didn't want Gerald to have anything to do with Percy Moore's daughter, lest the Fletcher name be dragged in the mud by association. If Gerald messed with his name, Alexander said, he would beat him until his head roped like okra. Good names were difficult to come by; he'd worked long and hard for his, and it was, this name, worth its weight in gold.

Gerald, wondering how much a name weighed, agreed.

The next day he avoided Josephine when he could and ignored her when he couldn't. It didn't take her more than thirty seconds to figure out what he was up to, and when she did, she was furious. Over the next three weeks she expressed her fury by hiding her hurt and becoming outrageous. Her drawl thickened and became almost incomprehensible. She wore heels and stockings to school and swept her hair off her face in a way that accentuated her beauty and made her look thirty. Drenching her arm in perfume, she carried it held before her at chest level. Iceman tried to make friends with her, but she was having none of these Montgomery boys. The only person she would allow in her company was her cousin, Jesus. But even he grew tired of being crucified, and Josephine was, finally, alone.

No one became better at laughing at her than Gerald. His jokes were the crudest and cruelest; when others poked fun, it was he who laughed the loudest; in the harsh, strained sounds was his fear that this acceptance by Josephine's tormentors was impermanent, that one day soon he'd be left outside again. When it was pointed out that he had originally befriended her, he held his breath and said that his father had made him do it until it was discovered that Josephine's father was a drunk.

Iceman was appalled and disappointed, and took Gerald to task. His guilt exacerbated by Iceman's tongue-lashing, Gerald stopped participating in the revelry. Iceman said that wasn't enough; he owed the girl an apology. Too weak to approach her in public, Gerald looked for an opportunity to speak to her alone. In church she never strayed from her mother's side and never looked in his direction. He called; she slammed the receiver in his ear. His letter was returned unopened. He began to go out of his way after school on the chance that she might be hanging around in her yard or on the porch. When the school year ended, he would occasionally walk down her street on his way home from the golf course, stand camouflaged behind the bushes on the undeveloped land across from her house. At those times, and at night, and when he awoke in the morning, the shame for what he'd done would clutch at his throat, and he would tell himself that the next day he would make it right. But except in church, he never saw Josephine all during that summer of the beautiful weather. From Sunday to Sunday she made herself a prisoner, alternating between mourning and rage, and a loneliness deeper than blue, taking what relief she could from the fact that at least she hadn't told Gerald her secret. Twice Gerald saw her father, a squat, heavyset man with graying hair, who, both times, was frowning. One afternoon he watched Meredith Malone, head bowed, leaving Melinda Mclain's house. He would not have paid any attention to this had it not been for the fact that it was July and Meredith was wearing boots and was wrapped in a blanket.

CHAPTER
17

"You came back," Meredith said.

She had seen him twice in twelve years; now she'd seen him twice in two days. She thought there was something profound in that. His suit was royal blue this morning, no tie; against his chest was hung a gold medallion. He hadn't been careful coming up the sidewalk. Bloody worms stuck to his left shoe. One was not dead. She watched it writhing.

"Children gone?"

"To school."

He saw that the house was spotless. Clean made the room look shabbier; dirt had hidden its true lack of splendor. She asked him to sit. He wouldn't. He looked at her. Her dress was green, too heavy for summer, too large for her wasted frame. She had not rinsed all the soap from her hair. The perfume she'd washed herself in was twelve years old, like the layer of yellow on her rotting teeth.

"You say Hosea, Jr. died?"

There was a wind in the air; it made her shiver and left in its wake a silence. She waited to be frightened.

"That's right."

"Right after I left?"

"The second time."

"Where's he buried?"

"St. Luke's."

"They didn't bury Negroes there in 1948."

"I say St. Luke's?" She smiled. "I mean Emmanuel."

He watched her, his gray eyes like a snake's. "People saying I took Hosea, Jr. with me when I left."

The wall that had confined her all these years, that had limited her vision and bent her memory out of shape, began to crumble. She saw a patch of blue sky, a sunflower, something wrapped in a blanket. She kept waiting to be frightened.

"Where is he?"

Meredith watched the tendon in his neck. It was pulsing. Wondering what it would feel like to lick his throat, she pointed to the back yard, to the patch where the sunflowers had not yet bloomed. The wall was crumbling, like Hosea's face. She began to chew her hair.

"You buried him in the back *yard*?" It was the first time in two days that his voice had carried inflection, and as she looked into his eyes she saw that they had lost their lack of intensity. Meredith laughed. When he asked what she was laughing at, she said at the funny way things worked out.

"Murder ain't funny. You can't go burying babies in your back yard."

Meredith knew you could; she'd done it. Give people a chance, she said, and the odds were they'd surprise you. One night they'd be there; in the morning they were gone.

He didn't answer. He *had* no answer, and she laughed again and spit her hair out, recapturing in the process her rage and understanding of desire. The weight of it in her palm made her fingers coil. She could feel its heat and frantic heartbeat, as if she'd reached out and plucked from the air some unsuspecting bird. Because she was enraged, her fingers ached to form a fist, but she wouldn't let them. If you do, she thought, you'll crush the bird. But neither could she open her hand, for then she'd lose it. She kept it at her side, curved like a supplicant's, or a claw.

When she'd worked all of that out, she discovered she was too furious to speak. He stood there with stricken eyes, smelling of after-shave and confusion, fingers searching for a hat brim to caress. Her wall was crumbling, all the blue sky, the anguished understanding of desire, lips bared with hate. There was only one thing left to recover, but that could wait. That wouldn't feel good. The hatred did. Since she felt good, she smiled. Hosea swallowed and said that leaving someone and killing them wasn't the same.

"Ain't it?"

"I didn't kill no one," he whispered.

"You didn't bury no one."

"Your *child*."

"Yours, too."

"How could you?"

Still smiling, wrapped in rage and blue sky, she told him. "You left the dresser open where you took your clothes. You dropped a sock on the floor. A long green one, a hole in the heel. I sewed it up and put it in the drawer for you. I got in bed underneath the covers, but every time I close my eyes the room was turning. So I kept em open, trying not to blink. You ever do that, trying not to blink?"

She took a long, deep breath, so deep she was standing on tiptoes when she let it out. "All the kids was sleep but *it*; I could hear the rustling. I got up and turned the light on. It was lying there, blind eyes all calmlike, like everything in the world was copacetic. I'm looking at it and I'm hurting. I didn't want to be the only one hurting. Everybody else sleeping or calm, or *leaving*, and I'm the only one hurting. I pinched it on the leg. He don't do nothing. I pinch it harder, he just keep still. I get a pin off the dresser and stick it to him, deep, and his eyes go wide, but he don't cry. 'You the cause my husband leave me,' I say. 'Who gonna fill this hole, *you*? *You*, big watermelon head? You go rub these titties and stick yo finger in my ear? *You* go dry my wet?' He make a little whimper sound. 'Shut up,' I say. I stick em again. He hollering, make my eyes hurt. I take the pillow off the bed and shut em up."

The last stretch of wall gave way with the sound and tremor of an earthquake, shattering what was left of her protection. There in the rubble, as the dust cleared, lay the last thing left to be recovered. Sorrow reached out to her. It was beautiful and rare, stronger than hate, mightier than desire. She began to weep as she had not wept in all those years.

"Oh, Jesus, Hose-ee. He didn't even fight me. You know how you used to play putting the pillow over my face, and how when I couldn't breathe I'd start to fight you, and then you'd take it off and we'd . . . we'd . . . ? He didn't even fight me, just lay there letting me do it, like he knew it was his fault. I was scared to look at what I done. I hold the pillow, hold the pillow . . . Then I took it off, and his blind eyes open like they see me. . . ."

She cried out and fell to her knees, wrapped her arms around his legs. "Hose-ee. I didn't even remember to close his eyes. I wrapped him up and carried him out back and put him in the ground, and I didn't even remember to close his eyes. What I'm going to do?" she sobbed. "Sweet Jesus. What I'm going to do?"

He was like a rock. "Nothing."

"Nothing? I killed my child. I got to pay. God *knows* I got to pay."

"There is no God," Hosea said. "And you've already paid for it. Just keep your mouth shut and go on like you been. And get up from there; you messing up my suit." He gave her money. "Get your teeth fixed."

Once people had begun to ask about the son he'd taken away, Hosea knew something was wrong, and he'd invented a story to protect Meredith. He said he'd had the child placed in an institution, where he'd died seven years ago.

When he left Meredith's, he was under control; he stepped carefully around the earthworms. Driving back to the house he and Alice had rented, he thought again of that day in 1948 when he'd run headlong into life's well-kept secret: it had no meaning and there was no God.

Despite the impact, which had given him blinding headaches until he'd stopped wearing hats, he'd found that he could not totally escape the effects of his long, intimate relationship with religion. Reserved in the most private pocket of his heart was a small, but nagging, doubt that perhaps man was *not* unanswerable to any but himself; someplace in the universe there might be a limit. For twelve years he'd lived with this imperfect disbelief. Bereft of the rituals of family and church, he'd created his own, designating one activity as his symbol of uncertainty. He who had left his wife and seven children, who daily broke the law, who sold substances that shipwrecked human life, created for himself a limit: one thing would be taboo, which he would not violate until he was certain life really was as he'd seen it.

Now he knew. He was not bound except by himself; he could go beyond his limit. He was free.

Alice was in her bedroom when he got home, stretched out with a box of chocolates and six fashion magazines. Hosea called a greeting to her from the hall, then went into his room. He took off his suit and hung it neatly in the closet. Socks, shirt, and underwear went into the hamper. Naked except for the gold medallion, he walked into his partner's room.

Jesus, he's beautiful, Alice thought, and licked her

fingers. He began to pick up the magazines from the bed, throw them on the floor. The room was awash with sunlight; he closed the drapes. But it was important that he *see* what he was doing, and he turned the lamp on.

"What's up, sweet man?"

"Give me the candy."

She handed the box to him.

"Get up."

Chocolate smeared her face and fingers. There was a smudge of it on her pink tent dress. Hosea lay on his back across the bed.

"Take your clothes off."

"Hosea . . . ?"

"Take your clothes off."

When she was naked and awkward and confused, he looked at her. The only thing rising was his disgust. There must have been 280 pounds of gray-white flesh in front of him, a red beehive of hair, a black, volcanic crotch. She was his partner. She was responsible for taking him from being an elevator boy to the man he was today. As a result, he respected her and was grateful. It could be said that he cared for her. But, as a woman, the only thing she had going for her was the fact that she kept herself clean and didn't smell.

"Come here."

"Let me wash first."

"Come *here*."

He moved to one side of the bed, held on while the other side sank, then pulled himself into her arms. Her mouth was moist, chocolate sweet, nibbled like a child's. He put his hand between her rubbery breasts; it disappeared. Propped on an elbow, he kneaded the flesh of her belly where it hung like a sack from her frame, finding pockets of perspiration in every fold; it turned her powder to paste. Tentatively, her sticky fingers danced along his spine. Her breathing was ragged. But there was nothing happening in him except disgust.

"You got to help me."

She helped him. When the beast which had no conscience stiffened, he rolled on top, searching through the maze of meat for the opening. He found it, long and hot and slick; he aimed and plunged.

"Uuuhh," she said. "My *God*."

It ain't bad, Hosea thought, holding to the pillows of her breasts. All the shifting meat demanded that he make adjustments, but once he got the knack, there was nothing to it. Not bad at all. He had one last clear thought before the feeling got to him, and that was wonder that such a big woman could be so small in there.

When it was over, he answered the inevitable question before she asked it. "Because there ain't no standards. No limits. No God."

Alice, deep in the purple of her postcoital dream, asked how the three were related. Annoyed that she didn't share his insight, Hosea said he wasn't in the habit of explaining the obvious.

Alice didn't answer. She was staring into the featureless face of the gold medallion, smitten by an inspiration only slightly less stunning than what had just happened to her.

All during the night after Hosea left the fourth time, Meredith lay in her bed unable to sleep. She'd gotten herself together enough to fix dinner for the kids, and then she'd locked herself in her bedroom, where she alternately wept and stared at the ceiling until her eyes felt as if they'd been scored with sandpaper, and it seemed that all the tears were gone. At one point she got up and went to the mirror, where she studied the toll twelve years had extracted from her flesh. Baring her gums, she ran a finger along her teeth, discovering the devastation neglect had caused there. Her hair, in whose abundance Hosea had loved to hide his hands, had lost its sheen and was thinning; as she combed her fingers through it, a fistful littered her palms. There was a hollow in her throat deep enough to nest a bird's egg, but too hard, defined by sharp bone and cartilage; no egg could survive in such a rocky place. Her nose was pinched, her cheeks sunken. Above the eyebrows her forehead furrowed like ground broken up for planting. And her eyes, *look* what had happened to her eyes. There used to be lights there; at some point when she wasn't watching, they'd turned the power off.

She got back into bed, lay on her stomach. This was her punishment, twelve years lost, and with them her youth and beauty. The punishment was just, for youth and beauty and her sexual power were what she'd valued most; they were what she believed made Hosea love her. What else did she have? She was not smart or witty; even he had joked about her housekeeping, and she knew a dozen women who could make her Sunday dinner look like Tuesday's lunch. So that was her punishment and it was just, but what was his to be? What loss would he endure beyond that of soft-brimmed hats his fingers still searched for, and who knew if that was really loss; perhaps he'd left off their wearing in the same way he'd abandoned her. What *was* to be his punishment, how would God leave his mark on him, how would he shrivel, for what thing taken would he moan, weep, regard himself with horror?

Then she thought of the watermelon-head boy whom she'd murdered, and she found that she was *not* cried out, tears still lapped at the bottom of her desolation. She did not weep for the child as living flesh, or for his condition, but because she'd hated it, been aghast that such ugliness had come from her. From the very beginning she'd directed toward the baby everything she understood of malice. Six girls, and how they'd wanted a boy, and how could it not be perfect? She'd killed it because it was the reason for Hosea's leaving, but she could not have killed if she had not hated it so perfectly and wished it dead.

With the profoundest sense of awe, she realized that once again God had worked in His mysterious manner, which was to give her what she'd said she wanted. Even though she hadn't prayed for it, God knew her heart. Besides, what was prayer anyway but a fervent longing (it was too late to be dishonest), a concentration of desire on the condition not possessed? Yes, God had given her what she'd wanted, but He hadn't let her see the price tag. And now she was paying; had paid and would pay until they shoveled dirt into her mouth. Even then her debt would be outstanding; she simply wouldn't be around to make the payments. She'd be waiting in a hole for Judgment Day, when she would find out if she'd finally been forgiven.

So this was her punishment, and it was just, and she accepted. But she lived in the world, and there were two laws that governed it, God's law and man's law, and she had yet to answer to the latter. This frightened her; she began to tremble so violently she thought her bones would break. She knew that man in devising his judgment would be much less private, much more impersonal, than the Lord had been.

Still, that judgment must be faced. She could not do it alone, however, and nine weeks later she rinsed the soap from her hair, wrapped herself in a blanket, and went to see the pastor. When Meredith finished her halting story, the pastor asked if anyone had seen her bury the child.

"Norman Fillis did."

The pastor grunted. Norman was as crazy as a bedbug. If he hadn't said anything in all these years, chances were that he'd forgotten. She looked at the pitiful woman before her and experienced a sharp distaste for men. Then she sighed and wondered why the Lord was testing her. First, there was Hosea's coming back with a fat lady who'd be at home in a circus. Instincts told her Hosea was up to no good, and that, as usual, whenever a black person stirred up trouble, she'd be called in to make it right. Her cousin had just moved next door with a husband who was a roaring drunk and a daughter with a missing hand and a phony Southern accent. Rumor had it that one of her deacons' wives was messing around on the side. On top of that there had been all those earthworms, which had only recently disappeared, the visitation of which signaled impending disaster. She wondered how long it would be before the reason for the earthworms was disclosed. Back in 1948, when black people had inexplicably begun to die, everybody had blamed it on the racetrack. Today, more than a decade later, Melinda Mclain knew the real reason.

In the face of all this, she was not about to make a snap decision. She told Meredith to go home and not to say a word to anyone until the Lord had given some direction. Then she went into her bedroom, where she stayed for twelve hours, the longest she'd prayed since the birth of her child.

The Lord didn't answer. For months, in her daily prayers, Melinda Mclain faithfully sought assistance in the matter of Meredith Malone, but, though God spoke to her daily, He never mentioned the subject. Finally, she figured this was one affair the Lord didn't want man meddling in, and she let the matter rest.

CHAPTER
18

The summer of 1960 would be remembered in part for its beautiful weather. From July 29 to August 30, each day dawned in sunshine and high blue skies. The temperature never went above 85°, and there was a soft intermittent breeze that kept the scent of flowers in the air. The weather created a sense of well-being; folks moved languidly and said what a wonderful place Montgomery was to live in. On August 31, the tail end of the season's first hurricane snatched limbs from trees, downed electrical wires, and roused people from their torpor. The storm spent itself in a little more than eight hours, and on the morning of September 1, people began to clear the litter and to recognize that Norman was acting strange again.

The truth was that Norman had been acting strange all that August, but everybody had been too lulled by the weather to do anything about it. It had been some time since he'd disrobed; most recently he preached in public places. Since it was a free country, and the weather was nice, folks left him alone. Besides, his sermons were not objectionable. He preached of the miracle of flight and the properties of fire, one of which, he said, was that fire had taste. When three children suffered second-degree burns on their tongues, a few folks grumbled, but it was not until September, when the sermons began to writhe with images of death and destruction, that he became a nuisance. The time they were living in, Norman preached, was the Dispensation of Earthworms. It had begun in 1948 with the destruction of trees and the death of black folk. It would be marked by death and dissension and would not end until all the prophecies were fulfilled and Montgomery was poised for flight. In the meantime, the madman said, watch the children.

Nobody but Meredith, Pastor Mclain, and Hosea had the slightest idea of what Norman was preaching about, and they weren't talking. Since he'd made everybody else irritable by calling up the memory of the earthworms, it was easy for Melinda Mclain to make a phone call and have him put away again.

Josephine's records arrived, and she was placed in the ninth grade. Nobody engaged any more in serious taunting; they'd grown used to her. When, on three occasions, he approached her and was rebuffed, Gerald decided he'd fulfilled his responsibility. "I'm sorry," he'd bleated, but he might have been talking to a wall. He'd made his apology; he couldn't force her to accept it.

Grownups felt sorry for Josephine. Not only was she missing a hand, but also she'd gotten the bottom of the barrel when fathers had been handed out. Percy Moore's capacity for alcohol had quickly become legendary. Some folks began to mark their calendars on the few days he was sober.

One other thing people noticed: Alice Simineski, the white lady who lived with Hosea, had rented a bigger house and spent money freely, although neither had any visible means of support. No sooner had September opened their eyes to this than they realized that the fat white lady had begun to change.

Since the last of April, Hosea had been busy setting up his protection. By the middle of August, every member of the

153

police force was receiving a stipend. Several judges and the president of the town council had demonstrably improved their standard of living. Hosea had deposited large sums in each of Montgomery's four banks, and had hired Jackson Smalls Ltd. to construct a laundry, which would serve the community and provide a front for his operations. He'd been so involved that he'd failed to notice what Alice was up to. When he did, he rubbed his eyes and lit a cigarette, the first one he'd smoked in eight years.

With an abruptness that rivaled his relinquishing of hats, Alice had abandoned chocolate. The afternoon Hosea had made love to her was the best thing to happen since she'd discovered his ability to confront her ugliness without lowering his eyes. Not wanting to give this new thing up, she reasoned that if she were to make herself attractive, she wouldn't have to. By the third week of her diet she'd lost twenty-one pounds, but couldn't see it. Standing naked in front of her mirror, she wondered if the scale was working. She bought a new scale, which confirmed the weight loss, but failed to lighten her spirits. Despondent, haunted by the memory of chocolate, she talked to Hosea. She needed incentive. "Once every three weeks, if I can come to you. Okay?"

He agreed so quickly that she berated herself for not having negotiated a two-week interval. But the arrangement was made now. Whenever she was tempted to buy a box of Barton's, she'd consult her calendar. "Twelve more days," she'd say. Or, "Hold on for five more days, and he'll make love to you." She began to exist on fruit juice, lean meat, exercise, and sex. Miraculously, the pounds melted, revealing a face that hinted of extraordinary beauty. She began to imagine that this beauty was a flame burning perfectly in her bones, and that if she continued to diet she could reach it. She was 214 pounds on September 1, and figured she had ninety-nine to go.

* * *

No sooner had the memory of earthworms faded than folks in Montgomery faced a new concern: their children began to exhibit the strangest behavior. It started in November, when the captain of the basketball team began to date a white cheerleader. By December, black and white parents were wringing their hands; interracial dating had become epidemic. Gerald was pursued by a seventeen-year-old, Melody Coffman, who he swore had talked to Wanda. Melody would let him fondle everyplace but between her legs. Driven to distraction, finally unmoved by her tight-lipped kisses, he considered giving her up, and would have, except that almost everyone he knew, even Iceman, had a white girl, and he didn't want to be left out.

Black girls found themselves in a totally unexpected position. Some reacted by withdrawing; others fought with methods that resulted in two of them becoming pregnant. Emmeline Robinson wondered out loud where her Dorothy had learned about sex, since she hadn't told her. Ruth Potts, however, had thoroughly explained the consequences of the male appetite to Sheila. This was on the occasion of her daughter's first period, and she and Sheila had held one another, laughing and crying at the same time. Ruth had presented her with a gift-wrapped box of Modess, Jr. and a sanitary belt trimmed with lace. Now, in a gesture that shattered her daughter's heart, Ruth's hand moved from her hip to her forehead.

The fact that black girls were willing to make love to keep their boyfriends put pressure on the competition, and all hell broke loose when the cheerleader had to tell her parents she was going to be a mother. "No, you're not," they bellowed, and sent her away for a while. When she returned, she was subdued, hollow; the only thing baby about her was the blue of the case in her purse, and a small tube of what looked like toothpaste. Her basketball player had been snapped up in her absence, and she had to settle for the black quarter miler who anchored the relay team.

Black and white parents had the first joint meeting anybody could remember outside of the P.T.A., but the resolutions they drafted could not stem the tide. White fathers whispered to their daughters that colored boys were subject to rare communicable diseases and to genetic disorders which resulted in deformed and mentally deficient offspring when mated with whites. The more realistic white parents closed their eyes and crossed their fingers. Black mothers and fathers resorted to belts and ironing cords in an attempt to beat some sense into their daughters. As is usually the case with sex, there was more conversation than contact. Still, it was clear that, despite the efforts of adults, sex had arrived in Montgomery, apparently to stay. Every boy over the age of eleven carried a prophylactic. Gerald bought one for a dollar from a senior. For six months it stayed in his wallet, where it stamped a circle in the leather.

Had this been the extent of the strange behavior, Montgomery's parents might eventually have let it slide. But an alarming number of children had begun to drink beer and smoke cigarettes. Suddenly kids needed money; the county clerk was deluged with applications for working papers. Teenagers started going to the track. When a chapter of Gamblers Anonymous was established in Montgomery, half its clients were less than eighteen years of age.

Then it was discovered that some of the cigarettes kids were smoking had a strong, sweet-smelling smoke, the inhalation of which left them glassy-eyed and prone to giggling. Whether the cigarettes caused what happened

156

next is open to conjecture: black students demanded history and literature courses that included *them*. In spite of the interracial dating (or, perhaps, because of it), a group of blacks began to refer to whites as "devils," and some of the whites were in passionate accord. "Yes," they said, "we're devils. Call us names. Hurt us." Several white boys had a different reaction: they discovered style, began attempting to walk with rhythm, and experimented with the angles at which they cocked their recently purchased hats. At home they practiced saying, "What's happenin, baby?" in the mirror. Then they went to school and tried to talk to black girls and got their feelings hurt.

These same black girls refused to have straightening combs dragged through their hair, and soon black boys were insisting they be allowed to grow theirs beyond the length of military haircuts. Black barbers and beauticians panicked as they watched business fall off. The skin-lightener salesman got called into his manager's office to explain the sudden decline in profits. Perhaps a younger man, it was hinted, one with more energy, would do better. The salesman, convinced that what was happening was just a passing fad, began buying large quantities of the products and storing them in his basement. When he saw that to eat he would have to take a second mortgage on his house, he revised his appraisal and prepared a memo that proposed the revolutionary concept of products designed to enhance dark skin.

Meanwhile, Montgomery's children who had grown up and moved away began to correspond with their families about the world they'd encountered. Rachel Malone spoke movingly to her sisters of the ocean at Atlantic City. She had a good job. No, she didn't want to see her father, unless he was dead. Daisy Madison said New Mexico was dry and was it all right to take a bath with her husband. Shipped to Vietnam as an adviser, Andre Fillis wrote of a lush, green countryside, and a small, brown people who were the most beautiful he'd ever seen. He sent photographs, which Claire passed around to everyone. No sooner had she placed them in plastic sleeves than news arrived of Soapsuds' death in Mississippi.

Soapsuds had been working for civil rights. He'd been told that the job was hazardous, that he should not answer back to Southern whites, who would go out of their way to provoke him. A generation of young people would follow this instruction; Soapsuds, when the deal went down, found he couldn't. Smiling like the slave he'd never been, in his most respectful voice he cursed the three men out. Some of the curses had Swahili roots, but most were from Lithuania, Paraguay, and a certain isolated neighborhood in Harlem. All sounded like flattery; only a scholar would have known he was being invited to suck his own asshole, to lie with his mother, to eat the diarrhea of wart hogs. Soapsuds' mistake was in the mockery he allowed to darken his eyes, and the perfect articulation, which indicated schooling and humiliated his ignorant foes. On top of that, he was beautiful, and the men began to tremble for their women. Furious and awed, they sliced his tongue away. Then, with axe handles recently planed, they began carefully to beat his brains out, only to discover that his inability to scream left them titillated but not relieved. So they fired both barrels of a shotgun into his mouth. His colleagues collected as much of his head as they could find and sent him home to Montgomery. Not even Moses Duewright could make him presentable for viewing, and at the funeral the casket was closed.

It was the first time anyone could remember Soapsuds' father in a suit—a black, narrow-lapeled special from Robert Hall. Throughout the eulogy the deaf-mute sat holding hands with the cat-eyed Edna. At one point he leaned back and stared at the ceiling just above his head, his mouth wide, throat vibrating, and it was a moment before anyone realized he was screaming for his tongueless son. His wife, her face invisible behind her veil, pulled his head to her marvelous breasts, stifling his silent grief.

After they put Soapsuds in the ground, black people looked around and remembered Norman's sermons. They began to read newspapers and watch network news differently. The world had always seemed so far away, ugly and inevitable, like death, but far away. Now, just before the spring of 1961, it had moved in, camped at Montgomery's borders. Black people were not fooled by its sphinxlike demeanor, or by its bulk, each of which suggested an absence of guile. They knew the world was devious. They knew it was armed and extremely dangerous. In the midst of their wondering what defense would be best, Norman, who'd miscalculated by nine days, arrived home from the asylum. Two days later, Gerald dismembered his women.

In the bathroom, Gerald groaned and spattered his seed across the pages of the magazine. It had been a particularly powerful orgasm, for which he was grateful. Lately, his women had failed to arouse him to rock hard, fever pitch; his imagination had run out of positions to place them in, and erotic obscenities for them to whisper. Today, for the first time, he'd gone to bed with *two* of the women—the redhead with stupendous breasts, and the ripe-mouthed blonde—had lain between them sandwiched by flesh and was the recipient of the fruits of their competitive labor.

Now, as he washed his hands and cleaned up the semen that had missed the magazine and stained the floor

with small, pearl-colored drops, he heard the muffled ring-
ing of the phone downstairs. In his room, he placed the
magazine back in his winter boot and had turned toward
the hallway when a wave of dizziness and nausea drove
him to his knees. Almost immediately, his head cleared,
his stomach subsided, but he stayed on all fours, puzzled
by the power and brevity of what had happened. Did it
come from jerking off? Had all that pulling and rubbing
resulted in some mysterious ailment which God had
finally sent to punish him? It was the feeling he got after
his father, well rested, had really been into beating him,
but whereas then he was dizzy for hours, too weak and
sick to his stomach to walk, this had lasted no more than a
couple of seconds. Cautiously, he pulled himself to his
haunches. When this movement caused no disturbance,
he rose on one knee. Satisfied that for the moment God
had engineered no permanent damage, he stood. He felt
fine, physically, but the air had changed, seemed thick.
The sunlight falling into the hall from his sister's room
carried dust particles that were not colliding; they hung
in the corridor forever bound, like the flecks in his mother's roasting pan. Suddenly he was afraid, not of being
driven to his knees, not because dust did not collide in
sunlight, but because he knew that something terrible had
happened; he had lost something that could never be reclaimed. Whatever it was was downstairs. He began to
inch down the carpeted steps, pressing his body against
the wall, as if, were he to sneak up undetected on calamity, he could change or contain it.

"Gerald?" Abigal called. "Gerald?"

He didn't answer.

His mother appeared at the bottom of the steps. She
gazed up at him without surprise, as if she were accustomed to finding him in the shadows on the staircase,
wrapped in thick air, pressed against the wall. Delight,

her eyes grave with not-understanding, clung to her skirt. Still Gerald did not move or speak; the three of them stood for a moment, frozen. Abigal's arms fluttered at her sides, rose in twin arcs toward him, hovered. Then they fell, shattering what he only later recognized as hope.

"Gerald? Iceman's dead."

His brain began repeating, "Iceland's head, Iceland's head," over and over, faster, not allowing any space between the words. "Iceland'ssheadIceland'shead." If he could keep the nonsense going, nothing would be true. But his brain failed him; like an automobile in the middle of a desert, it sputtered, ran out of gas. "Iceman's dead." He looked at Delight. She smiled at him, sang, "Hi, Gerald."

"Come here, baby," Abigal crooned. Woodenly, he descended, surrendered himself into her arms. She held him; Delight, giggling, clutched his leg. He was thinking how he was as tall as his mother, how her breasts mashed against his chest. They were soft and full and only for his father. He tried to remember when his mother had last held him like this. It must have been a long time ago; surely he would have remembered these breasts. His father yet lived. Curious and numb, he pulled back from his mother to look into her face, searching for the woman who, despite having lived with him all these years, was a mystery. He'd never, for instance, seen her weep. There had been times when her eyes had filled with sadness, or sparkled with tears of joy, but he'd never seen her weep. Did she never, or did she wait until she was alone? Where was his father? Where was Iceman? Iceman's dead.

"How?"

She told him. Something began to move in Gerald, something infinite began to splinter, leaving him with despair, but no tears to express it, grief, but no lament. And he wanted to cry, to shake the earth with his screaming. But he was contained, held rigid by the thickening air.

"I want to be alone," he said.

Abigal, baffled and frightened by this reaction, nodded. He turned, trudged up the stairs. In his room he closed the door and sat on the bed. He was cold and empty. Alone.

"Ice," he whispered, rocking, head buried in his hands, "why weren't you careful? How could you leave me by myself? Why weren't you careful?"

Iceman was dead. And he, Gerald, was in the bathroom, jerking off into the picture of a white broad's face while his friend hung burning from a wire. He was sinning and God had made him pay for it. It wasn't fair. Why hadn't God caused him to die, he who had wished it so fervently? Why hadn't He made him blind, or maimed him, taken his speech, caused sores to erupt on the surface of his skin, driven him into the wilderness to live with beasts? Why get back at Gerald through Iceman, whose life was defined by gentleness and love?

Furious at God, furious at himself, he went to the closet, retrieved the magazines. Inside, on the soiled pages, were the women he'd loved, about whom he'd never told his friend. Iceman was dead. He stuffed the magazines into the back of his pants beneath his shirt, marched down to the kitchen, where he gathered matches, and went out into the back yard. It was March, spring not yet arrived; the afternoon was suddenly overcast and smelled of rain. He dropped the magazines to the grass, arranged them, lit the corner of a cover. The flame came quivering to life, curled the paper, died. He tried again. Again the flame petered out. The magazines were too thick to burn easily. Trembling, he began to rip them up, tearing smiles from faces, breasts from the cavities of chests. Pink vaginas that glistened and gaped like wounds he dissected without compassion or remorse. Curved buttocks met splayed toes, eyes came face to face with hairless armpits. After he had ripped and torn and torn again, he set fire to the pile and watched the flame catch, leap, consume his dreaming. When it had all turned to ashes, despair rushed from his throat to crush him. Falling on his face, he beat his fists against an earth God had taken six days to create and an instant to make uninhabitable. There he lay until the rain began to fall, and Abigal, moaning, "Jesus, Jesus, Jesus," came to drag him back inside.

CHAPTER
19

Iceman died the way he had lived, demonstrating kindness. His last recipient was an elderly white woman whose cat had been treed by a dog. On his way home from the pizza parlor (where he'd devoured three slices), Iceman stopped, drove the mutt away, and went up the tree to retrieve the kitten, which had edged its way to the end of a limb. There it had chosen to panic as the plump, bespectacled black boy inched toward it. The branch swayed with their collective weight, brushed against the telephone line.

It was a pretty kitten, black with white markings, and it began to shrink as Iceman's outstretched fingers waved inches from its nose. "Come on, kitty," Iceman cajoled, "come to me." The cat made itself smaller. Iceman stretched his arm until his side ached, but the cat remained just outside the limit of his reach. Wondering how much weight the limb could take, he shimmied another three inches toward its end, holding his breath as the branch sighed and bent, brushing once again against the wire. He was tired and sweaty, and a little nervous as he glanced, despite himself, at the asphalt street below. To make matters worse, his glasses kept slipping to the end of his nose. Now the day darkened as the thin disk of sun slid behind a cloud.

"Be careful," the woman called, thinking that she should, as was her instinct, have called the Fire Department. But the cute little colored boy had insisted he could do it.

Clinging to the limb, Iceman considered how close he was to the object of his mission. He considered the time spent, the arduous journey. It was a lot of time and effort for what should have been accomplished in a minute. Then he did a foolish thing. He lunged for the cat. His fingers touched fur, but the abrupt movement set the tree limb violently in motion, threatening his balance. The cat chose that moment to drive its claws into Iceman's hand. When he jerked back, cursing, his glasses slipped. Frantically, he reached for them; as he began to fall he grabbed for the telephone line, grasped it at a place where the insulation had worn away.

His first reaction was to pull his hand back as he would from a hot stove, but he couldn't. Then he groaned at the sweet, sick feeling in his groin. Something hot and hard smashed his body, and he vomited the undigested pizza. That was the last thing he was conscious of: the slightly sour taste of tomato sauce. The force of the shock ripped his locked ankles from the limb, and he was hanging in mid-air to a wire he didn't know he couldn't let go of. Blue smoke seeped from his nose and mouth, and his flesh bubbled, oozing grease like the cooked meat he refused to eat. To retrieve him from the force that powered Alexander Graham Bell's invention, they had to throw a switch at the company, temporarily placing three hundred phones out of order. Only then did Iceman release the line, dropping thirty feet to the fire net they held below him. In public, the phone company said Iceman had no business being in that tree in the first place; in private, they discussed the necessity of raising rates to recover the expenses of the lawsuit Ezra Poole slapped them with. Eventually they settled out of court for $75,000 and retired to the conference room, where they joked about the ignorant nigger who could have held out for ten times as much.

Iceman died on Saturday. Moses Duewright had the body ready the next day, and on Sunday and Monday, Iceman lay in state in one of the small viewing rooms at the funeral parlor. His parents decided to bury him without the thick glasses he'd always worn, the lenses of which had shattered when they fell. This decision was made after some discussion; it was the kind of detail that plagues the grief-stricken, who want, above all, to do right by the deceased. Finally, however, it seemed rather pointless to buy new glasses for the dead, and silly to bury him with empty frames. Since nobody could remember ever seeing Iceman without his glasses, there were a number of startled reactions to how good-looking he was. To Gerald, his friend's calm face seemed to belong to someone else, and he sat between his parents with his head down, refusing to look.

The funeral was held on Tuesday, March 21, 1961. There was weak sunshine; the temperature at one o'clock was 56°. There was no wind, unusual for this time of year, and the church was full. Most of the pews held black folks dressed in the splendor of mourning clothes (some of which were beginning to show signs of wear), but several of Iceman's teachers had come, and a small contingent of his white classmates, the last of whom gaped at the beauty of the singing and the uninhibited way Iceman's mother expressed her grief. Several of the songs the white children knew and they were so moved that they added their wavering, off-key voices to "Rock of Ages" and "A Mighty Fortress Is Our God."

Gerald sat next to his mother in the fifth row of pews. In the front, facing the congregation, sat the deacon board in its place of honor above and behind the casket. His father was there, iron-jawed and solemn, and when their eyes met, Alexander's hardened. Gerald had not spoken more than ten words since his mother dragged him away from the mutilated women, and he had only picked at his favorite foods, which Abigal, not knowing how else to console him, had carefully prepared. The boy's reaction bothered Alexander, who said that Gerald had to learn to handle grief, that death was common and certain, and woe to the man who allowed himself to be broken each time it called. Alexander did not say this unkindly; he'd been feeling good about himself. Jackson Smalls had made him a manager, and he was in charge of building the laundry for Hosea Malone. When Alexander remembered that his father had deserted him, it was to find himself wondering what his father's reasons were. He began to assume they were grave. Perhaps he'd killed a white man and had to run for his life; the excess baggage of woman and children would have meant his capture. Perhaps he'd been blackmailed or discovered his wife's unfaithfulness.

Soon after he'd invented these pleasant fictions, Alexander took to considering what it meant to be a father, and noted the relationships other men had with their sons. It seemed as if every time he went by there, U. L. Washington was playing catch with his boys. Jackson Smalls had a son whom he always kissed and put his arm around. Alexander wanted a closer relationship with Gerald, although he wasn't sure about the kissing. Buoyed by good intentions, he took Gerald fishing, but not only had the boy caught no fish, he'd spent half the morning trying to get his line untangled. Next, Alexander offered to teach him how to throw a curve ball, but discovered that U. L. Washington had gotten there first. Not to be outdone, he handcrafted an oak desk for Gerald's room, but while Gerald had respectfully thanked him, Alexander had sensed the gulf that lay between them. There was nothing, it seemed, for the two to talk about. To Alexander's credit, he was patient, and promised himself that he would be more selective in his beatings. He'd kept that promise; since the earthworms had disappeared nearly a year ago, he'd only whipped him ten times. But there had been no response. This upset Alexander to the point of causing him to lose sleep, but he held his peace until Gerald's reaction to his little speech about how men must face death—which was to regard his father with the most impudent, insolent, loathsome glare that Alexander had ever witnessed. He had reached across the table for Gerald's throat when Abigal's arm knifed between them.

"Leave him alone," she said. "Can't you see he's suffering?"

"He ain't crazy."

"*Leave him alone.*"

Alexander tried to close his mouth, but he couldn't. He fell back against his chair, laughing his "nothing funny" laugh. "I believe," he snarled, "you'd fight me over that worthless boy."

"I believe," she whispered, "I would."

Gerald stared impassively at the ceiling. Abigal, shocked and frightened, was, nevertheless, resolute. Alexander got up and went for a walk. When he came back, he didn't say anything. But he hadn't forgotten how his family had conspired to humiliate him. It was this he considered now as the minister rose and walked toward the lectern.

Pastor Mclain did not preach the funeral sermon. Mount Zion Baptist in Midstown, a sister church, had a young man who'd just been called to the ministry. His delivery needed to be refined—"seasoning," the Mount Zion pastor called it—and he was being farmed out to neighboring churches, where he could acquire experience.

The Reverend P. T. Bailey (P for Paul, T for Thaddeus) was a tall man of thirty-four, with a sallow, mournful face and a blue serge suit that was two sizes too large. This, combined with his almost painful thinness, made him appear as if he'd only recently been snatched from the jaws of famine. Sensitive to his appearance, he attempted to deflect his audience with larger-than-life gestures. His strength was his voice, deep and booming, startling those who heard him preach for the first time. Folks found themselves craning their necks to look behind him to see where all that voice was coming from.

Traditionally, sermons at black funerals are only secondarily concerned with the saving of souls. Their primary intent is the commemoration of the deceased and consolation of the bereaved. The Reverend Bailey did not agree with this tradition. The responsibility of his ministry, he argued, was to keep the righteous in line and to bring sinners to the altar; he wore his responsibility like his suit. No opportunity should be missed to bring God's message; at his daytime job, where he stamped holes in doughnuts, he preached in the bakery's parking lot on his lunch hour. Today he would commemorate, he would console, but he also planned to make folks tremble. The best way to get people to pay attention to the Word was to scare them to death.

Since death had brought all of them together this afternoon, the Reverend Bailey began, death would be his subject. Old, black, hoary death, death whose breath stank and whose sole redeeming quality was that it was no respecter of persons. When the earth erupted, giving up its dead, we would see black and white, Indian and Jew, African and A-rab, made indistinguishable by rotting flesh. We would witness side by side those of great gift and those of little, those marked by honor and those by shame. World-class athletes and cripples would rise together, men of great wealth and men of poverty. And see the children, teensy-weensy babies whose only sin was being born. Out of the shallow graves would come little boys struck down while playing ball, little girls in starched dresses, snatched up while jumping rope.

Did folks know where death came from? From sin. Way back in the Garden of Eden, when Eve sinned the first sin and seduced Adam into following her example, ever since then death had been man's measure. For man was sinful (and he turned, sweeping a long, bony arm to the sign), and it was written: The Wages of Sin is Death!

Knowing this, we are invested with a grave responsibility. We must teach the children that death is everywhere, in the closets, beneath their beds, in school, on the dark, deserted road, inside the television; in the very air, old death, fangs bared, was waiting. The fact was that death liked children most of all. Children were easier prey. They didn't kick and struggle and scream like grownups did. Children went easy, and quiet, and *quick*.

He clapped his hands, and the sound cracked in the silent church like a rifle shot. Two of Iceman's terrified white classmates began to cry. As yet unaware that he'd lost his audience, the minister said that if nobody believed death loved children best, look at what was lying in the casket there before him. Could he get an amen?

Norman Fillis, thinking that if this was preaching, John Henry was a white boy, did what everyone else wanted to do. He stood and walked out. The rest of the adults expressed disapproval by frowning, or by looking over their shoulders at the whimpering white kids. The absence of amens to a black preacher is like the absence of laughter to a comedian, and the Reverend Bailey, his mouth grown dry, decided to change direction.

But, he bellowed (and everybody except Iceman cringed), but Jesus, bless our Lord, retained dominion over death; if death called children, it was only because

Jesus allowed it to, because Jesus loved children and wanted them to be with him in Heaven. Jesus had loved Zacharias, he said (and folks looked at one another in momentary confusion, having forgotten Iceman's given name). "You think *you* loved him?" The Reverend Bailey pointed to Iceman's father. "Not as much as Jesus did. *You*, sister, bless your heart, you birthed that child, held him to your breast, worried when he was sick, beat him when he was bad. You think you loved him? Nooooooo, not as much as Jesus did.

"And you, Robert, devoted brother, you didn't love Zacharias. Unh-unh. Not like Jesus did. Ain't you glad he's gone where he's loved with a perfect love? Can I get an amen?"

Iceman's brother was looking up at the minister with his good eye closed. His name was Richard.

"Ya'll can't say amen?" the panicked preacher pleaded. "God's word don't move ya'll none?"

Gerald surged to his feet. He did not know he was going to do it, but he was standing, glaring at the Reverend Bailey with a malevolence he ordinarily reserved for his father. A murmur swelled in the church. He could feel his father's infuriated scowl, but when he turned from the minister's astonished face, it was not to look at Alexander, but at Josephine. She was staring at him, her arm held at her chest. His mother was tugging at his coat. An usher reached for him, said, "Come with me, son. It's all right," and he allowed himself to be pulled into the aisle and led into the basement. He sat there, calmly awaiting the consequences of his deed. His mother came down. "You all right?" He looked at her, neither acknowledging nor ignoring her question. She sat next to him, held his hand until the singing started, until six men lifted the coffin to sturdy shoulders, carried it to the waiting hearse. The basement began to fill with mourners, who gathered their coats and prepared to leave for the graveyard. His father's face was clenched. "You wait till I get you home." Gerald stared into his eyes, on his face an expression so blank Alexander had to sketch the malice for himself. Swollen with rage, he would have beaten him right then had it not been for all the people who whispered and looked at Gerald with sympathy. His mother touched him; he stood, followed her outside. The sun was brighter now. People were pointing and grumbling, and he looked across the street. On his porch, wearing a pale-blue sheet with red stripes, Norman Fillis had begun to preach.

Back in August, fire had told Norman that the earthworms were a warning, that Montgomery would be visited by calamity and strife, and that the children would conspire to set their parents' teeth on edge. He would have liked to have been around to see some of that, but he'd also discovered the date and circumstance of Iceman's death, and he didn't want to subject himself to that experience, coming as it would hard on the heels of Soapsuds'. The death of young people bothered Norman; it didn't make sense to him. In addition, he had a special feeling for Iceman. Gerald was his chosen one, but Iceman he respected—for his gentleness, his heart and curiosity, and for the purity of the friendship he provided to Gerald. He knew what Iceman's death would do to Gerald, and that it would be a complicated, troubled time. Better to go away until all of it blew over. Knowing that nothing was as annoying to people as a prophet, he began to preach of the bad period ahead, and they sent him back to the asylum.

But he'd gotten his dates confused. Instead of returning a week after Iceman's funeral, he got back two days before. That is why he was present to hear the Reverend Bailey's sermon, a text so inappropriate, so complete in its failure to celebrate Iceman's life, that he got up and went home, where he prepared his own. It took him ten minutes to work out the presentation on three-by-five cards. Then, convinced that black was not the color, he searched through his closet for something suitable to wear. When he could find nothing, he decided to create an outfit, and took a sheet from the bottom drawer of the chest where Claire stored them. He undressed to his underwear, wrapped the sheet around him, and went to wait on the porch.

When the church doors opened and people stood shading their eyes against the sun, Norman imagined he was in Africa. Only the presence of the cars, the hearse, the magnificent oak trees, told him otherwise. In the field next to the church, long grass stood motionless. He heard the lowing of cattle, the swish of a tail that sent a fly spinning into eternity. And how African the people looked, with their dark and beautiful faces, especially the three men who broke from the crowd and hurried toward him. He began to preach.

His introduction consisted of his obligatory references to flight and fire, and then he cried, "His name was Iceman. Consider his example." That was as far as he got. Pastor Mclain, who'd had enough of travesty for one afternoon, had dispatched three of her deacons. Gently, they led Norman inside, where he considered impressing them with his ability to fly.

When the deacons came back, everybody got into cars, and the procession, headlights burning in the day, snaked to the graveyard. There, amidst green grass and gray stone, the simple eloquence of white crosses, they encircled the hole in the ground. The Reverend Bailey had been relieved of his duties, and Pastor Mclain spoke movingly of Christ's great promise—though flesh was born to die, the spirit lived forever; one day Iceman would rise. Then she intoned, "Ashes to ashes, dust to dust," and tossed her white carnation. It hit the casket and exploded. Petals rained, the pulleys creaked, Iceman descended as his mother shrieked. The first shovelful of dirt struck the coffin with a hollow thud. All of them who had approached the grave in columns, orderly and discreet, broke ranks, fanned out, went back to the waiting cars, traveled home to put away their veils and black attire. The women made dinner, and the men did whatever men can find to do in the hour after a funeral. Alexander, furious and humiliated, told Abigal to take Delight for a ride; he had business to attend to. When she refused, he smacked her. It was the first time in their fifteen years together that he had laid a hand on her in anger, and she closed her eyes. A thin line of blood trickled from her mouth. She licked it. Delight began to cry. Abigal picked her up and marched outside. When he heard the car pull away, Alexander went to work. Gerald stood there, refusing to weep, taking his beating like the man his father wanted him to be.

CHAPTER
20

Gerald played hooky the rest of that week. He would leave the house in the morning as if he were going to school, but he spent the days hiding in the woods behind the town barn. Some of the time he thought about Iceman and the vast emptiness his friend had left, but most of the time he focused on himself. It had never before occurred to him precisely in these terms: he had a life. This life, although affected by family, church, and school, did not *belong* to anyone but himself. Even though it could be made miserable, as his father had made it, though it could be taken, as Iceman had had his taken, still it was his own; he must control it. He did not experience joy or hope at this understanding; on the contrary, it made him solemn. He resolved to take care of his life, to respect it. In the months ahead he threw away his cigarettes, bathed daily, began to wear rubbers in the rain. In an effort to determine the limit of his intelligence, he easily made the Honor Roll. This last achievement impressed his teachers and his father, all of whom had long insisted that he had potential but did not apply himself. When he listened, he found that their congratulations were for themselves; one of their predictions had finally borne fruit. They did not know that neither praise nor imprecations could have reached him; he was beyond them now, had created a distance. He believed that he was different from other people and began to think of himself as special. When he looked for experiences that supported this, he wept at how dismally few there were. His grandfather. Iceman.

Norman Fillis. The first two he'd loved, one for the course of an evening, one for an abbreviated lifetime. Both were dead. He wondered if loving things made them die. He decided not to take any chances and resolved to love no one.

Alexander, incensed by the rhythm of Gerald's life, the angle at which he held his head and rebuffed his good intentions, sought to penetrate the distance with beatings, but while he bruised Gerald's flesh, it was as Iceman had said, he couldn't touch him on the inside. After a while the beatings stopped. Then Alexander once again tried to reach him through what passed as kindness and concern. But Gerald had wrapped himself in sadness, and wouldn't let him in.

Contained, rigid, he was working hard toward being self-sufficient. But he knew that at least one piece was missing; he had yet to convince Josephine to accept his apology. He didn't think there was a chance for friendship, but there was a chance to regain this loose end of his self-respect, a commodity as important to him as his intelligence. For a month after the week he spent in the woods, he assaulted her barricade; for a month she looked right through him and would never allow them to be alone. The old Gerald would have given up; the new Gerald saw it as a challenge and persisted. One afternoon in June he walked up the sidewalk and knocked on her front door.

"Who?"

"Me."

"Me, who?"

"Gerald."

"Go away."

"Let me in, Josephine."

"My mama ain't home. Neither my daddy."

"Josephine. *Please*."

She cracked the door. Her hair was up, pulled severely back from her forehead. "What you want?"

"To talk."

"Nothing to talk about."

"I'm sorry."

"Sorry?"

"The way I treated you. I was . . ."

"Green," she said. "Pea-soup green."

He nodded.

"Swamp green, puke green, and now I know what you want. You sad. You got no friends now. You come to me."

She'd opened the door a bit wider. He could see all of her face, the mockery that couldn't quite contain her pain. He knew he was going to win. This did not make him feel joy, but neither did it surprise him.

"I want to be your friend." As he said this, he realized that he could, such was his control, at any moment cry. He considered what the effect might be and let it go. "Please, Josephine. Please be my friend."

The girl with one hand watched him weep. She understood why he had done to her what he had. In the privacy of her heart she had long heaped scorn on herself; she was a freak. She had yet to be convinced of her beauty, and had, in the South as well as the North, ceased being shocked that humans, adult and child alike, found in her an opportunity to express their meanness. Still, it hurt. Putting yourself down was one thing, dealing with this cruelty in others was a second. And the others were legion; this was why she carried the arm in front of her, not to flaunt it, but to keep a cruel world at bay. She had thought that Gerald was different, had been drawn to him because the depth of suffering in his eyes approached her own, signaled a kindred spirit, and she'd lowered her arm, waiting for the proper moment to tell him the secret no one in the world but she and her father knew. But Gerald's suffering had made him weak; despite its reputation, suffering did that, and later she knew that his apology was insincere. After Iceman's death he'd changed, and she sensed he was really sorry. Yet, she'd waited. When you'd been hurt so badly, you wanted to be sure.

So his tears convinced her, not of how she felt—she'd never stopped loving him—but to open the door all the way, to pull him inside and put her arms around him, to croon in a voice mothers use to soothe children frightened of the dark, a voice that was Southern in diction, but stripped of exaggerated accent.

"You loved Iceman, didn't you?"

Iceman's dead. The words branded him, made him dizzy. He did not want to accept or understand them. "Yes."

"I knew it when you stood up in church."

"That was for you, too. To show I wasn't a coward."

"You hurt me. I couldn't never let anybody hurt me like that again."

"I won't. I promise."

"Gerald, I love you."

He wouldn't lie. "I'm empty," he said.

"I ain't asking you to say nothing."

She kissed him. He tried to make his lips speak of his regret, of tenderness and affection, but as her mouth opened, welcoming his tongue, as she traced her fingers across his face, her breathing grew ragged, and his cock grew hard.

"Come upstairs," she said.

"Your folks."

"They don't get home before six."

"Josephine?"

"Come on."

His hand in hers, he followed up the staircase. Her

room was pale yellow, trimmed in white. There was a window with curtains of tan, which muted the sunlight; she faced the window. When she pulled her dress away from her upper body, the wings of her shoulder blades made his heart fly. A magical movement of her hands, a toss of her head, her hair fell free. When she was down to her cotton underwear, she said that she appeared to be the only one with no clothes on, and he entered what seemed the interminable length of time it took to get his sneakers untied. She jumped into bed, burrowed under the covers, from beneath which she tossed her bra and underpants. He undressed to his shorts, took the two steps to the bed, marveling that he was not frightened; a little nervous, but not scared. When he got into bed, they took his shorts off together. One part of him was with her, another stood alone, watching, thinking how he'd come to apologize and was ending up getting laid. He stretched his body along her length and groaned at how good it felt.

"You got protections?"

The question confused him, occupied as he was in attempting to swallow her breast. "Protection? Yeah." He retrieved the solitary prophylactic from his wallet. Josephine regarded it with suspicion.

"How long you had that thing?"

He laughed, amazed that he could, amazed that she laughed with him. God, he felt good. Ten minutes later, softening in the hot grip of her body, he felt even better. Except that it had been too quick. He lay with Josephine's head cradled in his arm, telling himself it didn't matter that she hadn't been a virgin.

"How you feel?"

"Red," she answered. "Gold. Like the sun going down."

"We better get up before your folks come back."

"We got time."

He tightened his arm around her. The condom on his deflated penis began to cool; there was a heaviness at the tip that he found uncomfortable.

"Where you going?"

"Bathroom. Take this thing off."

She swallowed. "Was this your first time?"

"Yes."

His back was turned. He didn't see that her face was moving. In the bathroom he removed the rubber, held it up to the light, then flushed it down the toilet. When he walked back into the room, Josephine said, "It wasn't mine."

"I know." He sat on the bed. "Blue?"

"Wasn't Blue."

She was looking at the window where the sun came through, as if the glow she'd lost had gone to join that insubstantial light. He felt in absolute control. "Green?"

"It ain't funny."

"Okay."

"I just wanted you to know, that's all. You wasn't the first."

"What's wrong?"

She said to the window, "I *wish* you was."

"That's all?"

"If you knew, you'd hate me. You'd be sorry you ever touched me."

He touched her shoulder. "I wouldn't."

"You would."

"What do you want me to do?"

"Nothing."

"You can tell me if you want. It won't make any difference."

"Really?"

"Look at me. I promise."

"You won't hate me?"

"I won't hate you."

"Hold my hand."

It was cool, damp.

"I can't," she said.

"Okay."

"I'm scared."

"Josephine . . ."

"My daddy."

"Your daddy what?"

"My *daddy*."

"Your *father*?" He stood up.

"You're hurting my hand. You promised." She began to cry.

"How? When?" he sputtered. "I mean . . . was he drunk?"

"Always when he was drunk."

"You tell your mama?"

"No. But she know. Least I think."

"And didn't do anything?"

"Unh-unh."

"Why?"

She shook her head.

"Why'd you let him?"

She shrugged and reclaimed her hand, wiped tears from her face. "He's my daddy."

"Jesus, Josephine."

"I won't let him no more," she said. "I won't. He ain't done it since we moved here nohow." She reached for his hand.

He slumped back to the bed, feeling excitement, disgust, and an absence of disbelief, remembering what he'd overheard an old black caddy say at the golf course: most people had no more business with children than chickens had with Cadillacs. He would never have children. Then he began to imagine what it was like with her father.

"What you thinking?" Josephine asked.

"I want to again."

"You got more protections?"

"No."

"We ain't got time no way," she said, and hopped out of bed to begin dressing. On the inside of each thigh was a long, rectangular scar. She said that after the accident, the skin had gotten infected on her arm, and they'd removed skin from her thighs to replace it. The graft hadn't taken.

He watched her dress. He couldn't decide which was more lovely, her taking her clothes off or her putting them on. He reached for his socks, feeling powerful.

"I'll see you tomorrow."

"Yes." She smiled, harnessing her breasts. "Tomorrow."

"If he touches you, run. Call me."

"Run," she repeated. "Call you."

CHAPTER
21

Already defined by distance, by intelligence, and by three eyes, now Gerald was marked by his relationship with the girl whose hand was missing. His father was apoplectic, but managing the construction of Hosea's laundry was demanding, leaving him too exhausted in the evening to do more than make the most murderous of threats. The one time he had summoned the energy to beat his son, the effort had nearly broken him. He'd spent the next day in a daze that resulted in an error of judgment that set the project back a week.

When Gerald was not with Josephine, or at the golf course, he was reading one of the dozens of books he brought home in shopping bags from the public library. Reading made him forget and knowledge was power. Though he was calm and apparently controlled, the depth of his sadness was expressed in his eyes: deep blue, not yellow, was his color. Everybody said that this resulted from devastation over Iceman's death, but Gerald knew better. Sadness was what he'd chosen to become. Sadness made people leave you alone. But it also made you an object of pity, and in school, where he continued to excel, he cultivated an arrogance and a cutting tongue that made it impossible for anyone to pity him. This was the way he wanted it, to be unconnected, untouched; then nothing, nobody, ever again could hurt him. Even if a miracle occurred and Iceman came back to life, Gerald would be pleased to see him, but he'd go on camping out there in the distance, on the sad edge, where not even Josephine could come without permission.

For a time he entertained himself with thinking of Josephine's father and what he'd done, and he imagined running off with her. But this exercise always ended in suffering and ruin, for you had to make a living in this world, and he was not fifteen. For a while he waited for Josephine's father to rape again, after which Gerald planned to orchestrate the fiend's imprisonment and disgrace. One day he realized how contradictory this thinking was. He'd be insured acclaim; he wanted anonymity, the perpetuation of his distance.

He thought about what he felt for his lover and refused to name it. She adored him, but, more important, she looked up to and depended on him. She said he was the smartest person she'd ever met, a condition he'd arrived at, no doubt, through the reading of all those books. As with so many people blessed (or cursed) by beauty, she balked at acknowledging hers. Simply because he wanted to see if he could, Gerald set out to convince her. On the streets he pointed to attractive women, who, he said, couldn't hold a candle to her. He made her stand in front of mirrors while he held up photographs of models in magazines, comparing her eyes, her mouth, the definition of her cheekbones. She began to believe in her beauty, or, rather, she began to believe that he believed. Her arm descended from her chest, found her waist. Finally it hung at her side, where in stressful moments (someone stared, perhaps, or someone carefully didn't) it jerked with a rhythm that reminded him of the throats of birds.

At the end of the school year he began, weather permitting, to caddy six days a week. Half the money he handed to his mother; still, he had enough to keep himself and Josephine in pizzas, hamburgers, and ice cream. Since their sex life was active, a not insignificant portion of his earnings went to the purchase of condoms, which he bought one at a time, dividing his business equally among Montgomery's four drugstores. The problems with this method of purchasing were two. First, it was not economical. Condoms were thirty-five cents apiece, and three for a dollar; a dozen cost $3.25. Second, buying one at a time meant he and Josephine could not make love twice if they wanted to. This ultimately drove him to buy in bulk, for recently they had almost gone too far. A baby was the last thing he wanted.

Golden's was the biggest and fanciest drugstore in town. The clerk one afternoon was a big-breasted blonde, a senior at the high school, who, rumor had it, fucked like a rabbit. It had been a boring day and she didn't, to her dismay, have a date after work. She decided she was entitled to some fun.

"Prophylactics? That's a pretty big word for such a little boy."

"Is it? What do you call the ones *you* use?"

Her smile faded. "Most *men* called them condoms."

"Oh. Then give me some of those."

Five seconds later she asked, "What kind you want?"

"Trojans."

"Regular or lubricated?"

"Which are better?"

She was quick. "How would I know?"

"Lubricated."

"How many? One?"

"A dozen."

"Lifetime supply, eh?"

"Unh-unh. I'm spending the night with your mother."

"You little bastard. My mother's dead."

"May she rest in peace."

Mouth tight, breasts heaving, she dropped the condoms into a bag, handed him his change. "You got a fresh mouth for a punk kid."

"Look," Gerald said wearily, "why don't you quit? Can't you see I'm smarter than you?"

"Asshole."

"Did your mother have any children before she died?"

"Get out of here," she hissed.

When he went past the cosmetics counter, he looked over his shoulder at the stunning, red-headed white woman who was looking through a case of lipsticks. She wore a beige suit and an emerald-green blouse, and she was humming snatches of "What a Difference a Day Makes." She looked familiar, but it was not until he was out the door and had turned up Broadway that Gerald realized she was the lady who lived with the dope dealer.

Everybody knew by now how Hosea and Alice managed to live so well, but nobody made a move to stop them—this despite the fact that half the kids in Montgomery were "doing" hashish and marijuana, and some of the more adventuresome had begun to sniff the white powder they referred to mysteriously as "horse." Hosea had, in the beginning, been leery of selling dope to kids. The people whom he'd paid off would be hard pressed to protect him if the community took up arms against him in the name of the children. In addition, the kiddy trade was relatively small. His big money came from supplying the staffs and guests of neighboring hotels and the gamblers who frequented the racetrack. As soon as he heard the first voice lifted in serious protest, he planned to cut the children off.

But no one so much as asked a leading question. The track had weathered a few tough years before taking off; now Montgomery was booming. Small businesses, big spenders, and people just looking for a job flooded the area, along with prostitutes and con men. White people were so deep in money and had to spend so much time researching tax loopholes that they had no time for children. Guilty, they made amends by buying sports cars and motorcycles, with which the children proceeded to terrorize the county and maim themselves. This behavior baffled the parents, who, when a psychiatrist opened a suite of offices in Montgomery, traded in the motorcycles for analysis.

Black people, except Hosea, did not reap nearly so much prosperity. Nevertheless, it was a time when the "trickle-down theory" was more drip than drought, and, collectively, black people's lot improved. Only a few families couldn't buy high-topped Converse sneakers for the kids or spend the extra dollar for belts on the back of chinos. Montgomery's black children began going regularly to the dentist, and they were seldom disappointed on Christmas morning, when living rooms groaned with bicycles, electric trains, and sports equipment. Occasionally, some ecstatic teenager would look through the window to find a secondhand Chevrolet, which needed only a little bodywork.

It is true that some of these children smoked and drank, that several got pregnant, and that most had no use for the church, but black parents took consolation in pointing out that their kids were in better shape than whites'. There was no objective reality to warrant this conclusion, just as there was no record of what black parents did when they woke into the void of three o'clock in the morning, wondering where their children were. Most of them probably prayed, since they didn't believe in psychiatry. In daylight they sought to hold the line against destruction by being stricter. But it is difficult to be strict with children if basically you love them and the rest of your life is going well. Children are, under these circumstances, delightful. If you can pay your bills and have a little left over, and if you can afford to go regularly to the dentist, you are just liable to let children alone and ignore their glassy eyes.

In this atmosphere, Hosea flourished and had time to concern himself with his family. His oldest, Rachel, was the only one who wouldn't see him. A contact in Atlantic City said she was religiously socking away money for the day her looks were gone. Angela and her husband were working their way up the ladder at IBM in Poughkeepsie. Hosea gave them a belated wedding present of a thousand dollars and made them promise to make him a grandfather. Susan Ann and Joyce lived in Montgomery and were employed as barmaids. They were good girls, a little fast, but knew how to take care of themselves. He sent them to enroll in secretarial and business courses at the community college; he wanted them to run the laundry when they had the skills.

The last two daughters had the marvelous legs that their mother had flaunted in her prime. Chrissie was sixteen and smart as a whip; Donna Lee, fourteen, was simply a knockout. Hosea took them on a two-day shopping trip to New York City and told them that if they made good grades, he'd send them to college. When he found out that Meredith had taken the money he gave her for her teeth and put it under the mattress, he had Chrissie and Donna Lee lead her to the dentist, where she was fitted with dentures. In July, he sent two men from Jackson Smalls to finish the addition he'd started in 1947, and ordered new furnishings for the house. Then he sat back and considered how well everything was going.

There had been one sticky period, and Hosea had been amused that here in the North, in the year 1961, white people were still capable of good old-fashioned racist attitudes. As long as Alice was fat and grotesque, nobody cared that they lived together. But when she lost all that weight, you'd have thought he'd run off with Jackie Kennedy. The irony of it was that he and Alice didn't sleep together any more. When Hosea was a kid, his grandfather used to point to skinny women and smack his lips. "The closer the bone, the sweeter the meat," he'd say, but Hosea was bearing witness that the myth was a lie. As Alice lost weight, her interest in sex diminished. Whether it was mind or matter, Hosea couldn't determine, but as the pounds were shed her love muscle grew steadily weaker, until finally it wasn't worth the effort it took to get his clothes off. They were still tight buddies and fifty-fifty partners, but, sexually speaking, they went their separate ways.

White folks didn't know that. He was a black man; she was a white attractive woman. They lived together; therefore, white people made assumptions, all of which made their knees weak. Hosea didn't know what would have happened if Moses Duewright hadn't formed a chapter of the NAACP. This audacity on the undertaker's part deflected white people away from Hosea's love life, and filled them with the kind of righteous indignation last witnessed when Pearl Harbor was coldcocked by the Japanese. There was no need for the NAACP to come to Montgomery, white folks said. Hadn't Negroes always lived where they wanted, drunk a cup of coffee where they wanted? Didn't they vote? Didn't black and white kids go to school together?

Moses allowed that these were true. But where were the black businesses, other than the funeral parlor, barbershop, and Ezra Poole's Restoration Company? Where were the black bank executives? Why was the town council, the Board of Education, and the teaching staff lily white, and the Police Department without a single man of color?

With deliberate speed, white people engineered the

hiring of a black police officer, two black bank tellers, and had Ezra Poole appointed to the school board. Then they slapped one another on the back, lit congratulatory cigars, and wondered what the ruckus was. It was Moses Due-wright waving an American flag at the head of a protest parade.

There was a lot of excitement, and everybody got caught up in it except Norman, who experienced a keen disappointment in black folks. He hadn't expected white people to listen to his sermons; most of them, after all, didn't believe in anything except Santa Claus. Black folks, however, should have realized that what was happening was nothing more than fulfillment of the earthworms' prophecy; the chickens were coming home to roost. And there were lots more chickens where these came from. Before it was over, the air would be thick with chickens.

CHAPTER
22

She was in a car. It was night, and she sat between her mother and father. Her hand ached, not the one her mother held, but the one that was missing, the one that should have been where the white gauze glowed in the dashboard lights. She'd looked at it once, then refused to look.

They were leaving one place in fear, of what, she didn't know; they were going to a destination not determined. Then she was in the back yard of the house she'd grown up in. Her father was chasing a white chicken. An airplane left a plume of smoke against the bright-blue sky; she could hear the angry buzz of its single engine, and she was laughing because her father looked so funny trying to catch the chicken. The sun collided with the blade, relentlessly silver above his brutal face, and the axe descended. Blood gushed into the sparkling air; the chicken's body began to run. Incensed that its departure had not been noted, the head clucked in a pool of crimson, and the door of the clock with one hand opened onto darkness. Nothing came out. "Cuckoo," the darkness said. "Cuckoo."

She awoke. That the fear subsided quickly was because the dream was so familiar; she'd been dreaming it as long as she remembered. Then she knew that her father was in the room. She couldn't see him; it was dark, sometime in the desolation just before the dawn, but she could smell the liquor, beneath that the odor of his body which would identify him in a crowd, would lead her to him though she were blind. He smelled, inexplicably, of peanuts. Now, she could hear his labored breathing.

"Daddy?"

"Hello, daughter."

"Daddy, don't."

"Now ain't no reason for you to be that way," he wheezed. "That Fletcher boy ain't turned you from your daddy?"

"Please."

She could hear him undressing; her eyes, grown accustomed to the darkness, found the thickness of his shadow way in the corner of her room. "You know," he said, his voice seductive despite the distortion of drink, "you know you your daddy's girl. Ain't nothin changed that." And he began to walk toward her. She watched the shadow approach, feeling no fear, only a singular aloneness and a deep despair. The fingers of her remaining hand clenched, and she locked her legs together.

"Move over."

"Daddy?"

"Move over."

She moved. The bed sighed as he got in and turned toward her; he sighed. His hand burned on her hip.

"Daddy, please."

"You know you love your daddy," he whispered, and began to stroke her belly. It had always amazed her that a hand so huge and heavy could move so tenderly across her flesh. That was the way he had demonstrated his love for her when she was little, when, at the end of the day, she flew into his outstretched arms. In this memory, the only one she had before the age of nine, there was the cuckoo clock on the window sill, bereft of bird, the long hand missing, the short hand on the four. They would sit on the couch, and he would stroke her.

Yes, she'd wanted his touch, but as a daughter; she'd never wanted this. Now, more than ever, she didn't want it. But the resolve she'd thought she'd have at this moment was nonapparent, and she reasoned, hopelessly, that there was nothing she could do. He was her father, he was in her bed; he smelled of alcohol and peanuts. She'd never cried except the first time, when it hurt; she didn't cry now. When his fingers sought entrance between her barricaded knees, she resisted but a moment, then spread her legs. He was her father, and she raised her hips when he pulled her nightgown up above her waist, higher, so that her breasts would be available to his lips; raised them again so his hands could cup her buttocks when his weight came bearing down. Then she reached between them for his rubber-covered penis, found it, rubbed the head against her opening sex. Always *she* had to place *him* inside of her, and she did it now, because she'd always done it, and he, breathing "It's been so long," drove into her, slowly, gently (he was always gentle), penetrating, not her flesh, but her sadness, bringing, for the first time since the first time, tears to her eyes. She turned her head so that the full force of his liquored breath would not beat into her nostrils. Only when he insisted did she begin to move, pretending the piston inside her belonged to Gerald. When she couldn't bend her imagination to this duty, she told herself that none of it meant anything, and she began to repeat in her head words to a song in whose vague promise she found some consolation: "It'll all be over, bye and bye."

When it *was* over and her father had gone lumbering off to Gertrude's bed, she lay fingering the throbbing hole in her body. As she'd forever done in the emptiness after his leaving, she struggled to re-create the parts of her life that were missing. Something was wrong with her memory; it had been cut off—everything before the age of nine was

193

darkness except for her father's touch and the one-handed clock whose bird had gone away, and the dream, which, her mother said, had no connection to reality. She had only her parents' memories to rely on, and they had told her how she'd been hit by a car as she chased, of all things, a chicken into the darkening road. Her hand had been mangled; the doctors had to cut it off. The accident had happened when she was seven—that, too, she did not remember. The first real memory after her father's touch was not of an event, but of a feeling; she missed something, missed it so terribly she could do nothing but cry. Then she understood the feeling, for her father returned from wherever it was he'd gone. She loved her father more than anything, and when he walked back into that room, she felt as if someone had turned a light on, and she need never, any more, be frightened of the dark.

That day she chose to mark as the beginning of her life. Her father was wearing a blue suit and a red tie whose knot had come undone, and he carried a doll without box or wrapping, a white doll with blond hair and cold blue eyes. When her father looked at her, he'd begun to cry. He'd sat her on his lap and stroked her, talking soft, and she could smell the liquor. He said he was crying because he'd made her suffer. This disturbed her; he stopped the stroking when he said it.

And where was her mother through all of this? Where, during the dark years and the years of light? And why, when her father was not around, did her mother say such vile and awful things to her? "You heifer," she'd hiss. "You pig."

That had begun after her father had introduced to her the pet between his legs, and insisted that nothing would delight him more than that she play with it. But, he gravely cautioned, it must be their secret. She must never tell her mother; if she did, he would cease to love her. He had no idea how this threat frightened her; if he had, she believed, he would not have made it. To lose her father's love would be to find herself thrust back into the darkness. She would be empty, without memory. She did not know this in language; she sensed it, much as she later sensed the reasons for her mother's malediction. By this time Percy was rubbing the pet between her legs, and when she was eleven the pet became a weapon and made her bleed. Because he was her father and she loved him, she pleased him, even after she knew that it was wrong. She didn't say anything to her mother, bore her hatred, knowing that while her father lived, she was safe from what she couldn't remember.

But it had to stop now, for she had discovered the suffering in Gerald's eyes, and she had promised never again to let her father touch her. Gerald must never know that she'd broken this promise; she would never allow it to be broken again. How she would accomplish this she hadn't known when she made the first promise; she didn't know now.

As the sun rose, she wondered if she could contract her mother as an ally. At times she suspected that her mother knew; at times she was convinced she didn't. But if confronted, Gertrude would have to respond and put a stop to it. What mother could endure having happen to her daughter what was happening to her?

She lay in bed until her father left for work, and then she dressed and went downstairs. Her mother was at the sink, washing dishes.

"Morning, Mama."

"Morning, Josey." Gertrude began to hum. Josephine watched her pitiful shoulders, the black, wrinkled skin of her neck. Her mother's feet stood in slippers with the backs broken down. Her heels were ashy. Perhaps she didn't know.

"Mama?"

"Uh-huh?"

Maybe it was over. Maybe it wouldn't happen again. "Nothing."

"Sleep all right?"

"Yeah."

"You know you got to do the wash this morning?"

"I'll start it now."

When she left, Gertrude dug her fingernails into her palms. "Hussy," she whispered venemously. "Black, ungodly, one-hand hussy."

Downstairs in the basement Josephine separated white clothes from colored. Maybe it wouldn't happen again. Maybe it was over.

That was on the first of August. Since she'd been eleven, she'd never spent any time wondering whether her father would visit her in the night. He either came or did not; she was neither surprised when he did, nor disappointed when he didn't. For the whole year since they'd moved to Montgomery, she'd seldom thought about it until she'd made love with Gerald. Now, she could think of little else. Would he come this evening, or tomorrow? What was that squeak on the staircase; who, in the middle of the night, had suddenly to use the bathroom? As she lived with this increasing tension, she discovered that she could not bear the most innocent of her father's touches, not a peck on the cheek, or the hand he'd grown accustomed to stroking across her butt. She realized the perpetual sourness of his breath, the lack of space between his tiny, red eyes, the thick ungainliness of his body. Signs of his filthiness, which she had never assigned to filth, were suddenly everywhere; she had merely to narrow the focus of her eyes to note them. He left the bathroom sink covered with

196

short black hairs after he shaved, and blood spots on the towels. Gobs of phlegm floated unflushed where he spit in the toilet. He didn't raise the seat when he peed. His clothes, which she'd washed for years and handled without thinking, she now held by two fingers, arm extended. Huge arcs of foul, peanut-smelling sweat darkened the underarms of his tee shirts. Handkerchiefs clotted with snot and spittle lived in his pockets, and his shorts were marked with shit stains. The evidence of his squalor made her look at what they'd been doing with disgust.

Would he come again? When would he come? How would she resist him? She was afraid of him now, trembled in his presence, cowered when he spoke. She felt that she'd always been afraid of him, that what she'd thought was love was terror. She'd pleased him because she was afraid. Of what? And why?

She began to concentrate on her life before memory, peeled layers of darkness only to find more darkness still. Nightly she dreamed of the midnight ride, the airplane, the chicken dancing across the yard.

For two weeks she moved wrapped in terror, curdled by tension, waiting for his visit. This time she would be strong, she would reason with him, maybe he would relent and tell her what lay behind the darkness. She wanted to talk to Gerald, but she was afraid he would discover that she'd broken her promise. She wanted to believe that she knew Gerald well enough to be certain he would understand, that he would not despise her, but she knew she didn't. There was something hard about her lover; there was a space inside him that he wouldn't allow anyone to enter. It was all right to have a little of that space, but his was too large; it threatened, finally, to swallow him. Yet, she loved him; he was all she had. He had made her believe that she was beautiful, that she was not stupid or worthless.

"Please, God," she prayed, "don't let him come."

Percy Moore came on the night of August 14, left his clothes in the hallway, crept across the bedroom floor, and slid into bed with his daughter. He was drunk, as usual, but he was also in a foul mood. Josephine had been acting like he was a stranger, like she didn't love him any more. Recently, in his presence, she wore a disgusted look, as if he were some no-count nigger off the street. This must not, he'd decided, earlier that evening in the bar, be allowed to happen. The girl had to understand who was boss; she had to experience a renewal of her gratitude. He laughed out loud when he thought this. It sounded educated, something a white man might have said.

Gone was his confusion concerning how what had begun as an effort to console Josephine had ended in his comfort. Gone was his resolve that he would do this wretched thing no more; that here, in a new town, he would make a new beginning. Now, bloated with alcohol and lust, angry, he gripped her thigh, digging his fingers into her flesh, then grunted with pain and surprise as her knee drove mightily between his legs. A curtain lowered across the space before his eyes; it was wet like mist, crimson like blood. Her aim was poor; he was hurt, but not disabled. He could not see her, but he slammed his fist into where he thought her face lay on the pillow, and he heard her whimper, "Oh." Then she was fighting like a madwoman in the darkness. The bedsprings squeaked. Percy grunted again, "Bitch"; her fingernails had scored his chest. Rising, he straddled her writhing form, began to drive his fist into her face. He put one hand around her throat, squeezed. "Be quiet, I say. Be still. Don't, I'll kill you."

The fear was real; he did *not* love her. She didn't want to give in, but neither did she want to die, and she knew that he would, if need be, kill her, even if it meant that in the morning he would weep. Then she would never know what lived back there in the darkness; she'd never know what the dream meant.

She was still.

"That's better," Percy whispered. "Much better."

She lay, thinking of clocks without hands, a white baby doll with ice-cold eyes, and that tomorrow was Gerald's birthday.

She stayed in her room late that morning; her mother called to her through the door, but didn't enter. In the mirror, Josephine considered the damage. The area around both eyes was swollen, purplish. She had a puffy lip and some discoloration on her throat. Rage visited her veins like molten rock, cooled and made her rigid. She did not think this morning about the life she couldn't remember; she thought about the life she could, the life that was menaced. What her father had done to her was, as it was benevolently called, "against the law." If she went to the police, what would be their response? Disconsolate, she thought she knew: they would not believe her. Even if they exerted themselves and spoke to her father, they would do it apologetically, and her father would deny it. Her mother was not to be an ally; one prayed she wouldn't be a foe. If Gertrude hadn't known, she certainly knew now; not even the heaviest of sleepers could have slept through all that noise, and her mother was *not* a heavy sleeper. Her mother knew and had said nothing, had done nothing. It was up to Josephine; nobody anyplace was going to lend a hand.

She thought of Gerald and *his* father. The world was full of fathers; why had she and Gerald been so cursed?

On television, in school, in magazines, families, and, by extension, fathers, were exalted, but nobody ever talked about the danger to the children. If you were not lucky, families were detention camps, insane asylums, dungeons without light. Children were clothed and fed and sent to school, but nobody cared about them on the inside. Then the children must learn to care about and protect themselves.

She imagined driving an axe into her father's skull. She imagined severing his penis and stuffing it down his throat.

They celebrated Gerald's birthday with a picnic in the woods behind the town barn. She made ham sandwiches and potato salad and baked a chocolate cake. They ate in silence, Josephine's eyes hidden by dark glasses. She was wearing a white cotton blouse with a high collar, blue jeans, and sneakers, and he asked what had happened to her lip.

"My daddy hit me."

"I thought," he teased, "you said you were getting too old for beatings."

"I am. But I didn't say he was beatin me."

"What happened?"

"Last night," she said, and faltered. "He . . . he . . . She removed her glasses and looked, helplessly, into his eyes. "I didn't let him. But neither could I stop him."

He was stunned by her battered face. "You were supposed to *run* if he tried that. Call me."

"How was I supposed to run?" she said hotly. "Him sittin on me with his hands around my neck. How? Where? And what were *you* going to do?"

His mouth opened, but he didn't speak.

"And why you got to make it sound like *my* fault?"

"I didn't mean to sound that way. . . . Did he hurt you?"

"Look at me! Yes, he hurt me. Hurt, hurt, hurt, hurt me." She began to cry.

"Josephine. Josephine. It's all right." He crawled around the food, took her in his arms. "It's all right." He remembered the afternoon Iceman had held him in this very clearing. "I love you," Iceman had said. It had helped to know that someone loved him. If he said that to Josephine, it would help her. But he couldn't say it. He had vowed never to love again.

Yet he had a responsibility to comfort her, even while he knew there was nothing he could do to make it better. Her condition was out of his control. What he couldn't control he wanted to leave alone. Because he could imagine her pain, but not her rage, because his sadness was for himself, he lied, resorting to a childhood fantasy he had long since ceased to covet. He said they could rid themselves of their fathers by committing suicide.

Her reaction was furious. "*They* the ones should die," she shouted. Her words reverberated in the clearing, drove birds calling up into the glistening air. "Not us. Fathers like that don't deserve to live. We ought to kill *them*. Not us."

"Easy."

"I don't want to be easy. Come on, Gerald. Let's do it. We can."

The idea had, apparently, disconnected her from grief. She'd pulled back from him, sat on her heels. Gerald felt inadequate. Hers was the superior idea. He'd offered romance; she plotted revenge. But he did not want to kill his father, not while he was so effectively punishing Alexander by refusing to accept his attempts at reconciliation. The truth was that he did not want to kill his father at all. Despite his heart's quiet insistence that it would never be, he had not given up hope that through some miracle, or mystery, one day his father would come to love him. One day his father would plant a kiss on his cheek like a seal ineffable, would take him in his arms and say, "Son. My son, I love you." Then Gerald could do anything: fly, or strike out Henry Aaron, or go fifteen rounds with the heavyweight champ. He'd walk down avenues of unknown cities, stop strangers in the street. "Hey," he'd say. "My daddy loves me."

But he didn't want anyone to know about his doomed and silly dream. Josephine revered him, and he needed her to do this. It was weak to need anyone, and foolish, for then the person would go away, but it took time to learn to stand alone. All of this went through his head in an instant, and he decided to play along, knowing that eventually she would allow him to make the idea his own.

"How," he asked, "would we kill them?"

"I don't know. Could we pay somebody?"

"You got any money?"

"Unh-unh. You?"

"Nope."

"*Think*, Gerald. You smart."

"Put a bomb in his car."

"We ain't got no car."

"Poison. How about rat poison? Put it in his food."

"Yes." She was radiant, had never, he thought, looked lovelier. Inside, his head was shaking at her childishness. She was no more going to kill her father than she was going to grow a new hand.

"Let's buy the poison today."

"Today?" He laughed. "On my birthday?"

"I guess not. Happy Birthday."

"Thank you." She'd get over it.

"I feel orange," she said, "purple." She stretched out

202

on the blanket and looked, adoringly, up into his face. Then her eyes clouded, and she said, "I wonder if I'll ever remember."

"What?"

She told him about her missing life.

CHAPTER
23

All during the next week, Josephine pestered him about going to buy the poison. All during that week he put her off. He was tired or he didn't have any money. They'd certainly do it tomorrow.

On Friday, the morning which had promised rain delivered a little after noon, and Gerald left the golf course early. When he walked into Josephine's house, she was jubilant. She ran into the kitchen and came back with an arm behind her, dancing around him as he peeled off his poncho.

"Okay, tell me."

In the palm of her hand sat a small white box, an ominous black X on one side. His first reaction was to drop his eyes so she couldn't see his anger. He felt incredibly tired. He'd failed to control this situation, and now it had gotten out of hand.

"You proud of me?"

"Yes," he lied.

"I did it by myself."

"That's terrific."

"Let's go get yours."

"Now?"

"Sure, now."

"It's raining."

She looked at him, piercingly. "You scared, Gerald?"

"It's raining. I wanted to spend the day with you. In bed."

"If we go now, we got plenty of time. It's only one o'clock."

He stifled exasperation. Buying the poison had made her feel good. Maybe all she needed was to prove to herself that they could do it. "Okay," he relented, and glanced at the box in her hand. He didn't know that much about poison. It seemed enough to kill six men and an entire community of rodents; buying another box would be redundant. But he knew she would respond to this suggestion with disbelief, and it was imperative that she believe in him if he wanted to regain control.

"Get an umbrella."

As they walked to Broadway in the gentle rain, Gerald made up a story he said he'd read in a crime magazine. A young woman had murdered her lover and been sent to prison. There, her fragile beauty had attracted the most mean-spirited lesbians, who forced her to commit unnatural acts before they raped her with a broom handle. The message was lost on Josephine. While she sympathized with the unfortunate woman, she was more interested in what the lover had done to drive her, justifiably, to murder. Gerald realized that he should have put the woman in the electric chair, but it was too late for that now.

When they reached Broadway, he asked where she'd bought the poison. "Hegman's . . . Why you going past?" Patiently, he explained that one had to cover one's tracks; if their fathers turned up dead from poison, it would be easy for someone to recall that they'd bought from the same store. It was exactly the kind of evidence police looked for.

"You're so smart," she said, and shivered with excitement. "Look, there's Norman Fillis. Acting up again."

Across the street, bareheaded, looking like a vulture with navigational problems, Norman perched high up in a tree. When they got to Donaldson's Hardware Store, Gerald told Josephine to walk around the block and meet him on the corner. There was a line of customers, and he had to wait his turn. When he came out, the poison in his pocket, Norman was standing on the sidewalk. Smiling, he looked at Gerald, but did not speak. Slowly, he began to shake his head.

Through that adventure, Gerald was able to delay Josephine, but after a while she began to pester him about a date. Gerald had thrown his poison away the same day he bought it, and he was thoroughly dismayed that she had embraced the fantasy so completely and so long. He'd been a child when he'd planned to murder his father; Josephine was sixteen, physically and chronologically a woman. Mentally, he'd decided, was another story. As August craned its neck toward September, his patience thinned, and finally he told her.

"What you mean?"

"I mean it's ridiculous. A game. And it's time to stop playing."

They were in her bedroom, had just made love. The sheets were tangled, the odor of sex hung electrically in the air. Josephine sat up.

"Is what he do to me a game?"

He said it sternly, like a father. "You know what I mean. It's a game."

"Ain't."

"It is."

Her face was breaking. She said, a little like wonder, a little like scorn, "You scared."

"Come on."

"You *scared*."

"Don't be a child."

"You never meant to do it, did you?"

"No."

"All this time you been *playin.*" In the street a car went past with a faulty muffler. She looked at the window, and into his unrelenting eyes. "Treatin me like a child." She shook her head. "Here I am hurtin, and you makin *fun* of me."

He was silent. He would let her have her say, and then he would make it better. She interpreted his silence as affirmation; her eyes closed.

"You never said you loved me," she whispered. Her eyes opened; they were changing colors; gray became light brown. "I know some people don't say it easy. But you don't even *care* for me. All this time you was playin, takin what you could. Like my *daddy.* How many boys in Montgomery get it whenever they want? That's all you wanted. Not me. *It.*"

She looked at her arm with the missing hand. It was rising. Angrily she reached for it, held it down. "And you know what? I knew, Gerald. A little part of me *knew*, but I didn't want to believe it. I was *stupid.*"

"I love you."

"Don't *never* tell me that," she said, and it was the tone, not the volume, of her voice that made him blink. "Don't never tell me that except you mean it."

"Listen. Be reasonable. You're not going to kill your father. You can't kill someone and get away with it."

She'd known all along that at the last moment her nerve would probably fail. But that was not the issue. What was important was that Gerald would have been with her until that moment. His support would have meant that he'd understood her need to feel she could take charge of her life, that having only one hand hadn't made her helpless. It would have meant he understood her need to dream. But all of it, for him, was nothing. For

207

him, she'd been an exercise, an experiment, a fuck. He didn't love her. He didn't even *feel* for her.

She was holding to her arm with an effort that made her muscles taut. "Go away now. Please."

"Josephine . . ."

"I got enough dark in my life that's missin, enough pain in the life I know. I don't need you addin to it."

"Josephine . . ." He summoned his sadness, tried to bring tears to his eyes, but he couldn't. To Josephine, it seemed that he didn't feel anything. Because she wanted to hurt him, she said the cruelest thing she could think of: "I wonder what Iceman'd say if he could see you now?"

She was back alone in the darkness. She stopped eating, slept fitfully, dreamed in Technicolor. Her arm, as if it had life of its own, continually sought to rise; continually she fought to keep it at her side. Now another dread was added to her anguish, for September had arrived to chill the nights and set the trees on fire, and in a week she would return to school, where everyone would know about her and Gerald. She regarded herself in the mirror and wondered if he had lied, even, about that: was she beautiful?

She despised Gerald. She missed him. Either thought could threaten her breathing, grip her heart in an iron hand. She could not, however, weep, as she'd always wept, in private, and this unsettled her, for crying was the only way she had to relieve her pain. She feared that Gerald's hardness had rubbed off, that the power he'd manifested over her would remain in this most subtle and hideous of ways. Now, when she considered the hour of her father's next appearance, she experienced an expectation shorn of horror and disgust. If her father came, as he most certainly would, her emptiness would be defined; there would be, at least, that boundary, that expression of her worth—he, after all, needed her. But this logic wilted in the face of what she knew. Her father had deliberately hurt her, and his need, however great, was base, born not of her value, but his disgrace, and she was but a convenient receptacle into which he poured his lust. She rediscovered beneath the devastation of Gerald's betrayal that she yet hated her father. This filled her with loss at the same time that it battered her with hope. She couldn't cry because she had deceived herself. She went back to the mirror. She was beautiful. She was not without worth. She wept for the fact that she could weep.

Her father would come again. If she'd softened toward him in the days after she'd sent Gerald away, now she did not attempt to hide her disdain, would leave rooms he'd entered, and never allowed herself to look into his face. He would come again. She could tell from the angle of his shoulders, the increased narrowness of his eyes; he was building himself up to it through a slow accumulation of rage. At night she lay waiting for the sound of his steps on the porch, the door which shut behind him, the creak his ascending body made on the trembling stairs. The knife was wrapped in a napkin beneath her pillow. She did not know if she could kill him, but she was determined to protect herself. She would point the knife at his heart, and he would know that she was serious and that his nights of crime were through.

This night he did not come directly upstairs. She heard him opening and closing cabinets, rustling pots; apparently he was hungry. The walls of her room began to speak of the confined and dangerous space she lay in, the door without a lock, the window, through which the moonlight sifted, high up above the ground. She was not safe in this room. It was a prison, the scene of her violation. Most of all, it was dark. That had been, she saw, her constant error; he could not work his horror in the light. She switched on the lamp at the side of her bed. But even in this soft and peaceful illumination the room was not safe. There was space in the lower level of the house, and a door she could run through.

She got out of bed, put her robe on over her nightgown, walked into the hall. She listened, but could hear only her own breathing. She tiptoed past the room in which, presumably, her mother slept. Then she straightened and walked boldly down the creaking stairs.

The living room was dark except for the light that spilled from the kitchen. She could see her father hunched over at the table. He'd left open the door of the refrigerator—it was humming—and he was looking at the wall above the stove with the intensity of a man watching ice melt. She recognized this posture; tonight he had drunk himself into a stupor so immobilizing it was a wonder he'd made it home. He was harmless when he was this way, boorish and foul-mouthed and stinking, but harmless. She walked past him to close the refrigerator door. The hum stopped; she heard the clamoring silence. He looked at her and sighed. "Evenin, daughter."

"Hello."

He belched; his chin fell toward his chest.

"Why don't you go to bed, Daddy?"

"What?"

"Go to bed. You drunk."

"Ain't drunk."

She ignored this and pointed to his plate, where, in unhappy marriage, chicken bones endured cold rice and greasy turnip greens. "You finished?"

"Huh?"

"You want the rest of your food?"

"Unh-unh." He mumbled something.

"What?"

"Want you."

He was looking at the wall, his face solid and stupid, and she didn't understand. Then the floor of her stomach fell away, and she was bolting toward the front door, beyond which lay space and moonlight. Though she moved with the quickness of a threatened bird, he was quicker. His hand on her wrist was a vise; she would have left her arm, pulled it from the socket of her shoulder, but she couldn't.

"Daddy, ain't gonna be no more of this."

He was not wasting words tonight, he was not prepared to speak of loving her, and in the face of his unfamiliar silence, she tasted terror and began to gag. When he stood and embraced her, she grunted, "No," and began to fight him. He drew his fist, paused, and struck her with all his might. The blow snapped her head back. Dizzy, sick to her stomach, she spit in his face, and his fist hammered again, wrapping her head in flame. He dragged her into the living room, smashed her to the floor. In the moment before she slipped into unconsciousness, she saw his face. It was calm, emotionless, the face of a man watching ice melt.

She awoke to a feeling that she was in water above her head. Something was holding her down, someone was trying to drown her. Frantically she struggled, until she realized that this was a dream; the weight was her father's body stretched across her own. Her nightgown was up around her throat; there was a wetness between her thighs. She realized how hot her face was and that she couldn't see out of her left eye. She pulled and pushed and rolled her father off, and he lay on his back, one knee up. Something was singing in her brain, a high-pitched, one-note tune of nonsense. Painfully, she stood, rearranged her gown, tied her robe. She couldn't put all of her weight on her left ankle. *Forever*, she thought. *Your life. Forever.* Grimacing, she limped into the kitchen, opened the cabinet beneath the sink. Steadying herself with her stump on the counter, she bent for the box of poison she'd hidden behind the king-sized bottle of Clorox. With the end of a spoon she punctured a hole in the box top, put the spoon in her pocket, and hobbled back to her father. There, she knelt, listening carefully to the singing. She tried to sprinkle the powder into her father's mouth, but her hand shook and spoiled her aim. The poison sifted onto his nose, his lips, his chin; little found the opening. She was wasting it, she was making a mess she would later have to clean up. She remembered the spoon, set the box on the floor next to her father's head. This was one of the disadvantages of having only one hand, she thought, as she poured poison into the spoon. Now, in addition, she had only one useful eye, and the spoon seemed to leap as she aimed for it. Her head ached. Some of the powder went on the floor. She set the box down. The spoon was full; she steered it toward her father's mouth. Her hand was shaking; she needed another hand to hold it; the poison was falling on his eyes.

"Damn it," she said. "Damn it, damn it, damn it." She needed two hands. You couldn't do anything with one hand. She sat back, breathing hard, thinking, You're not stupid. Think of something. There had to be a way to kill him. She thought of some heavy object, but she couldn't see anything that was small enough to handle. She remembered the knife.

There was no sense in going back upstairs to fetch the one beneath her pillow; there were knives available in the kitchen. She took the biggest and heaviest one she could find, and then she stood above him, trembling. He stopped snoring for a moment, sighed wistfully, and began to snore again. Short, soft, living sounds. She listened, found herself breathing to a rhythm matching his. To block the sound, she began to sing the one-note song that keened endlessly in her head. She was shaking so violently she knew that if she did not strike at once the moment would forever be beyond her. Whimpering, she fell to her knees, raised the knife, and plunged it. The sudden shock of steel meeting bone made her arm go numb, and she cried out. She raised the knife again, again she plunged, again she hit bone. She was sobbing now, thinking her father was not flesh, but rock, iron; she was terrified that he would awaken, that his eyes dusted with poison would open and accuse her. Again she raised the knife. This time as it fell she put all of her weight behind it, discovering a resistance no greater than that of butter, so yielding that she lost her balance and fell across her father's waist. He made two sounds, one a grunt like a question, the other as if he were clearing his throat. Resolved to take no chances, she righted herself and tried to pull the knife out to stab again. She couldn't move it. She tugged, but she couldn't; she needed two hands. The overhead light came on. She looked up into her mother's burning eyes. She looked at her father, at the knife in his chest, at the seeping blood that smelled like metal and pooled on the floor at her knee. The stump of her wrist was pointing down into the blood, was wet with it, and she looked, and remembered what had happened to her hand.

PART FOUR
1980

CHAPTER 24

She was sixty-seven years old, and lately the thought had begun to visit with a new insistency. She would not live forever. One day, perhaps in the morning, perhaps at night, in church, or on the street, or in the house that for sixteen years had known no children, it would happen. She felt it in her bones, in the tendons that connected bones together. One day the Lord would call: "Sister Meredith, it's time to go." Then they would shoot the fluid into her veins and return her to the earth from which she'd been fashioned. There would be the brief sleep before the Final Trumpet, brief because, in the same way she could sense her death, she knew the coming of the Lord was nigh. All the signs were right, the prophecies fulfilled—war and rumors of war, earthquakes in divers places, the great, great falling away from God. People were going crazy all over the place. They'd even shot the President and the Pope.

For twenty years Meredith had waited for her pastor to tell her what to do. She had waited through the acquisition of false teeth, through becoming a grandmother, through watching the back of her youngest as she walked bravely off into the world. She had waited so long that sometimes she forgot what she was waiting for, but lately this was all that she could think of. On Judgment Day, if she did not do what she must, she would have to face God with her hands behind her back, so that she wouldn't be distracted by the blood that stained them. But of course He would see, He who had eyes everywhere. What a pity to have kept God's law all these years, and then be turned away from Heaven because she'd failed to abide by man's. She could tarry no longer.

Before dawn on August 9, 1980, Meredith rose from her bed, dressed, retrieved her teeth from the water glass, and went out into the back yard carrying a shovel scarred with rust. Before she began, she asked Hosea, Jr. to forgive her, not for killing him thirty-two years ago, but for disturbing his rest. Then she began to dig among the flowers. As she labored, the eastern sky exploded, the frantic birds began to carol, and the sun hulked above the trees like a monstrous lemon drop. Meredith shaded her eyes. The day would be hot. Already there was a heaviness in the air that made breathing a little like work.

When she saw what remained of her child, her nervousness subsided. There were only bones and teeth; she'd expected flesh, rotted, but recognizable, and a sharp and putrid odor. She'd expected that his eyes would still be open, and that after all these years she could finally close them. But there were no eyes, only holes in the skull. And the skull was not as large as she remembered. Isn't that strange? she thought, and wiped a hand across her forehead. She was thirsty. In the house she drank a glass of water in three long gulps, then bent below the sink to find a large green plastic garbage bag. She was on her way out the door again when she reconsidered and detoured into her bedroom. In the bottom drawer of the chest were baby things more than thirty years old. Little undershirts, diapers, a teething ring. She took a soft blue blanket from beneath a snowsuit—a receiving blanket. She remembered the name and smiled.

Outside, she knelt at the grave, spread the blanket and began to reclaim her child: first the skull, then the fluted rib cage. She had not thought that the task would demand such precision, but the absence of tendon had left the bones to separate. She worked carefully. There were so many bones. Some were tiny.

In an hour, the grave was empty. The sun was merciless now, and she folded the blanket and slid it into the garbage bag. She had to make another trip into the house; she'd forgotten a plastic tie. This accomplished, she sat on the ground to rest a while. The sun had battered the birds into silence, softened the tar of Little Pond Road. She recognized, striding along its emptiness, the familiar figure of Norman Fillis, who, no doubt, was returning from one of the brisk walks he referred to as his "Constitutionals." When he saw Meredith, he waved and cut across her yard. The perfection of his bald head caught the sun, sent it slanting back into the day. He was smiling.

"Morning, Sister Meredith."

"Morning."

"We're in for a hot one."

"Suspect so."

He glanced at the hole in the ground and nodded approvingly. "The dispensation is drawing to a close. You ready?"

"I'm getting ready."

"He's soon to come."

"Yes, He is."

Neither understood that they were not talking about the same event.

Norman spread his arms. "I'll be a condor."

"What's a condor?"

"A bird. A big, magnificent bird."

"Well. I plan on being an angel. Reckon we'll both be flying."

Norman looked at her as if he'd just swallowed a goldfish. "Hmph," he said, and, turning abruptly, walked away. Had he been anyone else, Meredith would have been upset by his rudeness, but Norman wasn't "right."

He'd managed in recent years to keep himself out of the insane asylum, but that, she figured, was probably because standards had been lowered. Still, in spite of (or because of) his madness, he'd kept her secret all these years. The least she could do was put up with his funny ways. She stood and slung the bag over her shoulder, marveling at how light it was. She took it inside to her bedroom, where she lay across the bed, the bag held to her withered breasts. Three hours later, she began to walk to town.

She could, if she'd wished, have driven, for she'd learned ten years ago to drive, and Hosea had bought her one of those little cars Detroit had begun to build when the Arabs got peculiar. But this was her burden, and she wanted to bear it by herself. Jesus didn't have no red Chevette to carry his cross up Calvary. Neither, then, would she.

By the time she reached Freight House Drive, the sun was brutal. She found a slow, but steady walking rhythm, went past the oil storage tanks, and in a little while she came to the spot where the freighthouse had long ago burned down. Weeds choked the foundation. Wiping perspiration from her eyes, thinking she should have worn a hat, she went past the street of Iceman's electrocution, and came to St. Luke's, where Soapsuds and Jesus and Iceman were buried. Experiencing a sharp and poignant regret, she stopped and set her burden down. The cemetery looked inviting; the headstones blazing in the sun were right up on top of one another, neighborlylike. She wondered how Hosea, Jr. had gotten along all by himself out in the yard. If she'd been thinking clearly back then, she'd have buried him here, where he could have had some company. Iceman would have passed the time of day with him; he wouldn't have cared that Hosea, Jr. had a watermelon head. She picked up the bones and began to walk again, heartened by the thought that after all this was over, she'd have the boy put back to rest in St. Luke's. After she died, she'd lie down next to her child to prove she didn't hate him any more.

When she reached Broadway, the massive trees took the brunt of the sun, and she stopped worrying about not having worn a hat. The wide street was thick with cars and tourists moving lazily in the heat, and with clots of teenagers carrying huge black-and-silver radios, all at a volume that could have raised the dead. Most of the kids were black, and they made Meredith uneasy. Sometimes they made her feel like white people made her feel. This had less to do with what the children did, than with what they didn't. Didn't tip their hats, or speak, or move courteously out of her path. Most didn't even look at her, and those who did regarded her with the same indifference with which they watched the sky. When she got past them and the sweet odor of the cigarettes they smoked, she felt better, although her feet were beginning to hurt. She went by Duewright's Funeral Parlor, clucked in disapproval at the peeling paint. The man was making a lot of money; he ought to keep things up. Past the pornographic bookstore and Flynn's Appliance, the First National Bank, and there was the courthouse all blinding white and pretty, the ripe green carpet of a lawn. She stopped, arrested by the traffic light, and wiped her brow.

People who saw Meredith that day would remember the bag over her shoulder, that her head was bare, and that her apparel was distinguished by a disregard for style or comfort. She wore a long, green woolen dress with white cuffs and collar, a dress so heavy its weight tugged at people's eyelids and made them think the day was hotter than it was. On her feet were black patent-leather slippers, the shine of which had long since been defeated.

Miraculously, the seams of her stockings were impeccably straight. Given the rest of her appearance, gambling men computed the odds that had resulted in this perfection, and figured the payoff would have fixed them for life.

Meredith hadn't been to the courthouse since 1961. That was when the Moore girl killed her daddy, and Meredith had found herself interested in something for the first time since Hosea left. Each morning she'd packed a lunch and set out early, so she'd be sure to get a seat. The trial, everybody agreed, was disappointing. No dirt revealed. Josephine had sat through it all without speaking, on her face an expression she had borrowed from the stone lions that flanked the courthouse steps. Meredith noticed how each day the girl found something else to look at. One day it was the flag; another, the clock.

The defense was self-defense, the murdered man an alcoholic of lowest character, but the prosecutor argued that the bruises Josephine had suffered came from a family man desperately fighting for his life. Do not underestimate the strength and resourcefulness of the handicapped, the prosecutor said, and proceeded to read to the hushed courtroom from a book entitled *Bizarre Murders of the Century*. Both examples were illustrative. Each defendant was a woman: one, who'd had both legs amputated below the knees, had strangled her husband between her thighs. The other, paralyzed from the neck down as the result of a diving accident, had bitten through her lover's throat and watched calmly while he bled to death. In neither instance was a motive apparent, although in the first case an ungodly practice had been hinted at.

When the prosecutor finished, the courtroom buzzed. The defense was not aided by the fact that Josephine had been hammered into silence, not only by her deed, but also by the tongue-freezing memory of what had happened to her hand. And Gertrude, veiled in inconsolable black, a figure of pity, shut her eyes and confessed to nothing.

The poison was the prosecutor's most potent weapon; it spoke of premeditation, the knife being simply an afterthought, the panicked *coup de grace*. They said Josephine was guilty and sent her away. Meredith felt connected to the girl and wondered what hadn't been told. She knew you didn't kill someone without good reason. When she had her trial, she wouldn't sit there looking at a flag. She'd tell everything, starting with when they made love, and how Hosea had left the light on.

It was cool inside. She asked for the county clerk's office and was directed to a room across the front of which ran a long counter. There were two occupied desks beyond this counter; at one a white woman talked into a telephone, at the other a black man wrote hurriedly with a silver pen. Meredith put her bag on the counter and waited to be spoken to. Finally the woman hung up the phone and walked toward her, asking if she could help.

"Yes, ma'am. My name Meredith Malone. This here's my son."

The woman looked at the garbage bag, and then she looked at Meredith. "Excuse me?"

"This here's my son. I buried him in 1948. In my back yard. These his bones. I come to give myself up."

The woman didn't understand. The black man glanced up, then returned to his furious writing. Meredith explained everything again.

"My husband left me cause of him. I smothered him and buried him out back. I want to go to Heaven. I come to pay."

"Melvin," the woman said nervously, "this lady says she's got her son's . . . *bones* in this bag. Says she buried him in her back yard. In 1948."

"We don't handle that kind of thing here," Melvin said. "Tell her to take it to the police."

Relieved, the woman asked if she knew where the new police station was.

"I hope not far," Meredith said. "I walked all the way from Little Pond Road, and my feets is hurtin."

When Roland Birdsong completed his interview with Meredith, the DA called his campaign manager and told him to throw away the timetable. "Jim, we've got our ticket to the state legislature. I've got the biggest drug dealer in this part of the state. *Cold*." Then he called the chief of police and told him he wanted ten squad cars and twenty men equipped for riot control. He wanted them at Hosea Malone's house in fifteen minutes. Birdsong would personally make the arrest.

The police chief asked what the charge was.

"Obstruction of justice, accomplice after the fact to murder one, to name two. I've got my boys hitting the books. We'll see what else we can come up with."

The chief was upset. Thanks to Hosea, he had a substantial down payment on a Mercedes 450SL, and he was looking to Hosea to help him carry the monthly nut. This was not the first time some district attorney had conspired to have Hosea arrested, but the charges had never been this serious. Disguising his alarm with weariness, the chief sighed. "You got cause, Birdsong? Or you just sending me on a wild-goose chase?"

Birdsong told him about Meredith. Then he hung up and called both local newspapers. The chief, after phoning Hosea to tell him what was going down, summoned the desk sergeant who'd sent Mededith to Birdsong. For five minutes he cursed the man out, at the end of which he put the fifty-nine-year-old officer back on foot patrol.

By the time he got the men together the DA had asked for (although he refused to equip them with shotguns), he had a triphammer of a headache, and he sat disconsolately at his desk imagining his Mercedes turning into a Volvo. He decided he'd better drag his headache out to Hosea's to make sure things stayed under control.

When the chief arrived, Hosea, flanked by his lawyers, was giving a press conference, in which he called attention to the number of policemen it apparently took to arrest a solitary, unarmed black man. Nattily attired in a blue seersucker suit, a white shirt open at the collar, he said he was an honest businessman, a taxpaying citizen, and a grandfather. Alice stood wide-eyed behind him, wearing a black one-piece bathing suit.

Birdsong waited while Hosea spoke, and then he had two policemen snap handcuffs on him. They put him in a black-and-white, carried him to the station, and booked him. Bail was set at $10,000, which Hosea paid out of his pocket. That night, phones were jumping off the hooks in Montgomery's seats of power, and in the morning the headlines read: DA DROPS CHARGES AGAINST MALONE. WIFE CHARGED WITH THIRTY-TWO-YEAR-OLD MURDER OF INFANT SON.

Grimly, Birdsong called his campaign manager and began preparing his case against Meredith.

CHAPTER
25

Four weeks before Meredith collected her baby's bones in Montgomery, Gerald, in New York City, found the contraceptive jelly in his wife's straw bag. He put the tube in his pocket and staggered into the bathroom. As he stripped for the shower, he considered how ironic it was that the discovery had caused this detonation in his guts, the trembling, the sour stomach. Three days ago he would have bet a year's salary that Margaret was planning to meet a lover. He knew it in his head and in his stomach, he knew it like he knew his name. Proof shouldn't have affected him.

The nine-year-old, childless marriage was rocky, had been for some time. Recently, love-making had been infrequent, born less of desire than of physical need and habit. But on the night before she left for a two-day conference, she'd swept from the shower wearing the most powerful nightgown she owned, and, wordlessly, began to seduce him. In the morning, the diaphragm had been in place for nine hours; safety demanded but eight. She didn't take it out, left the case, but took *it* with her.

For six years, every time she went away, he'd checked the case. Always she'd left the diaphragm behind, tacit renewal of her promise that she would never again betray him with another man. He appreciated the gesture, even while he considered how inexpensive diaphragms were, how they were small and could be kept in other places, say, the drawer of her office desk. But he did not allow this observation to torment him; it was he, not she, who possessed the imagination. The truth was, probably, that such a scheme had never entered her mind.

She was a sales representative (by everyone's account, a damn good one) and had, for the last five years, been at IBM. She traveled a lot, all over the Northeastern seaboard, and she always left the diaphragm behind. Of course, there were other ways to make love, but there was little besides good old-fashioned copulation that Margaret had developed a taste for, and she'd compared the wearing of condoms to going to bed with your socks on. Six years ago she thought she was pregnant with another man's child, a circumstance that had driven her to a psychiatrist's couch, and he doubted that she would take a chance on using nothing. Ambivalent about becoming a mother, she refused to get her tubes tied; having had no children, an IUD was out of the question. Four years on the pill had, alarmingly, caused her vision to blur. She was reduced to the diaphragm, and this time she took it with her.

Now, as the water beat against his head, Gerald closed his eyes to confront the image of Margaret covered by a man whose face was hidden. Her face was taut with lust, dark with gathering blood, and out of her slack, exhorting mouth came short, hard exclamations of her passion. The image was familiar; so was the need it created to crawl, groaning, into the nearest unlit room. That was why he trembled; not that Margaret had been with another man, but that another man had caused her to writhe and moan, and cry out, as he, Gerald, did. That another man had made her come and come again ("I'm a come machine," she'd said), to go on coming until she screamed for the man to be merciful, to stop. Then, without transition, the scene changed, grew brighter, and he could see who his rival was.

The man was white. His face, if not handsome, was

interesting, an angular face that smiled a lot, but that was now ravaged by his agony. His name was Chester Stone.

Chester was a biologist who, when Gerald and Margaret met him at Cape Cod, was still recovering from a year old divorce. One weekday he had settled his blanket near theirs on the beach. For hours he had lain within touching distance, alternating, Gerald noticed, between reading and dozing. It was not until the tide began coming in and threatened their position that he spoke. Moving hastily away from the water's edge, giggling at the inelegance of their retreat, they exchanged names. Gerald liked him. He laughed often and easily. There was a sensitivity in his eyes and fingers. "Piano player hands," Margaret said, and lowered her eyes.

They'd gone to dinner, over which Chester told them the details of his broken marriage. The next day they met again on the beach, and for the rest of the week, until Chester shamefacedly excused himself, they were a threesome. Gerald realized he'd never seen Chester as an intruder. He liked the man. Six months later, when Margaret was afraid she was pregnant with Chester's child (she wasn't), Gerald began to despise him. For six years Chester had lived in Gerald's head, mostly in images which involved Chester sleeping with Gerald's wife.

Rona, Margaret's best friend, said that Gerald shouldn't imagine that Margaret was the same in bed with Chester as she was with him, that, sexually, people responded differently to one another, but he did not believe the difference was significant. He did not believe that Margaret believed it. Neither was into "recreational sex," but once they'd discussed having affairs and Margaret said that sex had to be terrific if the two people cared for one another. He'd never seen Margaret make love to another man (neither, he supposed, had Rona). He knew, however, how serious Margaret was in bed, as if each time she had to prove something, and he couldn't imagine her half-stepping through an encounter.

He stood beneath the driving water, thinking, as he always did when his world threatened to dissolve, about his father, and about how no one except Iceman had ever loved him.

He stayed in the shower until his fingertips puckered. As he stepped from the tub, he decided that he wouldn't say anything; she had her secret, he'd have his. He would keep his cool and control; he would smile and put a hole in her diaphragm, find excuses for not sleeping with her, then laugh when she became pregnant with a white man's runt. He rubbed condensation from the mirror and ran headlong into his devastated eyes. The collision rattled his rib cage. He turned away, removed the tube of jelly from his work-pants pocket, put the dirty clothes in the hamper.

In the bedroom he dressed: no underwear, faded jeans, and a tee shirt with the words "Malcolm X lives," a relic of his college days. The shirt still fit; around the age of thirty he'd begun to gain some weight, but basketball and golf and working on the garbage truck had whipped him back in shape. His eyes were clear now, and he walked into the living room. Margaret was on the couch reading the *Village Voice*. She was letting her hair grow, wore it straightened, pulled back in the briefest ponytail. He'd liked her better with an Afro; its roundness did things for her angular, coppery face. None of her features was outstanding (he thought her eyes were too small), but her face was intelligent-looking, and the promise in her faultless legs caused men to turn in the street for a second look. Although she'd been inclined to chubbiness as a younger woman, maturity had worked its magic; she was thirty and headed confidently toward her prime. He was looking at how her hips stretched the summery fabric of her skirt, so he did not know she was looking at him until she asked what was wrong.

"Wrong?"

"You're shaking."

He looked at his hands. "Nothing."

"Don't tell me nothing. You look like you've seen a ghost."

He hated the trite expression. There was a language; why didn't people use it? He hated her for discovering his trembling, for interpreting his silence as weakness. It was imperative that he speak; in the sound of his voice striking the charged air would be a handle he could cling to, a hard place where he could stand. But when he opened his mouth it was to be swept by panic and heat and impotence. He fought it with all the fury of a man fighting for his life, or his child's life, or his wife's. "I . . . I never thought . . ." He snorted, gripped his knees. "That I would go through this if you took another lover. Not after last time."

He wished he could have been more dramatic, more eloquent. Last time was six years ago. Apprehension had replaced concern on Margaret's face. He was waiting, he knew, suddenly aware of the traffic thirty-one floors below (a horn, a truck that backfired), for her swift and insistent denial, or for an expression of her disbelief that he had dared, after all these faithful years, to accuse her. He could almost hear the options tumbling in her lawyer's head: whether to deny or flare with anger, whether to allay his fears or to wring from him an apology. None of this, he realized, had anything to do with what she'd done, or hadn't done, but, instead, with his accusation, and his trembling. When her denial was not swift, he knew there would be none, and he despised her for not giving him that consolation.

"What," she said carefully, "makes you think I've taken a lover?"

He was better now. He knew what he was fighting. He could see it. "I knew it the night before you left. When you put on your sexy nightgown. You'd taken care of home. You could 'forget' and take your diaphragm. It was," he said, pleased with the wording, "well conceived."

"I don't know what you're talking about, Gerald. I don't think you do, either."

He reached for the tube. As he held it up, watching her shrinking eyes, he considered how everything had its price. There was a price for being wrong and a price for being right; both left you bankrupt. He unscrewed the cap, squeezed the milky paste into his hand, then tossed the tube across the room. It hit on her lap, stained her skirt. He looked at the mess in his palm, clenched his fist, and cleaned his hand on the brown carpet. "I believe that's called incontrovertible evidence. If you weren't so thrifty, you'd have thrown it away. Thus thrift makes liars of us all."

Her eyes closed. "I'm sorry."

If this was meant to comfort, it did not. "I'm sorry, too," he said.

For three days, neither went to work. They lived on yogurt, cheese, and orange juice. They talked from the time they woke up in the morning until she pleaded exhaustion and fell asleep in the middle of one of his questions. He accused her of going to sleep to escape him. He was battered and bleeding, but he didn't need sleep; his energy was boundless. In the afternoons they walked. They were living in a neighborhood waiting patiently to become a slum. Haitians, Puerto Ricans, Jews, Blacks, and Greeks mingled in the squalid streets. Their expressions had always seemed as incomprehensible as their speech; now women whose lives he knew were desperate glowed confidently, secure. The children had yet to be introduced to heartbreak. None of the men had recently had their manhood called so brutally into question. At times he hated Margaret; at times he wanted to crawl inside her, to possess her the way bacteria did. They made love; it was, they both admitted, incredible, but when they separated the confrontation began anew. She would not tell him who the man was; it was casual, she said, someone she'd recently met. He didn't believe her. She said she didn't want to talk about that, she wanted to talk about them. Why did he never say he loved her? He didn't share his feelings, always kept her on the outside. He didn't laugh enough. He said she didn't need to take her diaphragm if all she wanted was to laugh. She said he never allowed her to feel comfortable about having a male friend. He said you didn't fuck your friends.

"What was important was the friendship."

"Bullshit."

"Men are like that. It's hard to have the friendship without the other."

"Who was he?"

"Nobody you know."

"I want to know."

"Why?"

"It leaves a goddamned space, that's why. What I fill it with is worse than knowing."

For three days he badgered her, waited for her to cry out the lover's name while they made love, lay awake while she slept, hoping she would dream it. He had to know so he could control the images in his head: Margaret with her lover. Margaret, his love, his wife. He knew that he had helped to drive her to it. He also knew he couldn't admit it.

"Who?"

"It doesn't matter."

Her face, wide-eyed, ecstatic, stunned with lust.

"Who, who, who, who?"

On the fourth day she screamed. "It was Chester Stone."

She hadn't seen him in all those years, and then she'd run into him at a cocktail party, one that Gerald, characteristically, had opted not to go to. She and Chester discovered that their offices were only a few blocks apart. They began, occasionally, to meet for lunch, or a drink after work. They got along famously.

"I realized I missed his friendship. He always made me feel I was special, the smartest, funniest person he knew. We just talked. Anyway," she said, and looked away, through the window at the tops of tenements, "I mentioned the convention, and he said he'd be in Boston that week and why didn't we meet for dinner."

All the way up on the train she'd tried to figure out how to tell him she didn't want to sleep with him, that she only wanted to be his friend. She thought about turning around and coming back home when she got there. Instead, she called him at his hotel.

"I figured I owed him that. He sounded so happy to hear from me, said to come and meet him for a drink in his room. I said I'd meet him in the bar. He laughed and asked if I was afraid of him.

"There was a drugstore across the street. I didn't want to use *that* as an excuse. And I didn't want to take any chances. I went to his room. We were . . . together. We went to dinner, and I spent the night. I . . . spent the night."

"What a nice expression. You spent the night."

Her mouth tightened, her eyes grew smaller still. "Do you want to know about it blow by blow? Who touched who? Where? When?"

"I want to know why you did it. How could you do this to me?"

"I didn't mean to do anything to you."

"Tell me what it was like."

"This is not going to help us. Don't *do* this."

"Do you fake it with me?"

"What has that got to do with anything?"

"Do you? The truth."

"The *truth*." She laughed bitterly. "He wants the truth. Yes. Not a lot. Sometimes, when we aren't talking."

"What wouldn't you do?"

"Invade your privacy. Go through your belongings."

"How's that worse than lying?"

"I don't know. But it is."

"You called me in the morning. From there?"

"He was in the shower."

"You never got over him. You still love him."

"I love," she said wearily, "you."

"That's what you said the last time."

"I would have told you."

"When?"

"Maybe we should have had children."

"Sure, sure. We'd really be in great shape, wouldn't we?"

She sighed and looked toward the window, beyond which the most magnificent sunset he'd ever seen painted riots in the sky. For a moment the two of them watched the poison colors, then Margaret sighed again. "I don't know, Gerald. I just know I'm not a criminal, and you're trying to make me sound like one."

"How many others that I don't know about?"

Her hands were covering her face, muffling her voice.

"You don't want me to say 'none' to that. You want me to deny that anything ever happened. To make it go away." She looked up, her face ravaged. "Well, I can't.

"Gerald," she said, "we've got a lot of stuff to work out."

He felt abandoned, unloved, that someone whom he'd trusted had tried to destroy the life he'd so painfully, and against the greatest odds, managed to achieve. How could he work anything out with a person who could do that to him?

He said that to her.

Each went back to work. Neither found more than the merest relief in garbage cans or legal briefs; neither could forget what waited for them in the evening. Margaret insisted that she'd been driven into the affair by needs Gerald had refused to meet. He accused her of refusing to accept responsibility for her actions, and of failing to make him aware of her grievances.

They were in a hole. Each insisted that the other had dug it. They were in the hole together; they could only get out together. The price they'd set for returning to the surface was that the other capitulate and take the blame, which meant, really, to confess to loving poorly, or not at all. Neither was willing to pay that price.

Two weeks after he went through her purse, Gerald told Margaret he was spending the night in a hotel. When he came back, he expected her to be gone. To his surprise, she was. He refused to acknowledge his fright or his concern about where she was staying. He began to condition himself to her absence, filled days with work, some afternoons and evenings with golf and basketball. He read. Nights were the toughest; he was not accustomed to sleeping alone. But he would not allow his suffering to touch him. He treated suffering like the bully it was; he controlled it, refused to let it push him around. He had a week's vacation coming; he'd rent a car, maybe drive to Vermont, or Maine. To celebrate his survival, he went one afternoon to buy the biggest porterhouse steak he could find, a ten-dollar bottle of red wine, and prepared a feast. He'd cleaned up the kitchen and settled on the couch with a novel when the doorbell rang. A little annoyed, wondering which neighbor wanted to borrow what, he went to answer.

He didn't have any neighbors who wore lavender silk suits. This woman had a floppy straw hat, which hid most of her face. She stuck an arm out; it had no hand.

"Hello, Yellow," Josephine said. "I hope your wife don't mind some company."

Gerald stood, mouth open in amazement, and then he began to laugh. His surprise was ordinary. The sharp, exhilarating relief was something else.

CHAPTER
26

She'd spent six years in a correctional facility on Long Island, and during that time not a single person from Montgomery had so much as sent a card, much less come to visit. She asked if he remembered the story he'd told her that rainy day they'd gone to buy the poison, the one about the woman who'd killed her lover and been sent to prison, where she'd been abused. It was like that for Josephine in the beginning, until she learned to cope. She was a novelty, and she described in vivid detail the uses to which she'd put her handless arm. Then there had been one of those periodic cries for prison reform, and things had gotten better. A year after that she'd been sent to a minimum-security facility in upstate New York. She'd taken courses there, learned shorthand, and saved the money she made working in the prison laundry. When she was released, she possessed the staggering sum of $325. Everything else she owned was in a canvas Pan Am flight bag.

The world had changed in her absence; man had walked on the moon and created babies in test tubes—somehow these events had come to represent all the adjustments she had to make. She had no place to go. She knew she could not go back to Montgomery. So she'd caught a bus for New York City, where she'd never been, but had heard so much about.

As she talked, Gerald watched from the other side of the troubled space between them. She was larger than he remembered; her presence commanded space. No metaphor had been coined to capture her magnificence; her beauty could only be framed, in the way that her hair, long and electric, like an Egyptian headdress, already did. As she recounted the meandering bus trip through small towns distinguished by their sameness, he moved from his chair to sit at her feet, wondering at what point he would look unflinchingly into her eyes and begin to talk about what so far had been avoided.

"Well," Josephine said, "when I got off that bus, I like to have died. All them people, them buildings. And the noise. I didn't have the slightest idea where I was going, or what I was going to do when I got there. I walked over to a taxi, and when the driver asked me where I wanted to go, I realized there wasn't but three places in New York I could remember the name to: 42nd Street, the Empire State Building, and the Plaza. I told him to take me to the Plaza. . . ."

She'd gone inside, checked her bag with a startled desk clerk, and walked into the dining room of one of the world's most exclusive hotels like she'd been going there all her life. Television had taught her the standard behavior; she ordered a window seat, shrimp cocktail, sliced steak in bite-sized pieces, *very* rare. Certainly she wanted Hollandaise sauce on her broccoli. No thanks, she didn't care for wine.

"So there I was"—they were both laughing—"six hours out of the penitentiary, in the middle of the Plaza, acting white. And *nobody's* paying me any *mind*. I'm trying not to stare at the place; I mean it's *beautiful*, and this little white-headed man came over, a red face, about *this* high, and begging my pardon, asked if he could sit. Hell, I'd gone that far, I told him yes, and offered him a bite of steak. He said no thanks, but would I care for wine. Champagne, I said. The waiter came back with a bottle older than I am. The little man said forgive him, but he couldn't help but notice my arm. How had this "unfortunate" condition come to pass? I told him I'd had an accident. He wanted to know what kind. I said I didn't want to talk about it.

"He showed me his card. He was an art collector from California, in New York on business. He'd be pleased to provide me with an opportunity to view some pieces he had with him. They were in his room."

She crossed her legs and her skirt stretched, revealing her thighs. "Well, you know what I'm thinking. This cute old man's some kind of freak. But he pays for my lunch with a fistful of hundred-dollar bills, and I figure, hell, he can't teach *me* too much about freakish. Lord knows I could use the money.

"I got my bag from the desk, and we went upstairs to his collection. It made my skin crawl in one way; in another, it was a turn-on. All of it little statues of deformed people. Beautiful women with scars for mouths, a leg or a breast missing. Boys with perfect bodies and elephant heads. Weird sexual organs. People all bent up.

"I was standing there staring—that wine had gone straight to my head—when he started touching my stump. Nobody had *ever* touched me that way, so much *power*, and he looked right in the middle of my eyes. I swear I got weak in the knees; he could have had his way with me right then—for free. But he wasn't interested in that. When I told him I had no family, he said he would be grateful if I came to live with him. He had a few other human *specimens*, and he felt I'd be at home there. I would want for nothing.

"Well, to make a long story short, I went. When he found I could take shorthand, he made me his secretary. There were seven of us, not counting him, each one exceptionally beautiful in some way. Each of us had a job. The Chinese hunchbacked lady cooked, the gorgeous one-leg man from Switzerland kept the garden, the Lithuanian with the enlarged testicles (I wish you could have seen his *eyes*, Gerald) was the valet. Once a month or so, we'd be arranged in pairs, or groups, or all of us would be together, and he would sit and watch us make love. Always we had to pay special attention to the other person's deformity. It was strange at first, but after while I didn't mind. It was a little like making love to yourself."

She stopped, her eyes dilated. She was thinking of her tenure in that house, and how after the opiate of ease and splendor had lost its kick, she'd begun to feel trapped again. Her presence said undeniably that she was helpless, half-stepping around a life she was incapable of fully living. She was a freak, without value except for her deformity, and she wondered if she'd ever merge her parts, the one a figure of self-hate, the other yearning to walk the earth like any human, an object only of indifference in other people's eyes. She could not say through what alchemy the merger was accomplished, but one afternoon, just before the old man died, she'd stood naked, bone weary, in front of the mirror. It was after an orgy; her body was cool with drying sweat; semen flaked on her face, her belly, between her thighs; but it was not the fucking that had made her tired enough to die. It was the sameness: her guilt and lack of self-esteem, the walls of her life, which, despite her physical strength, moved inexorably closer to crushing her. She held her arm up, the one with the missing hand, spoke experimentally into the mirror. "I'm thirty-one years old. This is me. I accept it." When the bile of self-loathing rose in her throat, she choked it back and repeated: "This is me. I accept it."

It was not easy. Self-acceptance meant self-discovery: her beauty and ability to think, her fundamental value as a living, breathing form. But it also meant confronting the putrid side of her humanness, a process that, metaphorically, consisted of rubbing her face into her sharp, breath-taking stink, swallowing her shit, tasting the red-brown monthly blood. But once she grew used to it, she discovered the power in self-acceptance. She also came upon the contradiction—on the one hand, peace, on the other, a restlessness that could only be calmed by bending people to her will. There were, back in California, boys and old men and several women whom she'd driven to permanent confusion, whose spirit pieces she'd stepped around as she exited with no more concern than a pedestrian skirting puddles left by a summer rain.

She declined to judge herself, or ask questions, kept self-examination and doubt outside the circle of her consciousness; her decisions were snap. She demanded only that she not be bored, and she'd found that the surest way to avoid boredom was to fuck with people's minds.

Only one thing caused her discontent, brought her wide-eyed and gasping from a tortured sleep. She still dreamed of the axe, the airplane, the chicken pulsing across the yard. And there was only one way to stop its bloody dance.

"Anyway," she continued, "he died; he left me money, more, God knows, than I know what to do with. I hung around California for a few years, but after a while it wasn't any fun. I decided to come east. For two reasons. I've got some questions to ask my mother. That's one. The other didn't come to me until I was in the plane, someplace, I think, over Kansas. I called your mother from the airport, said I was an old friend. She gave me your address."

"So here you are?"

"Yup. What's happening in Montgomery?"

"My father died."

Her eyebrows arched ironically. "You finally killed him?"

"No. My life hasn't been as eventful as yours."

"Couldn't be. You never took chances. On the plane I realized why I hadn't thought about you all these years. I didn't want to confront the pain. I was afraid that it, more than anything else, would break me. But I'm stronger than I thought. I let myself think about you, and you know what I felt? Anger. Rage. I finally let myself blame you. You fucked over me."

"I was a child. A battered, mixed-up child."

"I was a child, too."

"You hate me, don't you?"

She reached for the glass of Scotch she'd from time to time been sipping, twirled the tinkling, diminished ice. "Maybe. I don't know yet. I hate having had to go through all of it alone. I hate that you never showed up at the trial, never sent me a card, didn't know if I was dead or alive, and didn't care. Maybe you did care, but you were too weak and spineless to show it. I remember how when Iceman died, you didn't even mourn *him* right. Iceman you loved. What could I expect?"

He still couldn't think of Iceman without pain or guilt. "I want to make that up to you. I'm sorry."

"You were always sorry. Oh, well." She yawned and stretched, and her braless breasts writhed against her blouse. "I want to hear about you, what your life's been like. But tomorrow. I've been clear across the country, and I'm tired. When's your wife coming home?"

"She's not. We're separated."

"Another man?"

"How'd you know?"

She grunted. "Then my being here works out well, doesn't it?"

"I guess so."

"You look different. What is it?"

"Age?" He shrugged. "We all get older."

"That's not it." She searched his face. "It's your eyes. The mark in your eye. It's gone."

"I had it removed. It was growing."

"It leaves your face empty."

He was stung, smiled to hide it. "I'll get it replaced."

"Surely not for me. You seen my mother?"

"You haven't been in touch?"

She shook her head. "I saw her last on the day I was sent away. She brought me some sanitary napkins. I had my period and she was afraid they wouldn't have any where I was going."

"She had a stroke. Three years ago."

"Bad?"

"Enough to keep her in a wheelchair."

"Can she talk?"

"Yeah."

"Good." She yawned again.

"If you're tired, we can go to sleep now."

"I'll sleep on the couch."

"There's an extra room."

"Great. Take my shoes off."

He looked at her, responding less to the words than the tone. It was matter-of-fact, the command of a woman accustomed to having her way. He bent, removed the pumps, which had cost several lizards their lives, gave them to her when she asked.

"Rub my feet. Oh, does that feel good. Harder. Take my stockings off."

He reached beneath her skirt on the outside of her thighs, found the garter snaps. He had some trouble; Margaret never wore the things, but finally he peeled the stockings down her legs.

"Look at me." Her eyes had less emotion than a dead man's. "You want me, don't you? You're hard and you want me."

243

"Yes."

She hit him in the face with the sole of her shoe. "Maybe tomorrow. I'm tired. Show me where I'm sleeping."

Dawn was breaking. Obediently, he led her to the guest room.

In the morning, he began to tell her about his life. He'd gone to Columbia University, where he majored in English. He'd been an excellent student, a considerable achievement given the times. The world was still trembling at the edge of the abyss to which Kennedy and Khrushchev had brought it. JFK had been assassinated; in August of the following year the murdered civil-rights workers were found in the wilderness of Mississippi. In February 1965, Malcolm X was slain.

Columbia had endured its sit-ins, shutdowns, and marches, and he had been among those shouting obscenities at the system. But he had done it from a distance, with the perspective of a man engaged in an important task and accomplishing his objectives simply by going through the motions. To be a full participant meant that he would have to join something, and he did not want to surrender his separateness. As a result, he made no lasting friends during his six years at Columbia, although he did acquire a wife.

Margaret was a freshman when he was a senior. She came from Boston, where her father was a psychiatrist, had grown up in a white neighborhood and gone primarily to white schools. This could have had a crippling effect on her, but her parents were solid, and taught her who she was. As a result, she was not awed by white people. She was capable of viewing them as individuals, which effectively stripped them of myth and mystery—

the former being that all white people were frightening, obscene, and powerful; the latter that they were, somehow, to be emulated. Her politics were well left of his, but while this caused her to argue with him, it did not cause disrespect. In fact, it was his isolation that had attracted her; she'd been curious that someone could stand so still, so untouched, in the middle of a storm.

As he talked to Josephine, in the bedroom, the kitchen, or on the living-room floor, he would massage her feet and experience the exhilaration and gratitude that comes from being allowed to tell one's life to another. Sometimes she interrupted with a question, a command to clarify, but mostly she let him ramble. She moved into his bed, but would not let him touch her. He did not go outside except once, for groceries, wine, and Scotch, and when he did, the sunlight blinded him, and he could not wait to get back to her. Not bothering to dress in the morning, she wore underwear and a tee shirt all day long. Today, the third day of her visit, she lay on her stomach, and he worked oil into the muscles of her back. It was one of the most fulfilling tasks he'd ever undertaken.

He had clung to the possibility that Alexander would come to love him, and when that had failed to happen, Gerald remembered how he'd rebuffed his father's attempts at reconciliation in the months before and after Iceman's death. After he'd left home for college, his relationship with his father grew increasingly formal, like the acknowledgments of divorced couples when they met in a public place. If circumstance bound them to the spot for longer, they spoke politely of the weather, or one another's health, discovering in that awkward moment that there was something they'd neglected, calling from another room. Whenever Gerald had fled toward his invented task, he took with him the conviction that his father had unforgivingly perverted his life, that he'd been made incapable of loving or being loved. This conviction expressed itself in the flatness of his eyes, in his aloofness, and in the frequency with which he slept with women he felt nothing more than lust for. His reputation grew: he was a failure as a lover. He was controlled, impenetrable, selfish, but mostly he was rigidly controlled.

So it was to his surprise and suspicion that Margaret had fallen for him so completely and begun relentlessly her attempt to pierce his resistance. When he'd completed his master's, he considered earning a doctorate, but discovered that he was tired of school. He went to work as a group leader for teenagers at a community center in the South Bronx. The pay was insulting; the kids were recalcitrant in the way of people who know they are doomed, but he accepted his responsibility and worked his butt off. Despite his efforts, kids continued to drop out of school, to become pregnant, to O.D. During this time he and Margaret were like two boxers circling the ring looking for an opening; he, the more cautious of the two, for the reputation was that her hands were stone. If the truth be told, *she* was the one looking for the opening. He was on his bicycle, hoping to weather, when it came, her lethal punch.

He paused, pleased with himself, not so much for the metaphor as for the extension of it. Josephine was on her stomach; he sat between her legs rubbing the backs and insides of her thighs, in his nose and mouth the narcotic of her odor: wet fur and autumn (shocks of dried corn, recently carved pumpkins); it had taken him two days to identify the smell. Sometimes he let his fingers get close enough to brush the pubic hair that curled from beneath her crimson underwear. The hair was a mystery, coarse, yet fine. He ran his forefinger lightly across the curve of her buttock; her muscles tensed. Her toes began to beat against the carpet.

"Am I doing something wrong?"

She turned over, her hair fanned; he thought of a cobra. "Fuck me."

Hard in that instant, he nibbled her stomach.

"I don't need any of that. Just do it."

She arched, removed her underwear; he crawled between her thighs. When he'd freed his length of iron, she rose to meet him. He entered, plunged, once, twice, three times; she cursed, "Bastard," tightened inside; he came.

"You can forgive your wife now," she said. "You're even."

He felt himself deflating. She told him to get off, to rub her temples, to continue his story.

In January 1971, he was drafted into the army. Margaret had badgered him to apply for conscientious-objector status, or go to Canada. Immobilized by a curious lack of energy, he'd done neither. The army had roused him from stupor; for the first time since he'd left his father's house he was being controlled by a force other than himself. This force fed him when it wished, punished him when it wished, had taken his freedom, and was licensed to take his life. He needed to do something to regain control. So he married Margaret.

When he got out of the army, Margaret was in law school, and he got a job teaching English in a community college. Summers they spent on Cape Cod. There, in the early seventies, black faces were few and far between, but after a while it did not bother him to be surrounded by white people. Most of them didn't notice him anyway; they were too engrossed in cultivating tans. The rest thought he and Margaret were exotic and invited them to their cocktail parties. There on Cape Cod had begun the season of his and Margaret's experimentation. They'd tried drugs, Ouija boards, yoga, and nude sunbathing, dabbled in paints, weaving, and pottery. For a period they were vegetarians and swore off white bread, refined sugar, and hard alcohol. Neither smoked cigarettes, so they were left with one vice they couldn't get rid of. They'd decided not to have children; later, Margaret changed her mind, but he wouldn't reconsider. He didn't want to chance doing to a child what his father had done to him.

Teaching frustrated him. His students approached literature in one of two ways—with unshakable resistance, or as though it were a series of puzzles with right and wrong answers. When he found his pleasure in reading diminishing, he went to work on the garbage truck, where the value of his job was unquestioned, and symbols couldn't stand the smell. At first the men didn't take to him. They weren't accustomed to a garbage man who read novels and played golf. After a while he earned their respect. He carried his share of the work, and his mouth was as foul as theirs when they discussed women and politics.

He was rubbing Josephine's stump when she asked if he'd ever wondered how it felt to have only one hand. He said he hadn't. She sent him for a towel and a roll of adhesive tape. When she finished, his hand was the size of a baseball glove, unwieldy, useless.

"Isn't this fun?"

He looked at her.

"Keep talking."

He talked, she listened, he rubbed his deformity. He was captivated by it; it generated a possessiveness, demanded, like a child or a toothache, his undivided attention. They ate, he talked, they went to bed. Sexually, she drained him, cared nothing about his pleasure. She went through his bureau, discovered the sexual novelty items he'd bought for Margaret (who'd never used them) and made him watch while she electrically turned herself on, crying out, convulsing, as she came. She said it was better than anything he could do; her arm was better than he was. Contorting her body, she showed him what she meant. When he came too fast, she cursed him; when he'd gone on for what seemed like hours, holding back with everything within him, she forced him to withdraw. On the fifth day of her visit, she made him wear a blindfold. He was her thing and he reveled in her ownership and the deformity she'd given him. He who had always taken responsibility so seriously, who had dedicated his life to self-control, learned the beauty and peace that could be found in submission. It was not that he had nothing to do; he did not have to *think* about what to do. Josephine told him when to eat and when to go to the bathroom. When to bathe. When to talk and to pleasure her. It was the feeling he'd had about the army, but without the dizziness or sour stomach; he'd *chosen* what would control him. He said he would divorce Margaret, he and Josephine would live together, he would make it up to her. She laughed and said some things could never be recovered. Then she taped his mouth with adhesive and put Miles Davis on the stereo.

On the seventh day, at ten o'clock in the morning, she said she was bored and ready for the two of them to go to Montgomery. When Gerald shook his head and began moaning, she ripped the tape from his mouth.

"I don't want to go to Montgomery. I want to stay here, with you."

She smacked him across the face, told him to take off his blindfold and pack. When she realized that his bound hand made this activity difficult, she undid the towel. It took an hour for him to become accustomed to bright light and the ability to speak. It was not until he was in the car, both hands on the steering wheel, that he ceased grieving the loss of his deformity.

CHAPTER
27

When they reached Montgomery, the digital indicator in front of the Mutual Fidelity Bank said it was 3:49 and 82°. Josephine told him to ride around a little, and he drove along Broadway beneath the canopy of friendly trees. She smiled wryly at the pornographic movie house, and said everything seemed smaller. He took her past the racetrack, the new high school, along Freight House Drive to Little Pond Road, past the church. Just before he reached his mother's house, he swung back toward town and headed back to Broadway. There he made a right turn past Hosea's laundry, up the courthouse hill, at the top of which sprawled the new complex consisting of the Traffic Department, the post office, and the police station. As they approached, the doors of the station burst open, and an army of blue-suited men dashed from the building toward the rows of parked black-and-white sedans. Red lights pulsated, sirens screamed. Gerald, not certain which way the policemen planned to go, pulled over to the curb. The cars roared from the lot, turned right.

"Follow them," Josephine said.

"Why?"

"It might be fun."

He had never been the kind of person to loiter at the scene of calamity, and he said so.

"*Follow* them."

The caravan wound to the eastern edge of town, where houses gave way to wooded land, then turned abruptly onto a narrow paved road marked MALONE

PRIVATE. The road climbed a hill that rose precipitously for some 150 yards, then flattened and became a circular drive half as wide as Broadway. Gerald heard Josephine's sharp intake of breath, and he had to admit that Hosea's mansion, while not exactly to his taste, was impressive.

The edifice was set at the back of the property. It was white, with great windows and a columned entrance. The roof was a conglomeration of architectural design; the domes and spires were painted black. The area in front of the house was the size of a football field. Miniature trees and manicured brush spotted the landscaped lawn. There were splendid flower gardens, marble birdbaths, life-sized monuments of Aphrodite and Venus. At the junction where road and driveway met stood a grinning statue dressed in red-and-black jocky silks. There was something not quite right about the figure; Gerald realized its face was white.

The police cars had pulled up to the front of the house, and the men had gone inside, leaving the door gaping. Gerald and Josephine got out of the car and trotted across the lawn. Behind them wailed another siren, this one more urgent, and in a minute a white-and-red ambulance careened around them and jolted to a halt. Two white-suited attendants rushed inside carrying a stretcher. A policeman in dark glasses appeared in the doorway, gripping the arm of a brown-skinned woman who looked to be in her late thirties. She was handsome, well-coiffed; one of her earrings caught the sun and glittered. The woman looked back over her shoulder. "I didn't mean to shoot her," she shouted. "I wanted him. Somebody make him pay for my mama." She looked familiar, but Gerald couldn't place her.

Hosea appeared in the doorway, holding a hand to his shoulder. He was wearing a white suit, immaculate except for the spattered blood. "Somebody make him pay," the woman cried. The policeman pushed her into the car, slammed the door. He got in the front seat, nodded to the driver; tires squealing, they pulled away.

Hosea, still clutching his shoulder, took two bewildered steps toward the departing vehicle. The attendants came out carrying the stretcher. A sheet covered it. Hosea was shaking his head. A policeman gently turned him toward a car. Hosea left in the black-and-white, the ambulance driver ground the gears and drove away, and the policemen who remained stood in small, tight knots. Gerald went up to one.

"What happened?"

Rachel Malone, Hosea's oldest daughter, had tried to kill her father, but Alice Simineski had stepped between them, taking, for her trouble, a bullet in the throat.

"She's dead?"

"As a doornail."

"Why?"

The policeman told him about the bones.

They went for a drink, and Gerald filled Josephine in on Meredith and the watermelon-head boy.

"Everybody thought he took the baby with him?"

"He *said* he did. I guess he and Meredith agreed not to say anything. Then, for whatever reason, she decided she couldn't hide it any more. But when Meredith turned herself in, they couldn't hold Hosea. He hadn't done anything, really, except tell a lie."

"She'll go to prison." This seemed to depress Josephine; she sat staring into her drink. "No wonder his daughter tried to kill him. He walks, she goes to prison at age sixty something or other. I'd have tried to kill him, too."

"For leaving?"

"Yes, for leaving. But mostly for what he'd done to my mother."

Gerald didn't answer. He was looking toward the end of the bar, where the bartender, smoke from a cigarette wreathing his face, tried to hide his interest in Josephine's missing hand. He wondered if the man had been around Montgomery nineteen years ago, or if life had been so kind to him that this was his first contact with human imperfection.

"Speaking of mothers," Josephine said, "I have to go see mine." She was watching her fractured reflection in the mirror behind the tier of bottles, where her hairdo appeared like stair steps converging above her eyes. Now the twang of country music invaded the blue-green air-conditioned room. The song was sad. Somebody'd left someone who still loved him.

"I don't like this town," Josephine said above the music. "It feels like death."

"It's Small Town, U.S.A. You're used to something else."

"I'm not used to anything. I'm scared."

"You? Of what?"

"Ghosts. Secrets. My mother. I don't know." She sipped her drink, then, abruptly, set it on the bar. "Let's get out of here. Get something to eat. I've waited this long, I can wait a little longer."

He stared at her. She was not the person he'd spent the week with. This woman was vulnerable, needy. He didn't want her. He wanted the strong one back, the one he could submit to and with whom he could lay his burden down. He tried to say this with his eyes, but all she saw was his curiosity, which looked like weakness and disbelief.

"You should have kept the spot in your eye. It leaves your face empty."

"I understand you have to hurt me."

"I don't have to do *nothing*," she barked. "It's just fun, that's all."

Now he wasn't sure what he wanted. He thought about Margaret, wondered where she was, and if she needed him.

Two hours later, a little after eight o'clock, Gerald pulled the rented Ford up to the house.

"Want me to come in with you?"

"No. Go on to your mother's. I'll call you in the morning."

She took her overnight bag from the back seat, endured his kiss. When he'd gone, she stood at the edge of the sidewalk, gazing up at her bedroom window. A chill attacked the space between her shoulder blades; she shivered it away. Old black folks, she knew, would have said someone had stepped on her grave. But it was the beginning, not the end, of her life that concerned her. She had some of the answers, but she didn't have them all. Those she had acquired had no reasons. She swallowed, considered walking back to Broadway and catching the first bus out of this Godforsaken place. Murder had marked her leaving, murder marked her return. Her eyes veered toward the rooftop, her shoulders slumped, as she confronted the real reason for her fear. What would her mother look like? How would Gertrude receive her? What would she say? Josephine licked her lips. Then she squared her shoulders, walked on up the sidewalk, the three porch steps, and opened the front door.

The room was dark. All the shades were drawn, as if at this early hour the occupant of the house had gone to bed. As she blinked, adjusting her eyes, the odor of a dry and heavy mustiness assaulted her. All her mother's rooms had always smelled of disinfectant. This one smelled of sickness and relinquished hope.

"Who?"

"Mama?"

"Who?"

"It's me, Mama."

The voice came from the kitchen. Josephine closed the door, ignoring the feeling that she was barring her escape. There was the spot where she'd killed her father, those the steps where her mother had stood with burning eyes.

"I'm eatin," Gertrude said. "Care to join me?" She did not look up.

"I ate already."

The kitchen windows had no shades, only thin, translucent curtains through which a gray light seeped. Gertrude, in a wheelchair, sat at the table. Her right hand held a piece of toast; the left lay gnarled and empty in her lap. She was wearing a robe the color of a summer sky. Her hair was pulled back from her face and tied with a bright pink ribbon. Josephine couldn't think of anything to say except to ask her mother who fixed her food.

"Breakfast I gets for myself. Dinner one of the church sisters brings me. How bout some tea? Care for a cup of tea?"

"Sure, Mama, I'll have some tea."

She went to the stove, added water to the kettle. Everything was where it used to be: the tea bags, the cups, the saucers. She lit the fire.

"You back, huh?"

"To see you, Mama."

Gertrude grunted. Josephine stood at the window, looking into a back yard bathed with dying light. Waiting desperately for the water to boil, she considered the irony of her despair. No matter where you'd been or what you'd

256

gone through, some part of you would always be your mother's child. She ached with wanting what she knew she could not have, which was for her mother to welcome her, to weep, to hold her to that wasted chest with the one arm that was left her. Someone had mowed the lawn out back. Someone had prepared a spot under the tree where her mother could sit in nice weather. She wished the water would boil. Maybe it was the stroke. Maybe her mother's brain was so damaged that she *couldn't* welcome her properly. Maybe Gertrude thought she'd sent her to the store, and Josephine had been gone for half an hour, not a quarter of a lifetime. The water began to hiss. Blinking away tears, she switched the light on above the stove and turned her back to it. Her body blocked the light; between the mother and the child stretched the darkness, into which the daughter, hand holding tightly to the counter, cautiously stepped.

"Mama, why didn't you say nothing all those years?"

She was listening for the answer in the way that people in a dark room strain to hear the beast, the man with the axe, the demon who has come to snatch the infant: head cocked, breath held, trying to *see* the sound, all the time measuring its capacity, and theirs, to kill.

"Why don't we," Gertrude said, "let bygones be bygones," and Josephine knew that the creature in the darkness was as afraid as she, would rather run than fight, was intent only on that destruction necessary to survival. Gertrude knew exactly how much time had passed, and, more important, why the light was being blocked. Yet it was the daughter who was shaking. The mother had weathered the first shock of this unannounced invasion. Josephine, who had come to conquer, now smelled the possibility of defeat.

"Mama, I got to know."

The kettle began to whistle. She turned the flame off,

prepared the tea, carried it to the table. "Mama, I got to know. I got a right."

Gertrude regarded her, stony, imperial, the first time she'd looked at her daughter since she'd walked into the room. Josephine looked back, searching for anything, hatred or pain or grief, but her mother's eyes, one drooping with paralysis, were as unreadable as the surface of a swamp. Then, unnervingly, Gertrude laughed. "Rights? You got rights? What about my rights? You took my husband."

"Mama, I was a *child*."

"You was a child when you started. After that you was a woman."

"Why didn't you stop it?"

"It's over," Gertrude said. She looked down at her plate, seemed, in that instant, to discover the mashed potatoes, carrots whipped into pudding, the chopped meat brown and strained like the silence. It was a silence that hummed seductively that some mystery was better left unsolved, that the light in the darkness could blind as well as illuminate, that while it marked your way it also could reveal you to your enemy. But Josephine couldn't stand the smugness of that humming; as it invited her to sing along, it mocked her in a key just beyond the upper ranges of her voice.

"I remember," she whispered, "what happened to my hand."

The head came, abruptly, up. For the first time the eyes registered emotion: astonishment and fear. "You do?"

"That night . . . it all came back to me."

Gertrude looked away at the wall above the stove. One side of her face moved into anguish. "I prayed," she said. "I prayed you'd never remember. I prayed so hard. Oh, dear, sweet Jesus."

"Tell me, Mama. I got to know."

CHAPTER
28

Times were hard in North Carolina in 1950. Percy, unable to get even menial work, was reduced to selling what fish he could catch in the streams and rivers that abounded in that corner of the state. He'd begun to drink heavily. Gertrude, who in no way held him responsible for their misfortune, was frightened. It seemed as if each week marked the disappearance of yet another husband. Some left in the dead of night without so much as a whisper; others promised to send for their loved ones from wherever in the West or the North they could make a new beginning. The results were the same; the men were gone, leaving the women baffled prisoners to the sullen eyes of their young. In the absence of fathers, boy children sought to fill the vacuum with the wind of their youth, and fell back dazed, spent, their gaping mouths sour with rage.

Gertrude, wondering by what grace she would be spared, began to imagine on Percy's face, and in the cast of his shoulders, the hesitation of a man gathering courage to hop a freight train. In the middle of her panic, she became pregnant. This compounded her fear, placed her, she said, squarely between that rock and its partner, the hard place.

It was not simply the question of another mouth to feed; had that been the issue, she would have found a way. What she was afraid of was that the child would *not* be born, and that this would certify for Percy the extent of his impotence. After Josephine, Gertrude had conceived four times in eight years, each of which ended in miscarriage. Some said that her inability to carry to term was a result of the difficulty of Josephine's birth; she'd been born feet first, and there had been an anxious moment when the midwife feared for the mother's life. Other people, most of whom were men, said it was Percy's fault; his seed wasn't strong enough. Not content with the scars these words left, they laughed when they said it. In public, Percy strutted and scoffed at the notion. In the corner of his heart reserved for truth and wonder, he believed.

Of course there was always the possibility that this time their labor would bear fruit. But probability suggested otherwise. And if the pattern was repeated, Percy, already battered by his failure to provide for a family, would be reminded of his inability to produce one. One morning she'd wake up, and he'd be gone.

Later, Gertrude recognized her mistake. She had denied her husband the right to confront the issue; she had made assumptions about his character, or, more accurately, his lack of it. But the moment was fraught with questions of survival. Hindsight was twenty-twenty; the chart of her future was blurred.

"They didn't have no clinics in those days. Wasn't no place to go except to Aunt Grace, who'd fix you with a coat hanger if you wasn't too far gone. Aunt Grace was gettin old—she passed on right after she worked on me —and she made a mess of my insides. Sick as I was, and bleedin, wasn't no way I could keep it from Percy. He'd never been no fool. I sent you outside. I'm in the bed, covers up around my neck. He stood there froze up like a statue, mouth openin and closin, and then he shut his eyes. 'This mighta been the *one*,' he whispered. I didn't answer. Seem like the room was spinnin. He turned his back on me and clapped hands to his ears like a man tryin not to listen. 'Why you do that, Gert?' he say.

'Why?' The room was spinnin. 'I'm *so* sorry,' I said. 'Please don't leave me.' He had his back to me. He shook himself and went outside. I held my breath till I heard him commence to choppin wood.

"I remember thinkin he should have had a wrap on; it was chilly. I put my hands on my empty belly and I began to pray, knowin the Lord was deaf on account of what I done, but prayin just the same. All the time I'm listenin for Jesus, I'm hearin that axe; seem like every time it fall my heart go *boomp*. The boomps get softer, like the axe bitin a pillow, and I dozed off. I remember dreamin bout bein a girl in Tennessee listenin to my daddy choppin, and then I was dreamin bout bein in bed between him and my mama cause the boogey man was at me in the night. In the mornin I wake up and listen at em talk. It ain't really light yet; maybe a old rooster callin out, and you feel safe. You a child, so you don't put it that way, but what you feel is that danger won't never leave its mark on you, you never gonna die. I wouldn't let my folks know I was awake, cause then they'd stop talkin and the feelin would go away. Daddy'd be sayin somethin, and Mama say, 'Hush yo mouf,' and I'm dreamin bout bein safe when I hear the screamin. First I think it's the dream, but I'm wide awake now and it's real. I near bout crawl to the window. The day had clouded up—I remember thinkin that—and then the sun popped out again, a weak sun, no warmth in it. You . . . you was runnin round the yard like a chicken with its head cut off, and your daddy was chasin. For a minute I thought he'd worked his mad off and you all was playin; he used to love to chase you thata way; but there was a *sound* to the screamin. Well, I forgot I was bleedin. I grabbed the blanket off the bed, wrapped it round me, and run outside. He'd caught you by then, was kneelin down holdin you with one arm, look to me like he lookin right down your screamin throat. He was holdin a hand by one of its fingers. First I thought it was a baby-doll hand, but all your baby dolls was white. And this hand was bleedin. Your daddy looked up at me. He looked like he seen death. All I could do was holler, 'No, no, no!' "

Gertrude had been looking at a spot someplace beneath Josephine's throat, but now, as the wail constricted her throat, her staring veered to the wall above her daughter's head. In the poor light her eyes made Josephine think of a blind woman's eyes. She wanted to reach and touch her mother's hand, but Gertrude sniffed up through her nose. Whatever was soft in her face grew rock hard, forbidding touching.

"I used to wonder how it happened. I mean was he gettin back at me through you. Not that he meant to do it—I know it was an accident—but that he just went on and let it. He tried to tell me bout it once when he was drunk, said how he chopped for a while and sat down and took a drink, choppin and drinkin, and you was playin, puttin earthworms on the block. He scolded you bout not killin nothing you wasn't going to eat, but you wouldn't quit; you was hard-headed that way. And he recollected he was thinkin of somethin—it never came to him just what he was thinkin—and the axe was way up high, real high, cause he was tryin to work his mad off, and when it come down, he saw your hand there and he couldn't keep the axe from falling. Said he tried to move it to another place, but like somethin had a hold on him, and he couldn't keep the axe from fallin toward your hand. Like I say, he was drunk when he told me, but I used to wonder if he was gettin back at me for what I done to *his* child by hurtin mine."

For a moment, Josephine misunderstood. "What you mean, Mama?"

"Percy Moore," Gertrude said, "wasn't your daddy."

"What?"

"Didn't you never wonder bout how light you was, and us so dark? He didn't want you to know, said since he was raisin you, why'd you have to. No, Percy Moore wasn't your daddy."

She tried to discover what she was feeling; she didn't have time. "Who was my father?"

"Your daddy named Abraham Sylvester Jackson, but everybody know him by the name of June Bug. He was near white, big brown eyes, black hair straighter than a white man's. Lord, that was one pretty yellow boy. When he started payin attention to me, I didn't ask myself why, I just went on and give him what he want. I was sixteen; he was twenty-one and goin to college. His family had moved up North; he stayed with his aunt, woman by the name of Geraldine, used to do hair. He left, she died, he didn't have no reason to come back, cept for me, and I was jet black and no beauty and pregnant to boot. Later I hear he moved to Philadelphia, then down to Georgia and was passin for white. Folks said he had a white wife with red hair, and three little red-headed boys. Heads just as red as that white lady what got shot today, though they say she used coloring. Sister Meredith's child done it, I hear. You know why?"

Josephine blinked. "It's a long story."

"Bet you it had somethin to do with a man. Whenever womens gets in trouble, you look for a man someplace." She nodded. "Anyway, last I heard—this was just before us come to Montgomery—June Bug was runnin for somethin in the Georgia government. Uh-huh. So that's where you gets your good looks from."

One side of her face moved. Josephine thought Gertrude was in pain until she realized her mother was smiling. "I wonder," Gertrude said softly, "if he's still pretty." Her face was tilted by the weight of an affection time had not diminished; her eyes brimmed, and as her daughter sat, astonished by this revelation, Gertrude shuddered in delight. Then her hand moved in a way reminiscent of how old people recover faded photographs, from where, until that moment, they'd lain beneath forgotten letters, birth certificates, the receipt that had outlasted the purchase it confirmed. "Well," Gertrude said, "Percy was crazy bout you, and what happened like to drove him out his mind. We got you to a hospital, but there was nothin they could do cept stop the bleedin. Nowadays they probably coulda sewed it back on, but back then . . . I don't know what they did with your hand, child. It always made me wonder; it *bothered* me that they mighta just thrown it in the garbage. For a while I didn't eat no pig meat on account of maybe they fed it to the hogs. You know how hogs eat anythin. Anyhow, you got infected, and they took skin from your legs and tried to put it on your arm, but it wouldn't take. Finally they just wrapped it up and sent you home. You didn't remember nothin bout what happened. Your daddy was in a state. He couldn't stand people whisperin he the man who cut his little girl's hand off, and finally we up and moved over to Northrop, bout fifty miles away. News hadn't traveled that far and I thought he'd have some peace. But he wasn't right; I don't think he ever got right. One day I come home from some day work and he gone. Didn't leave nothin but a old pair of slippers and that cuckoo clock he won at the county fair, the one you broken the bird out of. He was gone for eighteen months, two weeks and three days, and then he walked back in the door wearin a red tie and carryin a baby doll. He looked at you and bust out cryin how he was sorry and goin to make it up. I'm over behind you tryin to get him to hush, cause you don't know what he talkin bout."

"When did you find out about the rest?"

Gertrude frowned. "I don't know *when* I found that

out. I ain't never been no suspicious woman. One day I didn't know, next day I did, that's all."

"Why didn't you stop it?"

"Maybe I should've tried. If I had to go through it again, knowin what I know now, I would've. My husband just might be alive. But I didn't know that then. Them eighteen months was hard, girl. Wasn't never enough for the two of us, and neither one of us was no big eater. I had rent to pay, you was growin like you didn't have good sense, and you needed clothes to wear to school. Kids already laughin at you bout your hand; I didn't want em laughin bout your clothes. Sides that, I was still a young woman, and I had needs, if you know what I mean. But Percy Moore was my legal husband, and I wasn't about to leave my good name with some man who didn't mean me right. I'd already done that once. Besides, I don't know if I coulda got a man worth nothin. I ain't never been what you call pretty, and men don't got much use for a woman who can't make babies. When I got my husband back, I wanted to keep him. The older I got, the harder it was to think about him leavin. Which he would of done, you know. He wasn't the kind of a man could of lived with me knowin what I knew. That was one good thing about him. He had shame."

They sat in silence, Gertrude's eyes without rhyme, the right rapidly blinking, the left as fixed as an extinguished star. Josephine was thinking that now she knew, and so what? What difference did it make? Still, she struggled to discover her reaction to Percy's violation now that she knew he wasn't her father. There didn't seem to be a difference, although she thought there should be. Her mother coughed, startling her, and asked if Josephine would mind helping her upstairs. It was almost time for "Mod Squad." Gertrude said she never missed "Mod Squad."

"That way I can call the deacon and tell him he don't

have to come around tonight." Every night one of the deacons came to take her upstairs. Another came in the morning. The bathroom was on the second floor, but she had a chamber pot down here, which was daily emptied. A ramp had been built where the back porch steps used to be, and she could go out in the yard if she wanted. Once, she'd been caught in a sudden rain. Now she mostly sat on the front porch.

"You ready to go now?"

"Uh-huh."

Josephine wheeled her from the kitchen to the stair-case. Then she bent, put an arm around her mother's waist, and helped her from the chair. Gertrude was damp, smelled like milk an hour away from spoiling. She weighed practically nothing. "I can walk a little," she said. "Just steady me." Slowly, they ascended the creaking stairs, crept into the bedroom. Gertrude sat on the bed licking her gums; Josephine turned the covers down.

"What channel your program come on?"

"Eleven. But you don't have to do it. I got one of these." She pointed to a remote control.

"You want to wash?"

"First let me call Brother Harold. You be here in the morning?"

"I don't know."

While Gertrude talked, Josephine took a clean gown from the dresser. In the bathroom she collected water in a basin with a bar of soap and a face cloth. She undressed her mother to the waist, regarded the shrunken breasts with distaste. As she bathed the sour, wrinkled flesh, she considered the strong sense of duty that guided her hand, a duty that cracked her heart at the same time that it made her stiffen with scorn at her weakness. Gertrude was her mother, but she had not *acted* like a mother, so why should Josephine treat her with this deference? Because she was old and sick? The world was full of old, sick women; you could deny your life by doing nothing more than contemplating their needs. There was no logic to it; it had to do with the awful mystery of blood. Blood trapped the children; even when the failure of the parents should have resulted in the children walking away, forever, without so much as a good-bye. The blood made you prisoner as long as you lived; the death of the parents did not free you. Only the death of the children broke the bonds of blood.

She brought the wheelchair upstairs, placed it next to her mother's bed. "Where's the chamber pot?"

"Down in the hall closet."

It was a white pot with a blue design and it had a cover. She took it upstairs, held her face away as she emptied the foul-smelling contents into the toilet, washed the pot with scouring powder and Lysol, and carried it back to the closet. Then she went back into her mother's room, where, on the television, the Mod Squad chased two thieves down an alley.

"Everything all right?"

"Everything fine," Gertrude said, but she did not take her eyes from the television. "Your room's all made up; ain't nobody slept in it."

"I don't know if I'm staying, Mama. I'll let you know before you go to sleep. I'm going downstairs, maybe sit out back a while."

Gertrude grunted.

In the hallway, Josephine looked at the closed door of her room. She had been up and down the stairs, had passed the room several times, but had carefully kept its idea from her mind. Well, now it was in her mind, at the very center, and she did not know what all the avoiding had been about. Although the room had been the scene of her violation, it was not the only scene, and it was down-

267

stairs that the ultimate horror had occurred. She had walked where her father had lain with only the slightest of tremors. Not her father, Percy. Then she remembered the feeling she'd had the night she'd murdered her father (it was impossible to stop thinking of him as her father), the sense of being trapped, the same sense she'd endured in prison, and the strange old white man's house, and while she bathed her mother. She opened the door. It was a room with a chest of drawers, a window, and a bed, a room larger than she remembered. It seemed neither safe nor unsafe; it did not call out to her to enter, or scream a warning that to cross the threshold would mean resumption of her past. It did not seem as if anything had happened there, not with Gerald, not with her father. The room was stuffy. The pale color of the walls, the gauzy curtains were not to her taste. She closed the door.

Downstairs, she cleaned the kitchen, and then she went out into the back yard to sit in the place prepared for Gertrude. She turned toward the house next door, wondering idly how her cousin had coped with the death of her son. Gerald had told her how Jesus had revolutionized his name to Muhammad Something or Other and died in Cincinnati in a shoot-out with police. All the lights were off in Melinda Mclain's house. Gertrude's house was dark, too, except for the bulb left burning in the kitchen and the ghostly flicker of the television in the window of the upstairs room. Josephine felt like a traveler to a foreign land who had yet to pass through customs, at which time she would have to explain why all her bags but one were empty, and that cluttered with a broken clock, a red tie, a silver, bloodstained axe. She had lived here a little over a year, that was why she had no sense of returning home. What memories the place held were conflicting, like the memories of fresh-cut flowers in a second-rate hotel. As childhood recollections were measured, hers were brief. She had not grown up here, had only gone down, although for a season she had worshiped Gerald. But her real memories were not in this house. They were in a prison and the gilded rooms of a strange old white man's mansion. These were the places she would have to return to if she ever wanted to go home again.

She'd gotten, anyway, what she had come for: the answers to all but one of her questions. She'd confirmed her memory of what had happened to her hand. She'd learned that Percy was not her father. This discovery was like being told after all these years that her name was not Josephine, but Priscilla. It made her curious, in the way that an interesting face at an airport made her curious. And it made her experience a sharp, small, nagging regret, like that she encountered when the face disappeared into the crowd, or around a corner, taking with it, forever, the possibility of friendship or adventure.

Now she began to consider what she was going to do tonight, or in the morning. Prison life had taught her the futility of thinking in blocks of time longer than a day. She preferred operating in hours, and was most alive on the few occasions when life provided the opportunity to live it by the minute. It came to her again that she could go anywhere, to China, say, or Africa; money was no problem. She had yet to become accustomed to this phenomenon, found that it made making up her mind more difficult. There were all those options, so many of which were boring. She didn't want to be bored.

All around her, crickets were singing their monotonous song. She listened, watching the star-studded sky, which, black and limitless, endured the probe of satellites from an earth that, having yet to penetrate its own mystery, sought feverishly to unlock that of the heavens. Too bad they didn't accept almost middle-aged black one-handed women as astronauts; she'd love to fly around up there. She laughed at the image of herself in a spacesuit—it would be silver-colored with black racing stripes. Her helmet would have a faceplate of smoked glass, and she would make weightless love to a man who was not afraid of flying. She entertained herself with this for a while, long enough to cause her nipples to harden, and then she leaned back, waiting for something to come to her. When it did, she sat chuckling at her devilishness, nodding at how right it was. She got up and went inside, climbed the stairs to her mother's room.

"Mama," she said from the doorway. "I'm leaving."

"When you be back?"

"I ain't coming back."

Gertrude didn't answer.

"Mama?"

"Where you going?"

"Well, first I'm going to Georgia. After that I don't know."

"You going to find your daddy, ain't you? Your real one."

"I thought that might be fun."

"What you wanna mess *his* life up for?"

"I haven't figured it out yet."

Gertrude grunted.

"Good-bye, Mama."

"Josey?"

"What?"

Gunfire blasted in the darkened room. The light flickered across Gertrude's face, creating the illusion of movement. But her eyes were staring at the screen.

"How come *you* didn't say nothin?"

Josephine began to tremble. That was the question she would never be able to answer with any certainty. How could you want what you didn't want? How could you hate what you needed? There was only one answer

270

she could give; it was the one she'd always given. She gave it now, even though Percy was no longer related to her by blood. "I guess . . . because he was my daddy."

"Uh-huh."

"Bye, Mama."

Gertrude didn't move, didn't look at her. "Hussy. Black, ungodly, murdering hussy."

Josephine took a step into the room and stopped, paralyzed. She did not know which she most wished to do: wring from her mother's neck what little life was left her, or console and beg forgiveness. She poised there, straddling the threshold, realizing now that the stronger urge directed her toward consolation; the blood had once again won out. And she knew that to cross the room and touch her mother would be to enter willingly the gaping trap; whether it be a minute, an hour, or a lifetime, she did not want, any more, to be vulnerable to blood. She straightened her shoulders and spoke sharply to her heart. She would leave now, in this very minute. It was only a little before ten; there had to be a bus out of this place before dawn.

Halfway to New York City she told herself to stop worrying about what her mother had said. It was over, she was never going back, she would forget it. Then she remembered Gerald, and shrugged.

CHAPTER
29

At eight o'clock on the morning after Josephine left the last time, Norman walked out of his door to take his constitutional. As he settled into his brisk pace, he computed how soon his change would come. With Meredith turning herself in, and with the death of Alice Simineski, the Dispensation of Earthworms was coming to a close. Death and the destruction of trees had marked its beginning in 1948; death and disorder had marked its dominion. Soon, however, Montgomery would be returned to peace, and the Dispensation of Flight would begin. Black people would once more follow the example of their ancestors, and they would no longer die.

It had been an intense and prolonged period of tribulation, and the signs that defined the past thirty-two years lay behind him like bleached bones in a desert. Of all the carnage, the grinning skulls of children bothered him most; he could have spent a week reciting the names of fallen children. He wanted the town to erect a monument to their memory. He'd designed it and sent a sketch to the city council: a black stone, massive and irregular, out of which grew one small and broken wing.

Seventy-one years old, Norman was still fairly fit, for the habit of daily exercise he'd formed in 1948 had never been relinquished. Understandably, age had taken its toll. He would have been the first to admit that he'd never achieved mastery of flight (he could not, for example, negotiate great height or distance, and he'd never learned to dive). In the last ten years diminished strength had eroded what little expertise he had. Now he flew only once a month, careful not to go too high, or too far away from home, for fear his arms would fail and leave him stranded in a field outside Poughkeepsie. As flying became more difficult, he took to marveling anew at the prowess that had enabled black people to swoop all over the place so long ago. Those of his ancestors who had flown from slavery back to Africa deserved a page to themselves in the *World Book of Records*, to say nothing of Most Valuable Player Award on the planet's All-Time Wonders Team. For it was inescapable: the human body was not made for flying. It was a miracle that anybody had ever gotten airborne, much less stayed aloft long enough to cross an ocean. Soon, he would fly like that. He was waiting for his change to come.

Claire waited with him. Age had not treated her so kindly, but this, Norman peevishly concluded, was due to her stubborn refusal to exercise. While he had lost energy for flying, she had lost energy for life. Norman urged her to get up and do something, but she said she was old and tired and content to let the Lord's will be done. Norman didn't see what the Lord had to do with it. He accused his wife of living just beneath life's surface, which, like some listless fish, she would pierce only when impelled by hunger or a need for air. Once a month or so, in the way that Norman summoned energy to fly, Claire would emerge gasping from her blue-green silent world. Blinking against the light, she might remark how beautiful the sky looked, or suggest they call the children. On the best of those days, she would bake an apple pie, or be flirtatious, making suggestions more fitting for a couple thirty years their junior. But the next day she would retreat into the water and resume her waiting. She was waiting for the return of Christ, or her death, whichever happened first. There was nothing morbid in this waiting, for beyond each event was a series of bright and magnificent promises. No longer would arthritis twist knife blades between her bones. She would not have to endure the shortened breath and her heart's constriction when she waddled from the kitchen to the bathroom, there to sit straining at her bowel's bolted door. When Gabriel's trumpet sounded, she would lay her body down and become a spirit; she would call the gold-paved streets of Heaven "home." She had only, in this aching interval, to keep her mind on the Lord, and to beware the voice of the AntiChrist, which recently resounded in the land under the name Moral Majority.

So the two of them waited—she for death or the coming of Christ, Norman for his change. This change would be preceded by the event that would mark the end of the Dispensation of Earthworms: the return to Montgomery of the boy with the spot in his eye. Norman, in a ceremony he'd not completely worked out, would pass on the burden of his knowledge. In the meantime, he had to remain fit so that his transformation to a condor could be easily made. And he had to disregard the evil spirits which whispered in a voice sometimes matter-of-fact, sometimes mocking, that he was a madman who had never flown, that black folks were eternally earthbound and would forever die.

Neither Norman nor Claire knew the exact dates of the events waited for, but both could approximate. Claire figured she could expire in the next interrogative instant. Jesus Christ was expected to come around 2,000 years after his birth; assuming the accuracy of the calendar, there were twenty years to work with. The boy with the spot in his eye would return sometime after the seventh anniversary of his father's death.

It was peaceful, as well-kept cemeteries always are in sunlight. Gerald moved toward Iceman's grave like a sinner approaching an altar, at the foot of which, whether mercy was available or not, he'd make his overdue confession. Like that sinner, not totally repentant, he doubted that salvation was possible, and as he stood before the slab with Iceman's given name, he looked around to ensure that his foolishness would not be witnessed by anyone who could repeat it. He had come to talk to the dead; he had come to mourn, to commemorate, and to say good-bye. He pushed the foolish feeling behind the guilt that he had not once in all these years visited his best friend's grave.

"Well, Ice, I guess you wonder where I've been all these years, why I never came to visit. It isn't because I didn't think of you. I think of you all the time. I might as well say I don't blame you any more for going off and dying and leaving me alone. I know it wasn't your fault, and I'm ashamed of ever feeling it.

"But that's not why I didn't come. I was afraid if I came and stood here, like I'm standing now, I'd have to admit you were dead, and I was afraid of what that would do to me. Make me go crazy, or just realize how alone I was, which is maybe the same thing as crazy. Well, I'm here now, and it's not so bad. I'm a little shaky, but I think I'm going to be all right.

"I don't know if you'd like me now. I'm the opposite of what you were. I've taught myself to protect myself, to keep the world off my back. I don't let people touch me. No matter how kind they think they are, people always end up bruising when they touch. I've stopped loving. Maybe that's the worst thing that could happen to any-one; it's happened to me. I told myself that I wouldn't love because everyone I loved left me in some way, mostly by dying. I wanted my father to love me. He didn't, or at least not in the way I needed him to. I still can't face that, can I? The truth is that he *didn't* love me. That's why he couldn't say it. There he was on his dying bed, Ice, with two shot kidneys, and I'm ready to forgive him; all he's got to do is say he loves me. I'm bending over his bed, crying like a baby, saying, 'Daddy, Daddy, I love you.' You know what he did? He looked at me and told me to be sure to take care of my mother and sister. Dying, and his last words to me are about responsibility. I hate that word. If he could have made himself say he loved me, he could have freed me to love. Even if he didn't mean it. All his death did was leave me blaming a dead man for what had happened to my life.

"Well, I realized that all of this *control* I'd become famous for was really *lack* of control. I was hooked on the habit of not loving, and called it control. Hooked is the right word, too, Ice. You know how junkies steal from anybody? They want to do better, but they can't help themselves. That's the way it is with me. I don't love my mama, my wife, nobody. Not even my sister. I loved the *idea* that she loved me, not her. And I want to, Ice, I want to love somebody. I don't want revenge any more; I don't want anybody to make what happened to me as a kid go away. I just want to love. I'll even settle, for the time being, for not being loved back.

"Josephine was here. Showed up at my apartment and stayed a week, and then we came to Montgomery so she could see her mama. It was a weird week, Ice. I tried to show her I was sorry for what I'd done, and that I was willing to learn how to love, but I don't think she heard me. I don't think she *saw* me. I just came from her mama's house, and Josephine's gone. To Georgia, of all places. Didn't say good-bye, didn't even leave a message. I started thinking again about how everybody I loved, or tried to love, was always leaving, some kind of way, and I could feel that shell I keep wrapped around me growing harder. But I don't want that to happen any more, Ice. I'm going to do whatever I have to do to keep it from happening. I can't use the same old excuses to justify my bad habit. People die or leave all the time, whether you love them or not. They die if you hate them, or if you're indifferent. I thought about going after Josephine, sitting her down, and trying to make her understand. But I don't think it would do any good. Josephine's changed, and I'm not certain for the better. But I guess you can't go through what she did and not change.

"Now I've got to get it back together. I'm going to go find my wife. She's the only person left, except my mother and sister, that I've got a history with. Maybe it's possible to start again. Not all over. Just again.

"So, good buddy, I finally made it, a little late, but I'm here. Pardon my tears. You were the most important person in my life, and I never mourned you properly. Look at me now—I didn't even bring any flowers. But that doesn't mean I didn't mourn. I loved you, Iceman. For all these years I've missed the shit out of you."

Someone behind him began to applaud. Gerald spun, arms extended, prepared to grapple with a ghost. But it was not a ghost who stood there smiling, clapping still.

"Norman Fillis, you almost scared me to death."

"Forgive me. Your speech was moving. I'm sorry I missed most of it. I saw you from the street, a solitary figure standing in a graveyard. An apt symbol for this dispensation." He put his arms behind his back and nodded.

Gerald's heart was resuming a reasonable rhythm; the fear that had seized him was easing its grip. Still, the shadow of fright lingered, like that left in the unbalanced moment of awakening from a nightmare, when he struggled to distinguish what was real and what was dream. He rubbed his eyes, wiped tears away.

"Dispensation?"

"Of earthworms."

"Earthworms?" For a moment he found himself distracted by the whiteness of Norman's shirt; the sun beat against it and it hurt his eyes. The blue pants were frayed and faded. The sneakers had no tongues. "Earthworms?" he repeated. "The earthworms were twenty years ago."

"They *appeared* twenty years ago. Wasn't that a time, when there was no place left to step? My, my. But the Dispensation of Earthworms started before that, in 1948, with the destruction of trees, with the disrespect for animals, and the death of black folks. Soon it will end. Then Montgomery will know peace and liberty, and we shall enter the Dispensation of Flight. Black people will fly again. I," he said, and smiled brilliantly, "will be a condor."

Gerald blinked. "A condor."

"Marvelous bird, remarkable flying machine."

Gerald recalled that afternoon when Norman had spun his magic, when he'd worn bird flesh like a suit of clothes and had flown across the chasm. "Do you remember me, Norman?"

"Should I?"

"When I was a kid, you talked to me about black people flying. Out in the woods, behind the town barn. You made the birds come. Remember?"

Way in the back of Norman's brain, a bell began to clang.

"You said I was special, that I was chosen to be the one you passed your knowledge to. Who chose me? What's the knowledge?"

He was in the middle of a graveyard talking to a madman. He had just finished talking to the dead. The feeling, which he only dimly recognized, was hope. "What do you have to tell me, Norman? Tell me now."

"Who told you?" Norman asked, his voice low and menacing. "How did you know about that?"

"I was *there*. You jumped across the ravine. The fire siren blew, and I ran away. Remember?"

Gerald moved his head to one side, his body tensed and focused, willing Norman to recognize him. Sunlight fell across his face, struck a glancing blow against his cheekbone. The light fractured, and the left side of Gerald's head was wreathed in rainbow. A good imitation, Norman thought, remembering the moment before the siren, when disbelief had wavered and the boy had almost flown. An excellent imitation. But not quite perfect. It was a sure sign that the dispensation was drawing to a close, for the forces that conspired to keep Montgomery earthbound were trying everything in their power to steal his knowledge. They had sent this impostor, but they had forgotten the identifying mark. This imitation, so perfect in every other regard, had no spot in his eye.

Norman began to tremble. But he could not display the fear; he had to control it, he could not let them know how close they'd come to winning by deception. "Go back to those who sent you," he called, his nose flaring, his tone as sharp as a cutting blade. "Tell them the people will not be fooled. That they are sick of death and the destruction of their children. They are ready to *fly*. Your time is up. It's *over* for you."

"What?"

"Go!" Norman bellowed, and waved his arms threateningly.

"Okay, okay." Gerald backed away, his hands in front of him, palms facing the madman's withering glare. Norman didn't have a reputation for violence, but who knew what changes the passing years had wrought? He continued backing away until he felt it was safe to turn his back. Then he hurried through the crosses and tombstones toward his car, looking several times over his shoulder. Norman, his body slumped, had sat down on a grave. Gerald got in his car and made a U turn. Norman was standing, arms stretched toward the sky. Gerald checked his rearview mirror. When he looked that last time, Norman had disappeared.

He needed to be above it all. He'd had a close call; he'd been in the presence of evil, and it had left him shaken and feeling unclean. How hard it was to keep faith in the midst of forces that worked to hold you down, to keep you from flying for no other reason than that *they* couldn't fly, and they needed you so they could continue to feel superior. They'd built flying machines that went halfway to Heaven, but they were not satisfied with this accomplishment. They wanted to fly in the flesh. And rather than come peacefully to you, who held the key to flight, rather than learn from you and have everybody flying together, they sought feverishly to keep the secret hidden until the day when they could steal it and use it only for themselves. That would never happen. You could not steal the ability to fly in the way that the music, the sense of style, and the naming of things had been stolen.

He sighed. He needed to be above it all. How long before the boy with the spot in his eye returned and all of this would be over? He understood, suddenly, what Claire felt: old and tired, and just a little bit disgusted with the world he lived in.

He needed to be above it all, for just a few minutes, even though it was dangerous to go up without enough energy. But he would do it for only a minute. He gathered himself and leaped. He began to fly.

As he spiraled into the sunlight-intoxicated day, his spirits lifted. One of the magnificent things about flying was the freedom; another, the view. To the west, bright pennants fluttered in measured intervals along the grandstand wall; the racetrack circled an emerald. To the south was Hosea's mansion. The trees along Broadway leaned toward one another as if cocking their ears to a whispered conversation; only a ribbon of asphalt kept them from touching.

To conserve energy, Norman hovered, his arms outstretched, legs parallel and moving in a gentle scissors kick. There was the courthouse, bright with the gallant lions, and there was the new synagogue, on top of which a huge gold-painted star came to six spear-sharpened points. As he floated, Norman thought sadly of the Jewish people, who, promised their Messiah, had failed, according to the Scriptures, to recognize Him when He'd come. As he thought this, a chill passed over him; one of the star points detached itself and flew to stick in his skull. It was not painful, but it was annoying, and he tugged at it with his right hand. He couldn't get it out. Kicking his feet more rapidly to compensate for his occupied arm, he'd managed to get all five fingertips around the point when he realized he was in trouble. He released the star piece, spread his arms wide, knowing he was falling and that he had to stretch his body in a glide. But his arms were tired and his legs wouldn't hold their position, and now the rush of air past his plummeting mouth made it impossible to draw a proper breath. He summoned all the strength that was left in his seventy-one-year-old body, a body he'd trained all his adult life to respond in a crisis. There was nothing left but weakness and terror.

Falling at sixteen feet per second squared at the moment of impact, he hit the cupola of the courthouse a bone-shattering blow that dislodged the star point from his skull. From the cupola he dove to the ledge high above where the lions lay, hit it with his rear end, then, in a lazy, graceful somersault, flew to the sidewalk one hundred feet below. The gunshot of his body striking the sidewalk muffled the explosion of his heart, and had people on Broadway screaming "Sniper" and scampering for a place to hide. Nobody had witnessed Norman falling from the sky. Several had looked up to see him an instant after he left the ledge in that lazy somersault, and his death was ruled a suicide.

So neither Gerald nor Norman is here, and in the awkwardness left by their departure, sporting an arched brow of disbelief, arrives opportunity for reflection. Perhaps reflection is a poorly chosen word, for reflection, while it imitates reality, is not reality itself.

Some facts are mystery. There are, for instance, earthworms. Conversations with animals have been documented, and death has been known to take a holiday. In the country of their imagination, into which we are seldom permitted, madmen fly. One man's sleight of hand is another's magic. According to those given to such inquiry, a vast range of experience lies just beyond ordinary vision.

What you see is what you get.